THE DUKE AND MRS. DOUGLAS

"You've been less than honest with me, Mrs. Douglas."

"What do you mean?"

"I mean, you have been dissembling about the woolen stockings and other . . . unmentionables my aunt regularly sends me as gifts. You're the one who has been knitting them these past couple of years."

"Well . . . yes. But it would not have been seemly," she said primly, pulling her woolen shawl closer around her, "for me to have sent them to you myself, and you a stranger and a duke, and not even related to me. I merely sent them along with her ladyship's letters, without comment."

"I feel as if you know me intimately, for you know, never have my unmentionables clung to me so closely, nor been so superbly fitted to my form. The stockings caress my legs," he murmured. "The singlets mold to my chest like warm hands. How much do you know about a man's body, Mrs. Douglas?"

His slow gaze traveled down over her curves.

She should feel insulted, she thought, as a hot blush rose over her. It was almost as if with just his eyes he stroked her intimately. But instead of being insulted, all she felt was this suffocating wave of hunger. She wanted to fling herself into his arms. How had she come to this pass? How had she come to want him so very badly?

BOOKS BY DONNA SIMPSON

Lord St. Claire's Angel
Lady Delafont's Dilemma
Lady May's Folly
Miss Truelove Beckons
Belle of the Ball
A Rake's Redemption
A Country Courtship
A Matchmaker's Christmas
Pamela's Second Season
Rachel's Change of Heart
Lord Pierson Reforms
The Duke and Mrs. Douglas

Published by Zebra Books

THE DUKE AND MRS. DOUGLAS

Donna Simpson

ZEBRA BOOKS
Kensington Publishing Corp.
http://www.zebrabooks.com

One

"I hate Brighton. I despise Prinny. What am I doing here?"

Though the Duke of Alban had not intended to say that out loud, being alone and not inclined to talk to himself, he found that he had, and his voice echoed against the cautioning hush-hush of the waves on the shore, invisible in the blackness of the night.

But what *was* he doing in Brighton? He kicked at the pebbled beach, and a single stone skipped and hopped down the bumpy slope, stopping with a splash as it reached the waves. It had been an awful year, with a dismal, tedious series of melancholy events in the public sphere in the last twelve or eighteen months: first the Duke of Cumberland's murder trial, then Princess Amelia's death and the King's sad descent into madness. For a man who had once been the intimate friend, almost another son, of the old king, it had been a terrible time of great personal sadness. His last visit to the King had been a horrible failure, resulting as it did in the gentle old man vociferously accusing the duke of attempting to poison him and the royal daughters in some mad Napoleonic scheme.

Alban had come away from the King's rooms with the melancholy sense that nothing would ever be the same again.

And then there was, in June, the Regent's deplorably decadent and almost indecent celebration of his Regency; how could Prinny not see that any celebration was a scabrous assault on the dignity of the old man, his father, who raved in grand isolation at Windsor? Though in fact the reports had been encouraging, if one merely considered the health of the King. He was said, for a while, to be recovering from his prolonged weakness, but Alban had not personally heard anything for some time, and that was not encouraging.

His days of intimacy with the royal family were at an end, he very much feared—his only remaining ally was the Queen, and she was increasingly fretful and frail, so he only made matters worse by remaining in contact with her—and at thirty-four he felt old and weary. Following the Prince to Brighton was *de rigueur* for someone in his position, but the seaside town had been hot all summer, so hot it was dust-dry, with not a blade of green grass to be seen anywhere. And the entertainments at the Marine Pavilion were overheated, crowded, and tawdry, to Alban's jaded eyes.

The Prince blew hot and cold where Alban was concerned, sometimes treating him as a trusted friend and confidant, sometimes making cutting and poisonously scathing remarks at Alban's expense. They should have been like brothers, even though the Prince was much older, but Alban feared that was impossible because of the King's past clear preference for Alban's company over that of his own firstborn son.

Alban turned his head; was it his imagination, or did he hear footsteps on the scaly beach surface? Sound was deceptive on the beach at night, with the shush of the waves and the echoes of drunken laughter that seemed everywhere in Brighton. It was likely nothing, or at most some reveler looking for sobriety in the cooler air at the seaside. As if there were any cooler air.

It was damper, certainly, than the dust-dry breezes of the town, but cloying and sticky, like trying to breathe immersed in a treacle tart.

God, he wanted peace! How he longed for green grass and cool breezes and uncomplicated people! How badly he craved cleanliness of spirit, something he couldn't quite explain to anyone else, but which consisted of moral decency, a rectitude of action and thought and speech that he had not witnessed in a decade, he feared . . . or at least not in London or Brighton.

He should go away.

The idea seized him with a fierce longing that ripped through his soul.

He should go north, where it was cooler and greener . . . north, where life would not be complicated by the capricious whims of Prinny and the sad spectacle of a distracted king, frail queen, and tediously political atmosphere of distrust and treachery.

North to Swaledale and his hunting box and his Aunt Eliza. It had been months since he had seen her or . . . no, not months, *years*. In fact he had not been back since that dreadful time three years before when he retreated north after the news came to him that his runaway wife and her noble lover had drowned off the coast of Italy near Ravenna in a storm on the Adriatic.

How remiss of him. It was not that he had not been in touch with his aunt; he wrote often. But he had not been back. Perhaps it was time.

"There you are, Alban! You disappeared; I thought perhaps you had found someplace more entertaining, but instead I find you alone on the beach gloomily kicking up stones."

"Orkenay!" Alban greeted his friend, the Earl of Orkenay, with mixed feelings. The earl was an entertaining companion at the gambling table, and no one knew the insides of the hells and brothels of London better than he, but he was not a companion with whom to while away the hours in solemn contemplation. "I had thought you would be back with the rest, listening yet again to Prinny's fabulous tales of his successes on the Peninsular battlefields by Wellington's side, or of his famous exploits in the boxing ring."

"Careful, old man," the earl said, pleasantly. "Spies everywhere, you know."

In the dim silvery light of the quarter moon, Alban could see Orkenay glance around. "What, are you afraid Prinny's toads will see you talking to me? Better to return to the Pavilion then."

"Whoa, what is eating your vitals, Alban?" Orkenay gazed steadily up at him—Alban was taller than the earl, who was of average height, by almost a foot—his drawn, lean face pleasantly vacuous, as always. "You seem . . . overset."

"I'm just feeling captious and gloomy, I suppose. Leave me to my malaise."

The older man studied his superior in rank as best he could in the Stygian gloom. "Peculiar atmosphere, Brighton this year, what?"

"True," Alban conceded. "I thought it was just me. It seems . . . excessively tawdry this year."

"Always was, you know. You are just seeing it afresh, as it were."

"I suppose." Alban kicked again at the pebbles.

"It's true; it is always so. But this year after that spectacle in London—the Regency celebration, I mean—some of us are finding Prinny a bit much."

Finding his own thoughts echoed so closely, Alban blurted, "I have been thinking of going north."

"North?"

Alban glanced sideways at the earl. "Yes, Swaledale. I

have a hunting box there, and it is almost the season. Hunting starts earlier up there."

"I think it is a brilliant idea, Alban. You're right; this place is growing tedious. I would be glad to get away as well, and Yorkshire sounds . . . refreshing."

Was that an acceptance of an invitation that had not been extended? Alban gazed at the other man and chuckled. "Ork, old man, you do have a way of intruding yourself where you have not been asked."

"That," the earl said lightly, "is because I know that wherever I go I am welcome, for I am excessively good company. You don't want to go north alone, old chap, for you will brood. Not to be thought of."

Alban threw back his head and laughed outright. Orkenay was right; he was good company, and after all, a man could neither hunt nor visit with his maiden aunt twenty-four hours of the day. Even if he had not just released her, Alban would never in a thousand years have taken his latest mistress there; he would never take any woman to his hunting box. It would be an insult to his aunt. But still, a man needed a companion with whom to drink and gamble, and Orkenay was perfect in so many ways. "All right," he said, moving toward the earl and clapping him on the back. His arm over the other man's shoulders—given their disparity in height, they likely made an odd pair—he turned and together they strolled back up the beach toward the town. "North we shall go. I'll go back to my room and write a few letters. You, sir, must go take leave of the Prince, for he will miss your company much more than he will miss mine. He has hated me ever since he got it into his head that I wished to marry poor Amelia . . . as if I ever would have when she loved her Fitz to such distraction."

"You don't do enough to curry favor, old man," the

earl said. "No one seriously ever thought you wished to marry the princess."

"No, but Prinny pretended to think so, and pretended that it offended him gravely. And she in love with the King's equerry! Ridiculous. I never will curry favor with him, Orkenay," Alban said, his voice becoming flinty. "I *never* will. Not after his behavior to his father."

In the ordinary, yet agreeable, routine of every day, a letter from Lady Eliza's nephew, the Duke of Alban, was a pleasant distraction, Kittie Douglas thought as she handed the reins of the pony cart over to Jacob, the groom, after her weekly visit to the village. She retrieved her basket from the seat and, carrying it over one arm, strode into the gloom of the front hall of the house, sniffing appreciatively the aroma of freshly baked bread that mingled with beeswax polish and freshly laundered linens. Though she would have to watch her consumption of bread over the coming winter, she thought ruefully, looking down at her rounded form. Not enough exercise in the winter months and she would be as round as a plum pudding come next spring. She would not give a fig if it were only her looks that suffered, but excessive girth left her short of breath and she enjoyed her walking and gardening too much to make it a discomfort rather than a pleasure.

All of life was a balance of pleasures and pains, she thought, taking off her bonnet carefully and handing it to Prissy, the maid. Too much of the first, and one was sure to suffer the second. "Where is her ladyship?"

"In the morning parlor, ma'am," Prissy said, with a curtsy.

"Could you see that the packages Jacob will be bringing to the back door are handed directly to Cook,

Prissy? There is some fresh tongue and a ham for to-morrow's dinner."

"Yes'm."

Kittie moved serenely to the parlor and opened the door, pausing as she always did on the threshold. There was Lady Eliza Burstead sitting near the window, her face turned to the warmth of the sunshine coming in through the gauzy curtains. The knowledge that she had a letter to read her from her beloved nephew, Alban, was a distinct pleasure; Lady Eliza had been so very kind and was now more friend than employer, though Kittie was careful not to presume on that friendship. Any pleasure she could bring her was a blessing.

"My lady, you should have come into the village with me. Mrs. Connaught was asking after you."

Lady Eliza turned toward her companion. "Then she must have another letter from her daughter," she said, tartly, "for all she wants to ever do is discuss young Jemima's confinement. I am sick to death of the subject."

"I think you're right. She looked out her window as I passed, and I was not able to move on for at least fifteen minutes. Jemima is still not delivered of her child, but Mrs. Connaught is convinced it will be a boy this time."

"She has been convinced of that for the last eight times."

"How true." Kittie moved toward her employer. "I have more wool from Judy Boxcroft. Her dyes are a little thin this time, but she has managed a lovely blue that I have never seen before." She set her basket down and pulled out the letter, turning it over and tracing the ducal seal.

"Blue, yellow, green, it matters little to me."

"I know. But I have something here that *will* matter to you." She placed the letter on Lady Eliza's lap.

The woman picked it up and turned it over and over in her hands and then traced the seal on the back as well, her sensitive fingers finding the grooves in the lion rampant. "It is from Alban," she cried in satisfaction, handing it back to Kittie.

"It is!"

"What does he say?"

"Tea first, and then the letter."

"Tyrant," Lady Eliza said, tartly.

"Nevertheless, unless you plan to try to make it out yourself, you will have to await my pleasure, and my pleasure will come once I have a hot cup of tea before me."

Tea procured, she settled at the table by the window from which she had drawn back the curtains to allow in more of the early September sunshine. She broke the seal on the letter and read out loud the salutation, but skipped over the duke's thanks for the latest knitted stockings his loving aunt had sent. Lady Eliza did not need to hear that.

She read on. "He says, 'Brighton has been tedious and blistering hot this summer, and I have decided not to stay into the autumn. In fact, by the time you read this I shall be' . . ." Kittie squealed and jumped in her seat.

"What is it? What is wrong, Kittie?" Lady Eliza reached out and touched Kittie's face, tracing the lines of her mouth and eyes. "What is it?"

Kittie leaned forward and let her employer trace her smile. "It is good news, my lady. Very good news indeed. His Grace is . . . well, let me read you his own words. Where was I?"

"'In fact, by the time you read this I shall be' . . ." Lady Eliza repeated verbatim.

"Ah, yes. 'By the time you read this I shall be on my way up to Swaledale. I have decided to open the hunting box this fall and am arriving with a group of friends. We shall be spending at least a month, and perhaps longer'."

Lady Eliza was silent for a few moments, and Kittie looked up from the rest of the details of the letter, concerned by her employer and friend's silence. Her breath caught in her throat. Trailing down Lady Eliza's cheeks were two fat tears, and that from a woman who never cried, not even to mourn her quickly eroding sight.

"My lady, are you . . ."

Turning her face away, Lady Eliza mumbled something, and then said, more clearly, "If he is bringing friends, then we must prepare for a couple of dinners, at least, here. Tell Cook. Alban likes beef and mutton, and has a special fondness for trout."

"My lady . . ." Kittie hesitated.

"What is it?"

"I . . . I suppose . . . remember we spoke of this? I was having a couple of friends come to visit in the next couple of weeks; remember my two widowed friends? I should go and write letters to postpone their visits . . ."

"Nonsense. If Alban is bringing gentlemen, then a couple of your friends will balance it out nicely and give the gentlemen a reason to come here to the cottage," Lady Eliza said, sardonically, her tears drying swiftly on her cheeks. "They might ordinarily avoid an old blind aunt of Alban's, but if there are women, they will come."

Kittie laid one hand over Lady Eliza's folded hands. "I'm sure His Grace would need no further incentive to come to see you but your own self. Anyone who knows you will always love your company."

"You are a good girl, Kittie," Lady Eliza said. "Leave

me now to think; I will have a few lists for you to make over the next couple of days, so run along. Is that all there was in the letter?"

"Yes," Kittie said, conning over the rest of the missive. "I will read the rest to you by the fire tonight, but really all he says is that he will save all of his other news and court gossip for his visit. And of course, he gives you his love." She folded the letter, slipped it into her pocket, and took her leave of Lady Eliza. She had much to do, but first—

First, she climbed the narrow staircase to her room on the third floor and crossed to her dressing table, taking a velvet pouch out of the drawer. She sat on her bed and spilled out the contents of the pouch and chose one item.

It was a tiny painting of a very lovely young woman; she had black glossy hair, the color of a raven's wing, and wide gray eyes. Around her neck she wore a necklace of brilliant sapphires. Her expression, caught by the talented painter, was of wistful hope and limitless optimism. Kittie laid it back down on the dark coverlet and picked up the next item, a letter. She unfolded it and once more read the lines she had read a hundred times in the last three years.

This letter should come as no surprise. You will well know why I am leaving, Alban, for you have been Inconceivably Cruel in your behavior over the last years, and Jonathan has convinced me that you will never treat me with the Kindness I deserve. He loves me, and will see me Suffer no Longer, and so he is taking me to Italy. Where you have ever been Sarcastic and Cutting and Brutish, he is Gentle and Sweet and Kind. I think that I never Loved you, after all, for I could not have Loved you and yet think of you now with such Revul-

sion. I wish you every kind of Catastrophe. Good-bye.
Signed, Your Wife In Name Only, Catherine.

Kittie folded the letter, pushing it back into the black velvet sack. She lay back on the bed and thought over the last three years that she had been in Lady Eliza's employ. As her ladyship's sight had deteriorated, she had taken on the task of reading to her the letters she received from various friends and most importantly, from the duke, Lady Eliza's nephew.

And she had often sat in the dining room and stared at the Duke of Alban's painting—albeit it was of him as a very young man—over the sideboard, tracing in his handsome face and large dimensions the man who wrote entertaining and yet loving letters to his aunt. How could he be one and the same with the man who was written such a hateful letter by his wife, the same wife who ran away with a courtier and died in a boating accident off the Adriatic coast?

If she trusted her instincts, and she had had to since her own tragedies had almost overwhelmed her, she would believe him to be a good man, a kind man, saintly almost. And so very handsome. Regal. Courtly. Polite. Good-natured.

She sat up with a deep sigh. It would do her no good to moon over the man when she had not even met him. There was much to do if he was already on his way north and could arrive within, at the most, a couple of days.

But what would she do when she met him, this man who had become a demigod in her mind? She would have to rein in her wandering imagination or he would know in a second how she felt, and how intimately and how often she had thought of him.

She would certainly have to tamp down her wildly imaginative nature, for in her mind he had become a golden idol, almost, and it was impossible that any living man would live up to her expectations. Or was it? Maybe he was everything she imagined, and then what would she do?

Two

A long, loud groan was the first thing Alban heard upon waking, and yet surely he was alone. Or was that . . . the duke opened his eyes on the sight of his inn room and the bright stripe of sunlight that bisected the chamber through the almost-closed curtains. Yes, his bed was empty other than his own self, and yes, that had been that same self groaning so loudly.

He swung his legs around and sat on the edge of the bed, holding his aching head in both hands. The room whirled around for a moment and then settled, as he kept his eyes closed. What had he done?

He remembered his friends, the private dining room of the inn they had stopped in outside of Harrogate, then there was the obsequious innkeeper and the pretty barmaid who had been assigned to them exclusively. He remembered playing cards long into the night with Orkenay, Fitzhenry, and Bart, and many tankards of ale, followed by many bottles of wine, followed by—

Followed by the barmaid on his lap, a few rounds of a local song, "When North I Came a'Questing," which he taught his companions, and a tickling bout with the giggling girl, a redhead, if he remembered. He did like redheaded girls, despite what fashion would say.

Alban opened one eye; the room had stopped

whirling and that was a good sign. It was a simple room, done up in some Yorkshire landlady's idea of elegance, with the ubiquitous touches in the Swaledale region of knitted coverlet and homespun curtains.

There was a tap at the door and a redheaded maid came swishing in with a pitcher of hot water. She curtsied, crossed to the dressing stand, and poured the steaming water into the ceramic bowl on the top.

Alban watched her; was she the same girl who had served them in their dining room the night before? And did he have anything to apologize for? For he was not one of those who thought that his elevated position excused every kind of behavior.

"Tea in a tic, Yer Grace," the girl said, her cheeks turning pink from simply having to address a duke, it seemed.

Hmm, he remembered the redheaded barmaid as a forward lass, not shy. "Good," he replied. "I shall breakfast in the dining room with my companions. Are they awake yet?"

She shook her head.

"Do I . . . uh . . ." Alban passed one hand over his gritty eyes. "I hope I did not offend anyone by my behavior last night. And yourself, miss, I hope I was not too free . . ."

"T'was m'sister who served you in the dining room last night, Yer Grace."

"Right. Of course. I hope I did nothing to affront the young lady, your sister, then. Please tell my friends that we will breakfast within the half hour. I don't want to spend too long, for we have a ways to go yet."

The girl curtsied and exited, and Alban crossed to the dressing table, splashed some cold water from the standing jug into the basin of hot water, and performed his morning ablutions. His head still ached, but he felt somewhat more human as he left the room, negotiating the narrow passage with some difficulty—it was not created with someone of his large frame in mind, certainly—and descended to the dining room.

He was grateful, as he sat down by the fire, that he at least did not have anything to regret as he would if he had awoken with a woman in his bed. It was too soon after dismissing his mistress, *la petite* Jacqueline, to even consider bedding another female. Much too soon. Betrayal tainted his memories of her, and although she had been surpassingly good at the skill all mistresses should be proficient at, he would not change how things stood. It had been time to end it. He missed her, oddly enough, even after finding out that she was passing on every scrap he told her to someone in Prinny's household; with whom she had been in league he might never know. But hearing Prinny relay a certain piquant piece of unsubstantiated—and false—gossip had been the one thing that had confirmed Alban's suspicions, for he had passed that tidbit on to Jacqueline with the knowledge that if Prinny did appear to know about it, then it confirmed the duke's worst fears.

His lovely, flirtatious, and skillful mistress was a traitor to him. He did not trust easily, and so betrayal stung like nettles.

Agitated by the memories, wanting forgetfulness, Alban stood and crossed to the window that opened onto the back garden. He swung open the casement, and a bird fluttered up from a morning feast on the pavement; a half-eaten worm wriggled around on it, and the hungry bird swooped back down and retrieved his treasure, then retreated to a more private dining area. Birdsong fluted through the misty morning air, and somewhere a cheery stablehand was whistling; it was "When North I Came a'Questing," and Alban grinned. They truly were in Yorkshire, and it was enough to make his heart glad. They were half a day's ride away from his hunting box and his Aunt Eliza. She would likely see them coming and would be out to greet them before they even stabled their horses. He remembered so well her long, loping stride from days gone by. She really was the most unusual woman, with the sensibility, sometimes, almost of a man. For she had no patience with whining, no time for tears, and a raucous laugh.

But how she loved children. And how she had loved him, even when he was fractious or impertinent, even when he was broody and impolite. She would simply glare at him, box his ears, and demand that he behave.

She had been the one stable force in his young life, for the seventh duke, his father, had been on one diplomatic mission after another, and his mother had been caught up in London entertaining or visits to Italy. He had spent more of his school vacations with Lady Eliza, the seventh duke's spinster sister, than with his parents. In that family history he was not unusual among his friends, but he was sensitive enough as a lad to wish it otherwise.

"Alban, what ho? Did you really have to send that redheaded termagant to awaken us?"

The duke turned to find his three companions groggily trooping in. It was Orkenay who had spoken, of course. He always was the most vocal of the gang. But of the three, he best knew his old friend Bartholomew Norton, third son of the Earl of Awnlea, and his boon companion from school days. When he realized his trip north would not be a solitary one, he had immediately thought of Bart, who had recently suffered a few setbacks that had left him gloomy. Bart knew Alban's Aunt Eliza from the old days, and would be glad to see her again.

But the third man who followed Orkenay and Bart

was almost unknown to Alban, and he couldn't imagine how Sir John Fitzhenry had insinuated himself in on the trip. Fitzhenry was a younger man, a baronet, good-looking and jovial, but mostly known by Alban as a hanger-on in the court of Prinny. So why did he interpose himself in this journey?

"I did set the lass on you all," Alban said. "I will not have you laggards lying in bed all day. We have a half day's ride ahead, and I prefer to ride well fed. I have ordered breakfast and they have promised to bring ale and coffee."

Orkenay groaned, and Bart was silent, as usual.

"I have already been out for a walk, Your Grace. Beautiful country, this part of the world. I have never been this far north." Fitzhenry had a cheery smile and it was obvious that he spoke no more than the truth. He had, by appearances, been up for a couple of hours.

"Then you will like my situation at Boden House, my hunting box. It is set in the prettiest hills for miles around."

Sir John Fitzhenry: There was a puzzle to give Alban pause. Was the young man trying to ingratiate himself with the duke? It was possible. He had many estates in his holding and many positions at his command, and gentlemen had in the past made the attempt to befriend Alban for the favors he could bestow. Few knew how he despised sycophants, but if a fellow proved to be steady, reliable, and worthy, he was not opposed to helping him along in his career. Fitzhenry had to this point not proven to be sycophantic, nor groveling. He would bear watching. In time he would inevitably reveal his reasons for pushing himself into this party.

As they ate, each devoting himself to the various dishes of kippers, curried eggs, ham, beef, mutton, pigeon, and toast, with jams and relishes accompanying them, there was silence, and before the half hour was up, they were on horseback again.

Alban thought ahead to his sojourn at Boden House. He could not imagine that it had been three years since he had been north, but he supposed that first, after the blur of misery over his wife's desertion, and then finding out about her death, he had existed in a kind of fog for a while. Not very manly to be so consumed by grief as he was for a time, but though he did not make a show of his emotions, he felt the pain of her abandonment keenly. Her death was a severe blow, coming as it did a mere month or so after she had left him.

It was then that he had retreated to Yorkshire, not even bothering with the usual folderol of opening Boden House, staying instead at his aunt's house on the grounds, Bodenthorpe Cottage. By the time he left Yorkshire to return to London she had roused him back into some semblance of himself, but in the three intervening years he supposed he had not even wanted to think about going back to the scene of so much despair as he had felt while there. He had been grateful to hear that she had retained a companion, for, stubborn as she was, Eliza would not even consider moving south, even though he could tell even in his abstracted state that her eyesight was failing a bit. It eased his conscience and made not going to see her easier, more shame to him, for he knew all the gifts he sent and his regular letters did not make up for his lack of attention.

That companion, a Mrs. Douglas—he pictured a widow of a certain age, upright, vigorous, and with a wrinkled, pursed mouth—had taken over many of Lady Eliza's duties, including the actual writing of the letters, though he could tell by the wording that they were dictated by Eliza. It was a good thing she did so, for his aunt's handwriting had always been atrocious, and she crossed and recrossed the page so many times it occasionally took his secretary to make out the words. In the months after his return to London, it seemed that they got much worse, the lines slanting crazily across the page, and it was a relief to be able to read the neat, elegant hand of the widow Mrs. Douglas.

The day was brilliant, with a clarity that turned even the most ordinary sight into a jewel; a rambling shack, in the brilliant sun and set against the cerulean sky, appeared to be an artist's picturesque setting. And the hills as they rose and fell, first cradling the Nidd, then the Ure and then, finally, as midday passed, the Swale rivers, were a glorious green, zigzagged with stone fences.

Bart was quiet as they rode, even when they stopped at an inn to partake of lunch. But Orkenay, of course, was talkative enough for all four of them.

"How far are we from your hunting box?" he asked as they rode along the Swale after stopping briefly at Richmond. He moved in his saddle. "I have not done this much riding for a decade or more, and I fear I ache. And I do not feel quite myself without the attentions of my valet."

"Not more than an hour," Alban replied, hiding his grin at the earl's grumbling. When he had proposed making it a riding tour of the moors, the earl had protested, but when Alban held firm he did not back out of the trip, as the duke had half expected he would. Instead he had sent his valet north with Alban's, ahead of them, with the full complement of servants and luggage. "We leave the Swale at Grinton and travel north a few miles along the Arkle Beck, and we are there."

"I never suspected this was such beautiful country," Sir John said, his tone awed as he pulled his horse to a halt and gazed around him.

Alban, with fresh eyes, took in their surroundings.

From the banks of the Swale the green hills rose in an emerald sweep of majesty, with dry gray stone fences—the builders had used no mortar, yet the fences stood for centuries—demarcating properties and fields and wooded copses dotting the slopes. "And you have only just entered; wait until you have seen Boden's situation."

"And met Lady Eliza," Bart said, the first words he had uttered in hours.

Alban cast him a swift look and was overjoyed to see color in his friend's pale visage and a sparkle in his blue eyes. Bart had always been of a melancholy cast, and though Alban had never understood his friend's long, brooding periods and occasional withdrawals from society, he valued Bartholomew too much to abandon him for that character flaw, if such it was. He thanked the inspiration that had urged him to invite his friend north with them, for Bart had been in one of his withdrawals, and this was rousing him nicely. Lady Eliza had always been good for him, and perhaps would still have that magic.

"Yes. My aunt is the most vigorous country woman I have ever known. It is she who taught me how to hunt, and that is why she has stayed north, I think. She could live anywhere she likes but she prefers this district, even though she was born and raised, of course, with my father at Alban Hall. She moved north when I was still a lad, so upwards of twenty years ago. She has never explained why. Just her preference, I suppose. She always did like the wild country."

Orkenay said, "Yes, I have heard many a story about Lady Eliza and her unique preferences."

It was said with an innocuous tone, but something in the earl's manner made Alban watch him for a moment.

"Regardless, gentlemen," Sir John said, breaking the

brief silence, "let's ride on, or we shall stand our horses too long. Mine is restive already."

Soon they turned away from the Swale and followed Arkle Beck, then even turned away from that humble stream. The sun had passed its zenith and was descending toward the west hills when finally they passed onto land belonging to Boden House. From above, on the crest of a long fell, Alban could see the wooded glades planted centuries before by his ancestors for their hunting pleasure, and the long road that led through his property.

"We're here," Alban said. "This is my land."

As they drew closer he felt the anticipation build, and he realized he had missed his aunt fiercely, though he supposed he would not have recognized the feeling if he had not been about to see her. She was a rock in a shifting world when he was but a boy.

As they rode along the fence-lined road, they passed the ruins, in the distance, of Mawkethorpe Castle. He stopped, as always, to gaze at it.

"What is that?" Sir John asked, riding up alongside Alban.

Alban supplied the name, and then said, "It goes back to before the first Duke of Alban was ceded this property. I always stop to look at it. It makes me sad, and yet inspires me. I don't know why."

"You don't know why it inspires you, or why it makes you sad?"

"Both, I suppose. But I always look at it," Alban said, pointing and tracing the outline of the ruined roofline, "and think that it is like a very old person. Look, the two windows left are like eyes, but they are just black holes. It's like the old fellow has gone blind, and I can't help but be sad."

"And yet it inspires you?"

Alban thought for a moment, then tried to explain.

"Because it has survived so long, even blasted and ru- ined as it is. It is so ancient, no one is quite sure how long it was there before it was destroyed in the wake of Henry Tudor's ascension to the Crown. They tried to pull it down, but it resisted, and so remains, unusable but somehow alive."

"You are a fanciful fellow, aren't you?" Orkenay said, riding up on the other side of Alban. "Are we going to arrive at Boden House today, by any chance? I'm per- ishing for a drink."

They rode a few more minutes, up another long slope, and then—

"There it is," Alban said to his companions. "There's Boden House."

They had halted their mounts at the crest of a long slope and gazed down at the valley on the other side. Boden House, a limestone manor house of ample di- mensions, was set on the hillside, clinging like a stubborn ram. Just beyond its mossy walls, a forest of beech and alder spread down, and a private road led through the woods to Bodenthorpe Cottage, a lovely little three-storey brick home with walled gardens and thick hedges, where Lady Eliza lived. Beyond that again, a few miles distant in the valley, was the village of Loxton.

"Gloomy," Orkenay said, gazing around at the fells that stretched on as far as the eye could see and disap- pearing into the mist. He shivered. "I still need that drink, but I think I shall ask for mulled wine. Damned cold in these hills."

Alban glanced over at him and chuckled. He still felt the excesses of the night before, but he never let it af- fect his plans for the next day. He might not have chosen Orkenay as his companion again if he had the chance to go back—there was something oily in the man's demeanor that had always made him uneasy—

but in that moment all he knew was that he was home, home in a way he hadn't felt in a long time.

Taking Orkenay's increasingly pointed hints, Alban rode on, followed by his friends, and soon they turned onto the long winding lane that led them to the hunting lodge.

Greeted by the staff and by his own valet, who had been sent ahead with luggage and orders to hire extra staff for the months he would be in residence, Alban left his companions to settle while he, impatient, exited Boden and walked through the woods to his aunt's house.

Would she be watching for him out the window? Or would she be out walking the property, as restless as always?

Of course, she didn't know the exact time, nor even the exact day of his arrival, so unless her serving staff had seen them coming she would be just going about her business. That appealed to him, stealing up behind her, mayhap, and covering her eyes. Of course she would know in an instant it was he, but how lovely to surprise her for just that moment.

He rapped on the front door but then entered, too anxious to wait. The hall was as dark as he remembered, but spotless, with brasses shining and the mingled scents of beeswax and the floral aroma from the heaped bowl of chrysanthemums tickling his nose.

A maid entered the hall and started, then curtsied.

He stared at her. "You have very much the look of Mrs. Ranulph, my housekeeper at Boden."

"M'mother, Yer Grace," she said.

"I have come to see my aunt. Where would she be?"

"In the front parlor, to be sure. She doesn't stray much beyond that after tea."

"Well, that is unlike her!" Alban said. "She always

loved to wander after lunch, up the hills and through the forest."

The girl gave him an odd look and didn't answer.

"I'll go in to see her, then. Don't announce me. I want to surprise her."

Three

Kittie knit steadily, but also watched her employer, who sat facing the window. Though she seemed the picture of serenity, Lady Eliza was fretful, and Kittie thought she knew why. The woman had not, in the time that Kittie had been there, said one word in any letter to her nephew about her increasing blindness. Why, Kittie was not sure.

From what she could piece together, the encroaching darkness had started even before the duke's last visit. When the duke did come north last and stayed at Lady Eliza's house rather than Boden, it was during the awful time following the duchess's abandonment of her husband and her subsequent death in a boating accident. Lady Eliza had likely not wanted to add to the duke's understandable sorrow during that time, but why not in the intervening years? Surely it was natural to share that information with her closest and most beloved relative? But no, Lady Eliza had remained sequestered for those three years, not even letting the news leak out to her other relatives; there were not many she was close to, for some reason Kittie did not clearly understand. That there was some mysterious sorrow in Lady Eliza's past Kittie had so far surmised, but what it was she had no idea.

Still, it seemed to Kittie that it would have been nat-

ural to confess her failing eyesight and ask Alban to
come up for a visit before it was gone entirely.

And yet she hadn't.

"Shall I ring for more tea, my lady?"

"No, Kittie. I shall float away if I have one more cup."

"Would you like me to read to you?"

"No! I can hear your needles clacking away, my dear.
Don't stop for me."

"But it would be no trouble . . ."

"No! Stop fussing, Kittie. I know what this is about,
and I will handle it in my own way."

Kittie fell silent and resumed her knitting. But her
heart would not stop thumping, and her fingers trembled. The duke was coming, likely that day or the next.
The very man whose portrait hung in the dining room,
and whose visage she had examined every day for almost three years . . . and he would soon be there. She
had conned over his letters, reading them to herself
much more often than even to her ladyship, and she
had oft examined the miniature of his wife and her last,
resentful letter. Having been married once herself in
a far-from-perfect union, she was looking for clues, perhaps, as to how their relationship had broken down to
such an extent that the woman had felt compelled to
take the extreme measure of abandoning her marriage.

What could make a woman married to not only a
duke, but the Duke of Alban, and not just any man, but
one of the handsomest, most sophisticated, kindly, gentle—from his aunt's reports, and who should know him
better?—men of his rank ever to grace that position,
desert him? Every man, woman, and child in
Swaledale, without exception, had only praise for the
duke as a landowner, gentleman, master, and relation,
distant or near.

And yet the social censure of abandoning one's husband was not a step taken lightly by any woman with a scrap of dignity, much less a duchess, and the daughter of a duke, as the Duchess of Alban had been. Something had made her life intolerable, but without knowing the lady, Kittie could guess all she wanted and would never truly know.

But she would soon know the man, the duke, would meet him and see him, perhaps daily. She glanced down at her knitting and felt a flush rise to her cheeks. She stretched out the lengthy stocking, one to fit the dimensions of a very large man, and thought that perhaps she would put this project away for the time being, for it would surely not be seemly to be working on the duke's stocking while the duke himself was present. Such intimate apparel had ribald connections in many a cruder mind.

She heard a commotion in the hall and rose from her chair, but not before the door swung open.

And there on the threshold of the room was the man himself, larger, older, even more handsome than his painting. She felt as though she would faint.

Alban paused in the doorway and drank in the homely scene. His Aunt Eliza he spied immediately, seated as she was by the window in the stream of sunlight. And then . . . he stopped abruptly. There was a lovely woman—glossy auburn hair, tall, voluptuous—half risen from her chair, knitting hanging loosely from one hand.

"Y—Your Grace," she stuttered, in cultured accents.

"Alban!" Lady Eliza cried, turning in her chair but not rising.

"Aunt Eliza," he said, and swiftly crossed the room in just a couple of strides. He bent over to hug her, overwhelmed by how glad he was to be there, and how happy to see her again.

Her fingers touched his face and hair as he hugged her to him and knelt by her side. For a moment he didn't trust his voice, but then he held her away from him and stared at her, drinking in the familiar angularity of her bony face and the homely hook of her nose, her iron gray hair coiled as always into a simple bun, and last but not least, her eyes. Always, her piercing gaze had had a way of finding the secrets of his heart, demanding that he share his sorrow or his happiness with her, his most beloved relative.

Her eyes. There was an odd silence in the room. He could feel rather than see that the young woman was standing behind him, waiting for something, some acknowledgment or word or release from Lady Eliza. He examined his aunt's eyes, wondering if their unfocused and hazy look was emotion, or—

"Aunt Eliza, are you quite all right? Is anything . . ."

She clutched his hand and held the back of it against her weathered cheek, rubbing it against the softness of her skin. "I am so glad you have come, Alban," she said, clearing her throat and speaking out.

And yet her voice was tremulous with emotion and husky. That was unlike her. Alban glanced over his shoulder at the young woman still standing there.

"Mrs. Kittie Douglas, Your Grace."

"You're the companion? I had imagined . . . but never mind." He turned back to his aunt and gazed steadily into her eyes. She seemed to stare back, and yet there was some subtle difference in her gaze, some lack of knowledge, some . . . lack of sight. The pupils were milky looking instead of clear black.

All the strength left Alban and he slumped to the floor at her feet. "Why didn't you tell me? When did this happen?"

"Alban," Lady Eliza said, tugging at his hand, urging him up. "Do not disintegrate on me."

"How long?" He pulled a chair close to her with his free hand and sat across from her, tightening his grip and staring at her.

But she seemed lost for words.

Mrs. Douglas came forward and knelt by her employer's side, and he was distracted for a moment from his discovery. There was something . . . soothing about the woman, her very presence. She was beautiful, but there was something more.

"It didn't happen overnight," she said, her voice gentle, "but did accelerate about a year and a half ago. We had been trying to save her sight by not taxing it too severely before that, but the doctor said there was nothing that could be done. It is some kind of degeneration of the eyes, the left worse than the right, but most of the sight is gone now from both."

Eliza reached out with her one free hand and found Mrs. Douglas's and squeezed it. The younger woman tucked a stray gray tendril from Lady Eliza's bun behind her ear, and the older woman turned her face and let her companion's hand briefly cup her cheek. Alban could see between the two women not just reliance and gratitude and devotion, but true love, as a daughter for a mother might have.

"Why didn't you tell me?" he asked, his voice harsh and grating against the warm quiet of the room.

Lady Eliza released his hand and sat back, straightening. But she didn't let go of Mrs. Douglas's hand, he noticed. It was like a cord of strength stretched taut between them, with a pulse of energy that flowed back and forth, giving both some needed vigor.

"I didn't want to bother you with my . . ."

"You could not confide in your nephew, the one who means as much to you as any son could, so you once told me? I don't believe you." He stood and paced, angrily. "What a selfish thing to do, not to allow me the time to come see you, for us to walk and talk as we used to before your sight . . ."

"Stop!" Mrs. Douglas stood, too, and swiftly said, "Are you most angry at Lady Eliza, Your Grace, or yourself? For surely you could have come up any time in the last three years without such a reason. Do not berate her for your own failings."

"Kittie, enough," Eliza said. "Both of you. I will not have you at daggers drawn over me. I will be honest, nephew, if you will come and sit down again and stop that infernal pacing. You too, Kittie."

Alban forced his ire back down, though that was not an easy task. But as the analytical cast of his mind once more functioned, he recognized that his outburst had been spurred by fear; fear of the vast change that had taken place in his aunt's life, and yet she had done it alone. Or, not alone, but with only a stranger for her companion.

And shame. There was a strong thread of shame in his eruption, shame that he had never asked after her health, shame that he had noticed so little on his last visit, so shrouded in his own grief as he had been, and shame that he had not made the effort to come see her long before her blindness had closed in.

Mrs. Douglas had already sat back down and was bundling her knitting into a cloth bag. Alban took the seat opposite his aunt again and searched her face.

"Is it total?" he asked.

Calmly, his aunt said, "For a while I could see some dim images in very strong light, but that is gone now. It is total."

"How did it happen?" He took her hands in both of his and cradled them.

"I have known for a long time it was happening. This

same thing happened to my mother before she passed away. I recognized the symptoms."

"How brave you are," Alban whispered.

"Oh, but I am not. I have railed, I have begged, I have turned away from God, accusing Him of all manner of outrages. But when all that was done, there was nothing left but acceptance. Kittie helped me with that."

He turned and caught the young woman staring at him with an expression of such earnestness and yearning that it caught him off guard. What beautiful eyes she had, big and very blue, and a beam of sunlight touched her hair just then, setting it aflame with coppery highlights. Her gown was blue, almost the color of her eyes but unfashionable; even as plain as it was, though, it couldn't conceal the loveliness of her lush figure. When she caught his returning gaze, she glanced away shyly. He felt an unwilling spurt of attraction, surprising since the object was a woman so unlike his usual amours. She was tall and voluptuous, built on a larger scale than any woman he had ever been attracted to before. His usual conquests were petite and slim, dark-haired and with olive complexions.

He tore his gaze away and returned his attention to its proper object. There was a smile on his aunt's face, a sly expression of smug self-congratulation that he could not imagine a source for. He dismissed his reading of her countenance, for it couldn't be right.

"She's beautiful, isn't she?"

"Lady Eliza!" Mrs. Douglas said, standing and pacing away in agitation.

"She is," he agreed, enjoying the companion's discomfiture as was his aunt. Lady Eliza was still the same, he was happy to note, in some ways, not loath to enjoy herself at someone else's expense. "So," he continued, still trying to adjust to this new situation, "what now?

Are you happy here still, Aunt, or would you like to move to London, where it might be easier to get around?"

"Easier to get around in London? Not true. I know this house so well I have no trouble navigating here. And even the garden . . . before my sight was completely lost Kittie and I set it up with stone markers along the path so I cannot go astray. And I have a pony cart and can even use it alone, for old Lily knows the way to Loxton with no interference from me, and once there I have acquaintance aplenty to help me."

"You don't drive to the village alone?" he said, aghast.

She chuckled. "I knew that would astound you. I said I *can* do it, not that I *do*. It was enough, I found, to simply know that I could do it. I go to the village with Kittie, for it is much more pleasant to be on her arm anyway."

"You seem to have accepted all of this," he marveled. "No matter what you say about railing against God."

"I have had time," she said, simply. "And what cannot be changed must be accepted."

"Are you sure it is permanent and irreversible?"

"I am. I went to see a very good man in Edinburgh a year and a half ago . . . *we* went," she amended, indicating, with a wave of her hand, Kittie. "He has seen this condition before and they simply do not know how to stop it from happening. I had spectacles at first that helped, but now . . ." She trailed off and shrugged.

"You knew this was happening even when I was last here," he said, troubled by his own self-absorption.

"I was having trouble with my eyes," she admitted. "But I wasn't sure it would end in blindness. My mother, though she had the same condition, died before becoming completely blind."

He sighed, weary.

"You have had a long journey, Alban. You must have come over here immediately as you arrived, or we would have had advance word of your arrival at Boden. Go back and rest. We will visit later, when you're more rested."

He stood, holding on to her hand, squeezing it, then releasing it. "I should go and see to my guests."

"Who have you brought?"

"One of your favorites. You will be glad to see Bartholomew Norton, I think. He is much changed from his youth, you know."

"What, no longer the melancholy poet?"

Alban laughed, appreciating as always his aunt's incisive character descriptions. "Well, I don't know if he writes poetry anymore, but yes, he is still melancholy. He's . . . he's in a bad patch just now."

"We'll make him feel better," Lady Eliza said. She reached out, and her companion was there in a second, taking her hand as she rose and then releasing it and stepping back.

"I brought two other fellows. One very witty gentleman, the Earl of Orkenay. I don't think you've ever met him." Alban remembered Orkenay's slightly snide tone when he spoke about his aunt, and he tucked that away for future reference. "And a young fellow I just met, a Sir John Fitzhenry. Seems a likely enough lad."

"We are to be joined by a party ourselves," Lady Eliza said. "Two friends of Kittie's were to come for a visit; she wanted to postpone them when you wrote to tell us you were coming, but I said nonsense. Two more ladies will be just the thing to even out numbers at the dinner table."

"I will know tomorrow what day they will arrive," Kittie said.

It was the first time she had spoken for a while, and he thought immediately how lovely her voice was, no shrill notes, just soft and clear. Again, that random spurt of attraction flared, and he watched her eyes, how her gaze slipped away from him and a pretty blush mounted her cheeks.

"I look forward to meeting your friends, Mrs. Douglas," he said, as he mused that there was nothing more enticing than a clear indication that a woman was attracted to and appreciative of one's self. She was attracted, and so was he. If it had not been for the fact that she was his aunt's valued companion, he would look forward to flirtation, then a conquest, then an affair. She was a widow, he a widower; if they had a brief and mutually pleasurable liaison it was no one's business but their own.

But he couldn't. He acknowledged it with regret. She was beyond reach, her position with his aunt much too important to jeopardize with an affair. After all, what would it say of her morals if she did acquiesce? He had no doubt she would—she was a widow, after all, and accustomed to a man's attentions, and yet mired in the Yorkshire wilds—but as long as she remained untouched, he could imagine her a companion fit for his aunt by virtue of her coldness and frigid morality.

The hypocrisy of that struck him, but he shrugged mentally and let it go. It remained; if he seduced her, he could no longer consider her a fitting companion for his aunt and he would have to replace her, and his aunt seemed to genuinely love the young woman. Ergo, she was forbidden to him.

He experienced a twinge of disappointed lust, and it made him think that perhaps he *was* ready for another woman, and perhaps for a woman as little like *la petite* Jacqueline as the luscious Mrs. Kittie Douglas. It was just that he was accustomed to having his pick of women, and when one attracted him it was not in his nature to forego the inevitable consummation of their mutual attraction.

But he was not a child, nor a lad, to take what he wanted when he wanted it and damn the consequences.

He turned back to his aunt after gazing steadily at the widow long enough to cause her considerable discomfort. "I'll come back this evening, if you like, Aunt."

"No. Come for breakfast tomorrow morning and we will discuss what you and your friends will do while you are up here, besides drinking, gambling and shooting, I mean."

Alban took her free hand in his and kissed it. "I didn't realize how much I had missed you until I saw you again. I should be soundly whipped for ignoring you for so long."

"You didn't ignore me, Alban," Lady Eliza said. "Not many nephews are as good to their aunts, I think. Letters almost every week, gifts, game, and the attentions of your staff at Boden; that is in no way being ignored."

"Hmm. I suppose. I still cannot believe that even Stuart Lafferty," he remarked, naming the Boden estate manager, "did not tell me what was going on . . . your . . . your blindness." He choked on the word. To say it in relation to the strongest woman he had ever met hurt. And yet she would despise pity; it would offend her if she found that he did sincerely feel sorry for her and her situation.

"It was by my express wishes. I said I would have him sacked if he told you. I wanted to do it myself, to tell you in my own time and in person."

"And I made you wait three years. I'm sorry." In a rare gesture—for him—he leaned forward and kissed her cheek. When he looked up it was to see Mrs. Douglas standing nearby and watching with tears wet on her cheeks.

Four

"So," Lady Eliza said, "breakfast tomorrow, and bring Bartholomew. I want to see him again."

He squeezed her hands and kissed her cheek once again and said, "I will be happy to bring Bart. Maybe you can cheer him up. Nothing I say seems to work."

Kittie, surreptitiously wiping the tears from her cheek, was amused by the surprised look on her employer's face and thought that perhaps His Grace had not been much of a cheek-kisser in past.

He bowed to Kittie and then strode from the room; he was gone, and she had survived, but not unshaken. She sat down by Lady Eliza and tried to compose herself. It wouldn't be easy.

Sighing deeply and adjusting herself uneasily on her chair, Lady Eliza took another deep breath. Perhaps she, too, was shaken. It had been an emotional moment for her; Kittie gratefully turned to her care for her employer and away from her own reaction to the duke.

"Are you all right, my lady?" Kittie said, reaching out to the woman and touching her hand.

Lady Eliza nodded once. "I will be all right. I do not think I realized how much I was dreading the moment when I would be forced to tell Alban until it happened, but it is over now."

"What was to dread about it? He obviously cares for you so much . . . it was impossible that it wouldn't hurt him, but he's a strong man."

The older woman shook her head, and her expression became contemplative. "I thought that was it. I thought it was just that I knew how much it would hurt him, this humbling experience of mine, but now I know what it was."

Kittie waited, choosing not to prod. Lady Eliza frowned, fiddled with her dress material, but finally continued. "I was always the one he could turn to, in past years. Alban's mother was flighty, vain, and though I suppose she loved Alban, she never stayed in one place long enough to show him. I despised her. My brother should never have married such a . . ." She stopped and shook her head. "So judgmental," she murmured. "I always was so judgmental. My fatal flaw, I very much fear, and the cause of much sorrow in my life."

"You shouldn't criticize yourself so!" Kittie said, squeezing Lady Eliza's bony hand.

"I am afraid there is much to criticize." She rallied and sighed. "But . . . I was proud that Alban began to turn to me. I gloried in always being the one who was strong and sure, there for Alban in ways no one else was. His mother continually disappointed him; he could never count on her. Though . . . perhaps if I had not always jumped in so swiftly she would have had time to react to his boyish crises."

Kittie waited.

"But now I am less than I was, felled by the encroaching blackness. It is pride, pure and simple, Kittie, pride humbled by nature. If I believed in a vengeful God I would suspect that he was singling me out for this particular punishment." She chuckled and shook her head. "But is that not *hubris*, too? To think I matter so very much? If I have learned anything it is how little I matter in the scheme of the world."

"You matter very much to some of us, and I think His Grace is one of those to whom you matter so very much."

"Thank you, Kittie, that was gracefully said indeed." The woman stiffened her back and shook her head. "I will be all right once I have had time to reflect. It is over. The worst is over."

"You should have told him what was going to happen when you first suspected. Then it would not have had to come to this."

"I know that now. But it is over," she repeated. "What do you think of my nephew now that you have met him?"

Kittie sighed. How could she answer? It had been a frightening experience in a way, to see the painting come alive, the man appear, and to see how much more he was than her wretchedly unprepared imagination had made him. A cool, pale portrait could not begin to do the living, breathing man justice. But whatever she said to his aunt, she did not want to reveal too much of how she felt. She dreaded appearing ridiculous.

"I think he loves you very much," she said.

"That is an evasion, my dear. What do you *think* of him."

"He's . . . so *big*," she said, in a breathless tone. "Most men are my height or shorter. He is vastly taller and . . . *big*." She meant big beyond the physical, big in every sense, big in the way of filling the room with his life essence, but it would sound beyond foolish to try to put those things in words.

But by the sly smile on Lady Eliza's gaunt face she very much feared the woman was reading behind the words, maybe more than she even thought she was saying.

"He has always been a large lad. And? How is his appearance?"

"He . . . appears different from the old painting of him in the dining room. Older of course, but more than that . . . different. His hair, though still brown, has gold streaks in it as though he has been much out in the sun without a hat. And his mouth . . . his expression is very firm."

"How observant you have been. What else? What think you of his character, and his behavior?"

"Other than my commentary on the purely physical aspects of the duke, I will reserve judgment until I know him better," Kittie replied. "You shall not coerce my thoughts until then."

"Very well," Lady Eliza said, by her grin appearing highly entertained. "Very well. I shall ask again, you know, as his visit wears on."

"And I may still reserve my judgment."

Alban retired early but had a restless night, although his serving staff had done the usual superb job and had the house prepared perfectly. He arose in the morning not truly rested but revivified just by the knowledge of where he was, and that he could walk out the door and there, around him, would lay the splendor of Yorkshire, rising above him in swooping fells.

Boden, nestled on the sloping side of one of those fells, felt like home. He had spent many happy times here, though none of them with his duchess. Catherine had disdained Yorkshire, claiming it was well known that Yorkish folk were little better than the Scots, and the Scots were little better than brutes.

He shook off that melancholy memory and went to

rouse his friend. He had told Bart about Lady Eliza's blindness over a glass of port the evening before, but that fellow had been surprisingly philosophical for such a gloomy gent. He had merely remarked that of all the people he knew in the world, Lady Eliza was likely the one person who could survive and triumph without crawling away in misery. If it happened to him, he would surrender and would likely just sit in a dark room all day and feel sorry for himself. Alban would turn to drink and rage. But Lady Eliza would find a way to turn it to advantage.

Very sage words from someone who knew her well. Alban was no happier about her lot, but it was not for him to deal with. He would, though, try to convince his aunt to come back to London with him, or at least to Alban Hall, where she could be properly looked after.

He asked a passing footman where Mr. Norton was, and was told he was out in the garden awaiting the duke's pleasure. Alban exited the house and was struck afresh by the grandeur of Swaledale, damned by some as grim, stark, and gloomy.

The fells, high, round-topped hills fit only for sheep and Yorkshiremen, were magnificently unchanged and unchangeable, oddly comforting in a world where people, with their petty concerns, could be swept away in a moment. It gave perspective to life. Alban felt as though he had been examining life through the lens of a microscope, only to look up and see the great wide world was still there, waiting for him to discover that there was more than his minute concerns.

He took in a deep lungful of fresh air and coughed. Lord, but it was fresh.

The very thing he loved about Boden was its age—it was hundreds of years old and had served as a hunting lodge for a courtier of Elizabeth's—but also its lack of pretension. It was a hunting box, with no aspiration to be anything more. The front door was porticoed, and there was a crushed white limestone walk leading around between hedges to the back garden.

Alban strolled and halted, not wanting to join Bart just yet. For one thing, Bart was fastidious, and Alban badly wanted a cigar before he went down to see his aunt. He heard murmuring voices somewhere, and idly wondered who it was as he strolled off the walkway and over the dew-jeweled grass. He could see that Lafferty was doing his usual excellent job; even though Alban had not been there for three years, the grounds were immaculate, with rolling stretches of green grass and impenetrable hedges. There were many projects that Lafferty had proposed over the intervening years and that Alban had agreed to, and he could see the outcome in the new pathway that wound back behind the house and would climb the fell to a spot where a small waterfall gushed and a new bridge was built by Lafferty's staff.

The voices were louder, and Alban recognized Sir John Fitzhenry's tones. He turned the corner of the house and there was the young baronet with one of the housemaids. Both started, guiltily, and Sir John waved as the girl scurried away.

"Your Grace, what a beautiful morning."

Alban, grinning, joined him. "One thing, Sir John; if you are setting up a flirtation with one of the maids, please do it in such a manner so as not to interfere with the household too badly. Help is hard to find, and Mrs. Ranulph will box my ears if one of the girls is moping from a broken heart."

He was overjoyed to see the normally unflustered young man turn scarlet.

"I was not flirting, sir, I was just . . . asking a favor."

"Is that what you young men call it? Anyway, have you seen Bart?"

"Yes. I know where Mr. Norton is." The younger man led the way around to the back of the three-floor gray house.

Alban was not pleased to see Orkenay with Bart. Something about the earl had always made him uneasy, but since he could never pin down a cause for his unease—Orkenay was always affable, courteous, even friendly—he forced himself to ignore his niggling distaste.

"Well, good morning, Alban, Fitzhenry," Orkenay called out. "Shall we depart? I'm looking forward to meeting your aunt, Alban, since you have spoken so glowingly of her."

Alban shot a look at Bart, who shrugged helplessly. Though the breakfast invitation did not specifically exclude the rest of his party, he had hoped to have the morning with just his aunt and Bart. And perhaps the beauteous Mrs. Douglas. Just to even the numbers, of course.

He sighed and stubbed out his cigar. "Very well," he said, not bothering to clothe his acquiescence in any prettier attitude. "Let's go then. I wouldn't want to keep her waiting."

Bart, intimately familiar with every inch of Boden property from long association, led the way past the stable, the cow byre, and the dairy shed. He commented on a few changes, but fell silent when he didn't get an answer from Alban.

Alban lost his surly mood directly, but still felt no inclination to chatter; it was too tempting to just enjoy the peace of the north country, the whole reason he had thought of Yorkshire when he was standing on the midnight dark beach at Brighton in the August heat weeks before. The way to his aunt's home was down the fell through a wooded glade. At the tops of the fells trees were wind-bent, like old women carrying fagots to town to sell for kindling. But down fell was different. As one descended, the earth literally thickened, gathering in rich folds on the lower slopes and in the valley bottoms. That was where farmers grew hay in lush meadows, followed, after haymaking, by acres of waving meadow flowers.

Two hundred years ago trees had been planted around Boden in planned copses, and in the intervening years thickets of hawthorne and bramble had grown up around them, impenetrable to humans but haven for rabbits, partridge, pheasant, and grouse. It made for a harmonious blending of the wooded glades with the sloping landscape. The trees were beginning now, in early September, to think about shedding their summer green finery for more somber hues of gold and umber. Pine needles and old leaf mold coated the path and crunched underfoot as the party of men silently wove through the forest.

"I can almost imagine Beowulf and Grendel battling in just such a forest," Orkenay murmured uneasily, glancing off into the thick forest around them. A rabbit, startled, leaped away from the path directly beside him, and he jumped with a yelp of alarm.

Alban chuckled. "What school did you go to, Orkenay? You do know that Beowulf is set in Europe and that the people in it are Danes and the like?"

As Fitzhenry and Bart chuckled, Orkenay sniffed in disdain. "Yes, well, damned gloomy place, these woods. Thought it suited the melancholic atmosphere of that kind of thing; you know, heroes battling and dying, that rubbish. Don't enjoy forests myself. Just pictured some kind of epic battle being fought among these oaks, that is all."

Alban was tempted to point out that there were no oaks around him, but thought he had tweaked Orkenay enough for one morning.

"I know what you mean, though," Bart said, glancing around as they wound down the path, the towering centuries-old trees closing in over their heads and obscuring the sunlight. "There is an atmosphere here of the ancients, but I think more like fairies and sprites, nymphs and brownies. Alban, is the fairy waterfall still here, and the cavern?"

"Of course, idiot," Alban said, affectionately. "Where do you think a waterfall and a cave would go?"

With a good-natured grin, Bart said, "I shall go to see it and make my wish as we did as lads, then."

"Norton," Sir John said, referring to Bart, "was telling us that your aunt has become blind since last you saw her. How difficult that must be for you . . . and more so for her, of course. And yet she still chooses to live here, in Yorkshire?"

Alban glanced over his shoulder at the young man, thinking how delicate a way the fellow had chosen to indicate that they already knew about Lady Eliza's blindness, and yet made it a passing reference. The fellow could be a diplomat, he was so tactful. "Yes, you will find that my aunt is an independent spirit. She has always lived by her own rules."

"So I have heard," Orkenay murmured.

Alban stopped and turned back to Orkenay, provoked into a reply by the insinuating tone of the earl's voice. "See here, if you have something to say about my aunt, or if you think you know something about her, why don't you just say it?"

Orkenay pulled back in alarm. "Your Grace, I only meant that I had heard that she was exactly what you say . . . an independent woman, not bound by rules. I am so sorry if I have offended you in any way, but no more was meant than just that. I would never impugn the honor of a lady in any manner; I should think you would know me better than that, Alban!"

Caught, and seeing the eyes of the others on him in puzzlement, Alban muttered an apology. How could he explain that the offense was not in the words, but the tone?

"Does she live here alone?" Fitzhenry asked, quickly filling the silence as they all turned back to the path and continued their walk.

"No, she has a companion, a Mrs. Douglas."

"Older lady?"

"No, actually, she is only about thirty, or even younger, I suppose."

Bart spoke up, over his shoulder. "Alban told me last night that she is very beautiful, and for him to say that . . . I know how particular he is about feminine beauty, so I expect something extraordinary in the way of feminine pulchritude."

"Don't know why I said that," Alban muttered, reluctant to praise her too vociferously, though just Bart's words brought back the eyes, the skin, and the lush form of the widow Mrs. Douglas, and the dreams of her that had soothed those hours of the night when he did sleep. But she was not at all his type of woman, and she would never do as a mistress for other reasons he had already canvassed. He would put that from his mind.

"We shall judge for ourselves," Bart said as the gloom brightened and the trees thinned. "Here is the cottage." He stopped at the edge of the clearing.

Alban had strode into it so quickly the evening before that he had not had a chance to drink in its quaint loveliness, made more so by the last blooms of the roses that trailed the garden wall and gate and adorned the mellow gold stone walls, touched now by morning sunlight. It was very much a woman's home, though he didn't suppose he had ever thought of it in that way before. At one time, many years before, it had been the huntsman's cottage, but when Lady Eliza left London and Alban Hall, she had chosen Bodenthorpe Cottage as her home.

"It's lovely," Fitzhenry said. "But I'm famished."

Alban, roused from his reverie, said, "Yes, let's go in."

Kittie, fussing with the roses in a vase for the dining table in the breakfast room, heard tramping footsteps, but surely it was more than just two men? Or could the noise be attributed to the duke's overlarge feet? She almost giggled at the thought, and then restrained herself. She had determined that the best demeanor to assume in the face of her overwhelming idiocy in the company of the duke was one of withdrawal. He was there to see his aunt, after all, not her. She would neither thrust herself forward nor make more than the most simple of answers to any questions that should happen to be addressed to her.

She heard voices in the parlor. That must mean that His Grace and Mr. Norton had been shown in and were greeting Lady Eliza. She took a deep breath and summoned the courage to sally forth.

Entering the room was a shock. It was filled with men, black-coated, brown-coated and green-coated men. She was about to withdraw and regain her equilibrium, but Lady Eliza, even through the din, had heard her footsteps.

"Ah, here is Kittie now. Introduce the gentlemen, Alban."

The duke turned to her and seemed without words for a moment, his brown eyes fixed on her. But then he said, "Mrs. Douglas, may I make known to you Lord Orkenay, Sir John Fitzhenry, and my very good friend, Mr. Bartholomew Norton. Gentlemen, this is my aunt's valued friend and companion, Mrs. Kittie—or is it more properly Kath . . ." He stopped, his face blanched, but then shook his head. "Uh, Mrs. Kittie Douglas."

The gentlemen came forward and bowed over her hand, one by one. But Kittie's attention was caught by the duke, who had turned away and stared out of the window. What was wrong?

Lady Eliza said loudly, "Kittie's name is just that, Alban. It is not a diminutive of some longer name."

Kittie gazed around in confusion, but the duke stayed by the window.

"We were admiring the roses outside the cottage, Mrs. Douglas," the duke's friend, Mr. Norton, said. "Is that your handiwork?"

"I do garden and I do tend the roses, but my passion is herbs."

The earl, his tone smooth, said, "I'm delighted to hear you have a passion. All beautiful women should."

Kittie gazed at him in alarm. This was not how she had imagined this morning. She stuttered into speech. "I . . . I th—think breakfast is ready, gentlemen. I'll just have Prissy lay two more place settings."

Sir John gazed at her and then at Lord Orkenay. "I think we were not expected, my lord."

Orkenay said huffily, "I should think we would be. We are Alban's guests too, after all."

Kittie interjected, "My apologies, my lord, Sir John; I think it was my misunderstanding, not His Grace's. I was . . . somewhat scattered yesterday. We don't often have the favor of company here."

The moment passed, the earl's indignation soothed by her reply. She led the way into the dining room, noting that Mr. Norton was assiduous in his care for Lady Eliza. It warmed her heart. He was a good man, she thought.

The men were clearly ravenous, with Sir John heaping his plate high in the informal atmosphere of family dining. The earl, she noted, was a fastidious eater, picking the most ornate dishes, while the duke ate heaps of eggs, rashers of bacon, and racks of toast. Mr. Norton, Lady Eliza's self-appointed aide, filled her plate and then his own. They held a murmured conversation, no doubt catching up on all that had happened during the years they had not seen each other.

In watching the men, Kittie ate hardly at all, but suddenly remembered, as a maid filled the water pitcher on the sideboard with well water, what she had originally planned for the meal. "Oh," she said, leaping up. "I entirely forgot, my lady. I had intended the gentlemen to sample the ale I made this summer. It is just ready now."

"Oh, yes, by all means, give the gentlemen some of your ale," Lady Eliza said.

Kittie shot her a suspicious look, for the dry tone gave away little, but it was often evident when the woman was laughing at someone. But—"Prissy, will you bring out the sweet cicely beer for the gentlemen?"

"Sweet cicely beer? What is that?"

Kittie turned to the duke, who was her questioner. "I found in the attic a box of old receipts from a long-past housewife. It's fascinating, really," she said, as Prissy brought out the brown glass bottles and tankards. "For it is a glimpse into the past. Sweet cicely beer is said, according to the receipt, to be especially good for the digestion."

"Is that so?" the earl said. "I shall certainly have to try it, then, for I suffer from dyspepsia."

The bottles were unstoppered and decanted. Kittie could see that the beer was an odd greenish color, but she supposed that was merely because of its herbal origin. The gentlemen, as one, held up their glasses, and the duke said, "To your health, my friends, and to that of the ladies, more especially."

They all downed hearty gulps, and one second later there was a tumultuous response.

"Faugh," Sir John said. "That is . . . pardon me, ladies, but I must say it is the most foul stuff I have ever tasted."

"Foul doesn't begin to describe that," the earl said, wiping his mouth with his sleeve and grimacing horribly. "It is loathsome, disgusting, poisonous!"

Kittie stared, and Lady Eliza began to chuckle, then roar with laughter.

The duke blinked, swallowed, and blotted his lips. Kittie gazed at him. What would he say?

"It is . . . not the finest brew I have ever sampled," he said, quietly, pushing his pewter tankard away as Mr. Norton did the same without comment.

Tears welled up in Kittie's eyes, but Mr. Norton's words dried them in an instant.

"Tastes like what I would expect a cure for dyspepsia to taste like," he said with a shrug.

Struck by the humor, finally, Kittie giggled, then laughed out loud, joining her employer, and finally joined by most of the men.

Five

In the drawing room after breakfast, Kittie felt that the laughter had broken the tension, for her anyway, of unfamiliar gentlemen surrounding her. After three years in virtual isolation at Bodenthorpe Cottage, she still found all of the male attention strange.

Mr. Norton was devoted to Lady Eliza and spent the morning at her side. Sir John, after sitting for a while over coffee, bowed and said, if his hostess did not object, he would like to walk the grounds. He had never been to Yorkshire and would like to enjoy the scenic views. Lady Eliza graciously acquiesced, but with a thoughtful expression.

The duke and the earl, though, seemed, strangely, to be vying for Kittie's attentions, albeit in different ways.

"How did you come to be my aunt's companion, Mrs. Douglas?" the duke asked.

"I have a distant relation in Richmond whose daughter was attended, at her lying-in, by a midwife who is from Loxton, and she knew that Lady Eliza was considering a companion. She helped us contact each other."

The duke glanced across the room at his aunt. "Why did she not tell me she needed a companion?"

Kittie, knowing how assiduous the duke was in his attentions in the past, and how that still had continued, even though by mail, simply shrugged. She couldn't speak for Lady Eliza and couldn't say why she had not gone through her nephew for help, except that it seemed to her it may have been tied into why she didn't tell him how badly her sight had deteriorated. "She's a very independent woman. Maybe she wanted to do this for herself. If you had chosen a companion, she would have felt obligated to keep her even if they didn't get on. If she did the choosing herself, she could find what suited her best. I came, we seemed to be compatible, and she hired me."

"And why would you become a companion?"

Kittie stiffened. It was akin to asking her about her past, her finances, and her motives, she thought. If she had not known from reading his letters that he only had his aunt's good at heart, she would have considered him very rude.

The earl strolled over just then. "Now, Alban, you must not dominate Mrs. Douglas's valuable time. She is too pretty a woman for the quizzing you appear to be giving her." He sat down beside Kittie on the divan and moved closer.

Kittie would have moved away, for the earl was pressing his thigh to hers and it was a disturbingly intimate attention from a stranger, as well as embarrassingly familiar behavior, but there was no room for a retreat. She adjusted her skirts and said, "His Grace was not quizzing me, Lord Orkenay. He is within his rights to ask me a few questions, given his concern for his aunt."

"Wasn't questioning you that closely, was I?" the duke asked, shifting in his seat, his large frame overwhelming the delicate Sheraton chair.

She felt his annoyance, but whether it was with her or the earl, she could not be sure. "I believe I said as much just now, sir." Kittie felt a wave of exhaustion pass over her. Her days were normally passed in pleasant boredom, and this amount of socializing was tiring and filled her with an uncertain anxiety. The two men were shooting dark looks at each other, and she didn't understand how she had become some bone to be pulled at by them both.

"My dear," the earl said, patting her hands where they were twined on her lap. "Do not let this one bully you."

He left his hand in place, the heat of it damp on her clasped hands.

"He has a morose cast of character lately, you know," Lord Orkenay continued. "I found him on the beach at Brighton—at night, mind you—staring out at the ocean. Just . . . staring. One would have thought that he had lost his best friend."

Did the earl not know that the duke had lost his wife at sea a few years before? Kittie thought that he must not know the details, or he would surely not make such a tactless statement. She shot a glance at the duke, hoping the earl's remarks did not raise old specters.

Alban stood and bowed. "I had not realized I was interrogating the young lady, Orkenay. Thank you for pointing out to me the error of my ways." He strolled away and stared out the window.

How resentful a temperament he seemed to have, Kittie thought. It made her wonder afresh about his duchess's last letter to him, and her contentions of cruelty. She watched him absently, noting the fine shape of his muscular legs and his commanding height and breadth. It would be overwhelming, she thought, to be loved by such a man in every sense, but certainly the physical. His duchess was a dainty woman, Lady Eliza had told her, fine-boned and delicate, and the miniature of her bore out that description, and added large gray eyes, jet hair, and a look of romance. She was lovely, though there was a hint of sadness in those fine eyes; whether that was the artist's invention, Kittie could not know.

A wider contrast between the woman in the picture, now lost at sea, and her own self could not be imagined. Though why it should even occur to her to compare his duchess to herself, she did not know. No, that was a lie. She did know. She had imagined for so long meeting the duke and had supposed him to be some perfect paragon of male virtue. And had pictured herself as his ideal mate, the woman who could soothe his agony over his lost faithless wife.

How foolish and romantic she had become in her isolation. Yorkshire had done that to her, for she didn't think she had ever been such a daydreamer before.

"What a bear he has become," the earl said in a pleasant undertone.

"Is he not generally like that?" Kittie asked, turning to her companion on the divan, happy that Orkenay had removed his hand. She surreptitiously wiped the dampness off against her skirt.

"Mmm, I would not say he is *never* like that. Does he have a resentful temper? Yes. But is he gloomy or generally ill-tempered?" He shrugged. "I can only say that in the Prince's company he is often gay and occasionally even witty. One must be one of those things for Prinny's sake, you know."

"No, I don't know. I do not travel in those circles."

"Ah, but you should," the earl said, pressing her hand *again* with an expression of fervent admiration. "You are beautiful, you know, quite out of the ordinary."

"You should not say such things, my lord," Kittie said, aware of the flush rising to her cheek. It almost seemed that the earl was saying she should be a countess, for surely one must be of that stature to be included in the Prince's court, she thought. The duke, to her consternation, was gazing intently at her from across the room. She was not accustomed to male attention, and had not experienced such sensations since the death of her husband many years ago. Then, male attention from Roger and his friends had been her due. Roger Douglas was merely the younger son of a baronet, but a *bon vivant* who enjoyed living beyond his means. To do so he had to gamble, and to do that, he had to find new people to gamble with. She was young and happy then, thoughtless and carefree. She had been raised to leave such worries to her husband, and so she had, to her ultimate detriment.

If he had been a better gambler, they might not have become so destitute, or if Roger had lived longer he might have recovered from the debt he was in at the moment of his death, which occurred because, it was suspected though not proven, in his cups he did not give way on a dark road, and so his carriage was run into a ditch.

But the past was the past. She had put that life behind her and felt that she was a different person now, wiser, stronger and certainly older. Though "wiser" was in doubt, given her foolishness over the duke this last while, for she realized that she had idealized him through his kind letters. No man was perfect, and to expect it was absurd.

"I should say it," the earl protested. "And you should hear, often, that you are a vital, beautiful woman worthy of adorning the highest society in the land. Your embarrassment is delightful and your blush gives you fresh beauty."

Kittie took in a deep breath. There was a time when she considered such attention her due, and there was no reason why she should not accept that now. She had missed it, she found, and there were other things she missed. Would she ever again enjoy the physical aspects of a male companion? Not if she didn't marry, she supposed. It was something to think about. Lovemaking had been a very enjoyable part of her union with her husband, and there were times . . . but she would turn her mind away from that for now. Right now, there was the earl and his kind words. She would relax and enjoy the attention. There was no sin in that. And one could not condemn a man for having damp hands. "You are very kind, my lord."

He had said nothing outrageous or rude, and she would unbend enough to enjoy his compliments.

Alban, bored and at loose ends, wearied of watching Orkenay flirt with Kittie Douglas. Instead he drifted toward his aunt. She and Norton were informing each other of all that had happened since his last visit, many years before. The third son of an earl, Bart had often been shunted aside in his family, ignored, virtually forgotten by a horse-mad father who was only interested in his first son, the heir, and his second son, the dashing military officer. Bart, with no particular talents aside from a fine mind, a tender heart, and an acute sense of justice, was considered the inferior in every way.

But Lady Eliza Burstead had recognized, in the lonely little boy who came to her home often with Alban on school vacations, a spirit that desperately required a woman's soothing company. Their friendship was cemented one summer when Alban, infatuated with a local maiden—at nineteen an older woman to his tender fifteen—spent all of his time waiting for her, talking to her, and watching her, and drifted away from Bart for a while, obsessed with the new sensations he was experiencing.

Alban later learned that his aunt took Bart under her wing, and that summer they spent hours together walking the fells, exploring caves, and talking. When Alban finally recovered from his infatuation—after achieving his objective, which was to lose his virginity, though he did not, to his surprise, actually have to take the maiden's—it was to discover that Bart had become a far different person; he had, in fact, grown up and become a young man of deep feeling and clever intellect, uniting with that a tender heart. He was calm and inflexible in his determination, and when they both finished at Oxford he took orders. Very soon after that he inherited a rather large independence, and so never needed to find a living, which was, perhaps, a good thing since his father had sold the living in his power in exchange for a particular hunter he was avid to own. But Bart had ever since exhibited the rallying effect of Lady Eliza's good sense and inner strength. Even when in one of his gloomy patches, he was philosophical and calm.

And now they were renewing that bond. It warmed Alban and reminded him of all the things he had missed about his aunt.

Lady Eliza, sensing his presence, turned her face up toward him. He gazed at her steadily, looking at her eyes, milky now, when once they had been so clear and steady in their gaze.

"Do not stare at me to pity, Alban," Lady Eliza said.

Bart grinned.

Alban sat down by his aunt. "How do you . . . how do you know such things?"

Lady Eliza frowned and shook her head. "I am not sure I understand, myself. It is a recent skill. But I do have some ideas on the subject. Have you ever watched animals, Alban?"

What kind of nonsensical question that was, Alban could not imagine, but he would humor her. "No, I can't say that I have."

"Hmm. Why am I not surprised by that? Bartholomew, have you?"

"Yes. My sister had always loved cats, though my father could not bear the creatures. I always rather liked them and they seemed to like me, often staying by me when I chanced to be sitting with my sister and mother. So though we had them in the house, Father commanded that he never see them. Although my sister didn't do any training that I knew of, the animals seemed to know just how to go about. Father would kick them if he saw them, so when we were all sitting in the drawing room, if footsteps were heard in the hallway, I would see the cats' ears swivel; if it was just a footman or another of the family, they would hold their ground, but if it was Father they would slink away under the divan, or find some other hiding place. And that before he ever entered the room. I have noticed that animals use so many more senses than just their sight—hearing, smell, even something beyond any of those other senses."

"Good boy!" Lady Eliza cried, reaching out and patting his hand. "And that is how I have learned to know things. I cannot even tell you how I learned, but it was as if as my eyes became dim, everything else sharpened. The breeze on my face, the sound of a voice and what direction it comes from, what height. All of it combines, and becomes knowledge. I test it always, I try to refine it. If I am to be in darkness for the rest of my days, let me not be in ignorance, at least."

"What a wonder you are, my lady," Bart said, taking her hand and kissing it. "You have accepted your blindness so readily."

Alban watched his aunt's expression, the lined face suddenly weary.

"No, it was not so easy. I never realized how much my pride would be involved in losing my sight, and how devastated I was the day I awoke to find that the last vestiges of my failing vision had slipped away in the night. That was a black day; if it had not been for Kittie . . ."

The breath caught in Alban's throat, and his heart spasmed in pain. He crouched by her chair, reached out, and took his aunt's hands into his own; though they were rather big and bony for a woman's, his own still engulfed them easily. "Why didn't you tell me?" he whispered, not trusting his full voice.

"I thought I was sparing you," she said. "But now I know I was proud. Too proud to write you a letter to tell you. It would have felt like begging for a visit, and I knew you had other worries, other concerns."

He was silent, guilt scratching at him.

"And I had Kittie to help me, after all. Perhaps it is easier for a woman to turn to another woman in a time like that. She saw my worst moments and helped me to find peace."

As he stood, releasing his aunt's hands from his grasp, Alban glanced over at Kittie Douglas. She was blushing prettily at something Orkenay was murmuring. What had she done to draw in a sophisticated man like the earl? Of course, he would never say anything like that to his aunt, for she was fond of the young woman, and with good cause, it seemed. But was the companion as altruistic as his aunt seemed to think? Or was she, which seemed more likely to him, looking out for herself, entrenching herself so much in Lady Eliza's household through her sly manipulation, that his aunt would not be able to do without her? Perhaps that was cynical to think that way, but in his experience, cynicism was usually well answered by the facts.

She would bear watching, he thought. She could not possibly be as good as she was pretty, no matter what she had done for Lady Eliza.

On the surface she appeared to be demure . . . retiring even. Even now he could feel the tug of attraction

toward her, and yet there must be some illusory force
there, for she was not at all his kind of woman. He liked
an intelligent woman, but no woman with sense would
be flattered by the attention of an idiot like Orkenay,
and she seemed to be enjoying herself far too much.
He also liked an alluring woman, one who went out of
her way to be attractive to him, who studied his needs
and wants and made herself available to him, without
being provocative or vulgar. Kittie Douglas was garbed
simply, as befit her station, he supposed, and she was
easily embarrassed, he would have guessed. Though
she seemed to be gaining ease as Orkenay persisted in
his flattery. But she was none of the things he looked
for in a lover.

He turned away from the sight of the earl and Kittie
Douglas—he found it oddly disturbing—and back to
his aunt and friend. But they were chatting quietly, Bart
confessing his growing desire to find a wife and marry;
he had never told Alban that, the duke reflected, but
maybe they hadn't really had the opportunity for that
kind of conversation in the last couple of years. When
they were in company, it was generally in a large group.

Had he really shut out all the people who cared for
him, he wondered suddenly? His aunt, Bart . . . in his
youth, they were the two rocks in his world. And yet he
had spent little time with either in the last three years.

Maybe it was time in his life for an evaluation of all
he held dear. He wished, suddenly, that he had not invited Sir John and Orkenay, but perhaps the two men
would be taken up with Mrs. Douglas and her two
friends, who were arriving within the next day or two.

And how opportune was that, he thought sourly. Two
more widows, with four eligible gentlemen. What a co-
incidence. Enough husbands for everyone, and one
to spare.

One to spare. Himself, certainly, for though there

were reasons aplenty for him to marry, he had not made up his mind to the task yet. He stared out the window. When he did marry, he supposed he would have to brave the Season and find a young thing trained to be dutiful and grateful to someone of his stature, should he deign to court her. It was enough to make him weary, the thought of the attentions a young woman would require, at least during courtship.

He turned and caught Kittie Douglas's eye. She had, it seemed, been gazing intently in his direction even as she listened to Orkenay, who leered at her bosom as he murmured in her ear. She blushed and stood, suddenly, made a hasty excuse to the earl, and exited the room.

Six

When she descended for breakfast with her employer, Kittie found that the message had come that she was to expect her two friends that very day. Among the feelings she retained from the day before, there was a tumult of excitement at seeing the other two of the Three Widows, as they called themselves, again.

Lady Eliza was already dressed in a pearl gray morning gown and at the table in the small wood-paneled breakfast room off the main dining room, and was making her way through the substantial breakfast she considered adequate for the start of another day. When first the older woman had gone blind, Kittie assumed her duties would include guiding Lady Eliza to the table and choosing her foods for her, but that was not to be. She descended every morning at eight-thirty with the help of her chipper maid, Beacon, and though she expected Kittie to join her there by nine, she didn't need any more help than that of her footman, Oliver, to make up her plate. All of her serving staff adored her, despite—or perhaps because of—her autocratic ways, and had adjusted splendidly to her new infirmity.

And so the lady was dining on eggs, toast, kippered herrings, and a horrible relish that Kittie could not even stand the smell of, but which the lady cherished.

"Good morning, Kittie," Lady Eliza said, as Kittie entered. "You are wearing the new green silk, I see."

Kittie stopped and held one hand over her heart, then said, calmly, "So, Beacon told you that?"

"No."

Reflecting as she sat down, Kittie tried to think how her employer would know what gown she was wearing. Some things had become almost a game between them since Lady Eliza had gone blind, and this was one of them. Kittie didn't mind, because it challenged her employer's senses and teased her own brain. Stimulation had been much needed at some points during the darkest days, and Kittie would do anything to keep Lady Eliza's spirits from sinking to the depths they had plunged that awful morning when the woman discovered the last of her sight was gone.

"All right, I cannot imagine how you know what dress I am wearing, unless Prissy told you, or someone else."

"No one told me," Lady Eliza said, blotting her mouth with her napkin and setting it aside. "But I know that your friends are arriving today and that Prissy would have taken you that message when she drew your curtains, so it stands to reason that you would wear the new dress for their arrival."

"Of course!" Kittie nodded, and Oliver filled her cup with chocolate. She took a piece of toast from the rack in the middle of the table. "The simplest explanation is always the best. That was a shabby trick, though, to say it that way, my lady. I . . . I thought perhaps . . ."

"That I had regained my sight. Kittie, you know better than to even imagine that possible."

"But you said you do still see flashes of things on occasion."

"Just flashes, my dear, of shadow and light, and even those are fading. Are you looking forward to your friends' arrival?"

"Oh, yes. I'm so grateful to you for—" Kittie stopped as her employer raised one hand. She knew better than to get too effusive. "Well, I *am* grateful, and you can't stop me from saying so. I don't think another employer in England would allow her companion so much." She smeared her toast with marmalade and frowned thoughtfully at it. "I think you will like Lady Severn. I'm afraid Hannah Billings may not be to your taste, but she is good at heart, for all her occasional depression and weepiness."

"We will discuss your friends at length, but first, I meant to ask you yesterday what you thought of my nephew's friends. You left the room abruptly before their visit terminated, and yet you and the earl seemed to be having a lively conversation. I did not see you much for the rest of the day, since Alban and Bart stayed with me."

Kittie was grateful for the delay occasioned by a large bite of toast and marmalade, which she chewed slowly. It had not been Orkenay's attentions that had made her flee, but the expression on the duke's handsome face from across the room. He turned and caught her gazing at him, and the expression on his face was a knowing sneer. He was not the man of the painting in the dining room, she thought. That man, and the man of his letters to his aunt, was considerate and kind, loving and giving, with a gentleness of expression and tone.

In truth he had an arrogance of mien that was most offputting, and when he spoke he was often sarcastic. He was very much the duke of his wife's accusatory last letter, as she told him she was deserting him. And yet Kittie could not help that her heart beat faster when he looked at her. It was most disturbing, but she could acknowledge her physical attraction to him even as she recognized his unpleasant characteristics. Perhaps his disdain would have a salutary effect on her. If it didn't, then she was very foolish indeed.

"You have not answered."

"What? Oh, I'm sorry. Uh, what was the question?"

Lady Eliza smiled and nodded. "Never mind. I find your silence almost as interesting as an answer would be. However, tell me now about your friends." She turned her head and raised her cup. "Oliver, more chocolate. And tell Cook she finally has it right. The chocolate is finally of the right consistency and taste."

"Well," Kittie said, swallowing another bite, "there is Lady Rebecca DeVere Severn. Her first husband was a dashing French *comte* who fell in love with her at first sight; she was only fifteen. Her family could not say no to such a good match, though Rebecca, from what she tells me, was very frightened to go back to France with him; it was a horrifying time in her life. He was lost in the revolution. She was a widow for the first time at sixteen."

"Sixteen! How sad to be widowed so young."

"Ah, but Rebecca was not one to be daunted. She was poor and had to live with a relative for a while, but she quickly decided that she needed a rich husband. Not only rich, though. Frightened by her experiences, she also wanted one who lived a calm, safe life. And so she settled on an elderly brewer who already had four children who were older than she, and married him."

"Did she never have children?"

"No. But she says her husband's grown children were very good to her, and their children have entertained her well enough. She still maintains a good relationship with them, even after her husband's death."

"I like your Lady Severn! She sounds like a very decisive character."

"She is." Kittie held up her cup and Oliver refilled it. "I met her when I married my husband—she was already married to her brewer—and we were all very gay together in London that spring we met. Rebecca has great determination, and she had decided that she wanted to be Lady Severn. She was Comtesse DeVere, you know, and retained her title even after marriage, but to many of our countrymen a French title is worse than no title at all. So she went about pushing and prodding her husband—poor lamb; all he wanted to do was sit by the fire with a pipe, but she forced him into court attire, and he made an address to the King— until he was knighted, and she became Lady Rebecca Severn."

"And her husband?"

"Oh, she allowed him to go back to his fire, then, once she had achieved her objective. He only died a couple of years ago. For all her social instincts, she was a very good wife to poor old Sir William. More nurse than wife for the last years."

"You said I should not like the other one so much . . . was the name Mrs. Billings?"

"I shouldn't have said it that way, my lady. I love Hannah dearly, but she suffers often from a depression of spirits. I just thought you . . ."

"Might become impatient with such a person?"

Kittie smiled. How perspicacious her employer was. "With your own troubles, I thought you might not sympathize with someone whose real trouble was a lack of any perceptible backbone."

Lady Eliza chuckled and put down her chocolate, finally. "You know me too well, Kittie, and it sounds as if you know your friend too well, too. But there must be something about her you value, or you would not care so much for her."

Kittie toyed with her plate, which was delivered as she spoke to Lady Eliza and laden with eggs and ham. "I love Hannah dearly. When . . . when Roger died five

years ago, Hannah took me in for a while. She couldn't
afford to. She has two sons, now twelve and thirteen—
they are currently at school, of course—and her
circumstances are straitened, to say the least, but she
took me in. She had only been widowed a year herself
and was still in mourning."

"I understand," Lady Eliza said.

Kittie felt that she did.

A clatter sounded from the hall, and a woman's
laugh floated through to the breakfast room.

"Rebecca!" Kittie cried, rising and racing to the front
hall.

Her friends had arrived.

"Kittie, dearest child!" Lady Rebecca Severn, glowing
brilliantly in a scarlet cloak that was, she assured her
friend immediately, "bang up to the mark," hugged Kittie fiercely as servants bustled in with trunks and bags.

Rebecca's perfume, enveloped in a velvet too heavy
for the mild autumn air, wafted around them. Although Kittie's heart swelled with joy at the familiar
embrace, she fought her way out of her older friend's
fierce hug and whirled, peering through the darkness.

"Hannah!" she cried. "Don't slink away, dearest,
come to me!"

Her friend, slight and pale, was leaning against the
balustrade as if for support. Kittie moved toward her
and Hannah fell on her neck, weeping.

"Oh, Kittie, dearest, *dearest* Kittie! I thought I would
never see you again! How I have missed you!"

Tears saturated Kittie's dress neck, and she looked
over Hannah's head to see Rebecca winking at her.

"For the first miles of our journey she cried because
we had delivered her boys back to their school. They
had to go early for some reason or another, I have no
idea what. It was a very affecting scene, I assure you,

with Hannah weeping and the boys sighing and me tapping my foot. Then she rallied for a while, but she has been crying again for the last fifty miles. And that was just because she could not believe you were . . . what did she say? Mired in such desolate country?"

Hannah gasped and straightened. "Rebecca, how could you tell her that?"

"Because it is true, darling, though so ridiculous. Yorkshire is frightfully romantic . . . like the dark forest of Germany, I always think."

"How nonsensical you are, Rebecca," Kittie said, hugging her again. "And how I have missed you. How I have missed you *both*."

"Ahem!"

Kittie whirled, to see her employer standing in the doorway to the breakfast room. "Oh! Lady Eliza, I wish to introduce . . ."

"Why do we not move to the morning parlor, Kittie," Lady Eliza interrupted, "while Prissy and Oliver take these ladies' luggage up to their rooms?"

Settling her nerves, Kittie guided them in to the parlor as Lady Eliza moved, on her own, to her familiar seat by the window. Introductions affected, Kittie added, "I must thank you again, Lady Eliza, for allowing me to have company in this way. I know how unusual it is and I'm very grateful."

"Nonsense," the lady said, briskly. "It has done me a world of good to have company, and the ladies will add to the mix splendidly. It could not be any better."

For a moment Kittie had forgotten the gentlemen, but she turned to Rebecca and Hannah, and said, "Yes, I have forgotten; Lady Eliza's nephew, the Duke of Alban, has opened his hunting box—that is Boden House, the estate you must have seen as you drove here—and he brought some friends with him."

"Friends? Men?" Lady Rebecca sat up straighter in

her hard chair. She was tall and dark-haired, with brilliant green eyes. Though not accounted pretty—her nose was hooked and her jaw too firm—she was remarkable in many other ways. "Are they unmarried?" she asked, her gaze turning from Kittie to Lady Eliza. "Are they good-looking? Are they *young*?"

"Rebecca!" Hannah remonstrated. She raised her voice and said, loudly, "Do not mind her, Lady Eliza. She is forward and pert."

Lady Eliza frowned. "I am not deaf, my dear Mrs. Billings, just blind."

Rebecca snorted and Kittie hid her smile behind her hand. Hannah looked disconcerted.

"And as to your questions, Lady Severn," Lady Eliza said, turning in the widow's direction. "Yes, they are all unmarried, to my knowledge, unless one of them has a secret wife hidden somewhere. My nephew is, of course, the duke, but his friends are, in order, an earl, the third son of an earl, and a baronet. They are all in their thirties, I think, except for the earl, whom I surmise from his voice to be somewhat older. I am the wrong person to ask about their looks, except I can tell you that Alban is exceptionally handsome, and that Bartholomew Norton is a very pleasing lad, though a little long in the jaw."

Rebecca gazed at her admiringly. "I think, my lady, that you and I will enjoy talking. I very much like your concision."

Hannah, her lip trembling, looked ready to cry.

"Oh, Hannah," Kittie said, moving to her and slipping an arm around her shoulders. "Lady Eliza did not mean to be brisk with you."

"It . . . it's not that." She sniffed. "It has been so long since we were all gathered. I am . . . I am so h—h—happy!" And with that she wailed.

"What is wrong, what's going on?"

That was Mr. Bartholomew Norton himself bursting into the room. He immediately crossed to Hannah and knelt at her side. "Are you ill, madam? How can I help?"

Kittie bit her lip. How could she explain that Hannah was crying over an excess of happiness?

The other men entered, too, at that moment. The duke said, "Heard some whimpering in here and Bart would not wait to be announced. Rushed to the rescue."

"Mr. Norton is a true gentleman," Kittie said, not bothering to conceal the asperity in her voice. "Mr. Norton, that is my friend Mrs. Hannah Billings. She is merely very happy."

The duke snorted, greeted his aunt affectionately, and then strolled to the window.

Kittie made the rest of the introductions and watched, in amusement, as Rebecca made a dead set for the duke, certainly the handsomest and most imposing figure in the room. Lord Orkenay joined Kittie, as he had the day before, and Sir John, his youthful face set in a cheery smile, sat down by Lady Eliza.

Conversation was general for a while, with no way to distinguish individual words or phrases in the pleasant confusion. Lord Orkenay was, unlike the day before, not behaving in any way that could make Kittie blush, and she was pleased at his attentions.

"Do you like living in Yorkshire?" he asked.

She considered her answer. "I do. There are disadvantages, of course. The winters are dreadful and it can be lonely, but it is so very beautiful."

"Do you find it so?" His forehead wrinkled, and he pursed his lips. He leaned back in his chair and crossed one leg over the other. "I cannot see the beauty. I know people rave about the picturesque aspects of the looming fells and wild countryside, but I suppose I prefer a tamer aspect . . . not so gloomy."

"And what do you consider that tamer aspect to be?"

"London," he answered promptly.

Kittie laughed. "London? I thought we were talking about picturesque countryside."

"London is beautiful this time of year . . . not so many people. Even the parks are clear of folks parading."

"And yet you came up here. Are you a special friend of the duke's, to make such a sacrifice?"

He shrugged. "We are part of the same set and we both followed the Prince to Brighton this year. When Alban suggested going hunting, I thought it would make an agreeable change." He leaned toward her and murmured, "I must say, now I'm very glad I did."

There was no other way to take that but as a compliment to her, and she smiled.

"You have the most delightful smile," he said, chucking her under the chin. "And you blush adorably."

Kittie shifted in her seat. There was no possible response to that bit of impertinence. She glanced toward the window and saw that Rebecca had the duke cornered and was flirting with him, reaching out occasionally to pluck a stray thread from his jacket and to touch his arm. The duke, clearly discomposed, was looking his haughtiest. He was using every polite method in his no-doubt formidable array of ways to freeze out a social-climbing mushroom, but as he didn't know that nothing would ever deter Rebecca once she was set on an objective, he was doomed to fail unless he was willing to be horribly rude in his aunt's drawing room.

Kittie would have bet that a man like the duke would consider that beneath him, to behave in any way not strictly decorous, and it appeared that she was right. He was frozen in distaste, but he was doing nothing other than trying desperately to ignore Lady Severn.

Kittie stifled a smile, wondering if a brewer's widow had ever had the temerity to flirt with the haughty and disdainful Duke of Alban. Judging from his demeanor of puzzled outrage, she would guess not.

"Mrs. Douglas, I am feeling a trifle annoyed with you, this moment."

"Uh, pardon, my lord?" Kittie's attention was reclaimed by the importunate earl.

"You have not been listening to a word I said, and I was telling the most delicious story just now."

"I'm so sorry, my lord, but . . . but I have to go talk to Cook about dinner tonight," Kittie said, standing. She could not bear any more society. It was a quirk of hers that at times so many people gathered together and talking, and expecting *her* to talk, would overwhelm her; an unbearable tension would build up, and she would feel as though her head were in a vice. A few moments of solitude, and she would be able to return to the company with a refreshed tolerance. But for now, she just needed that few moments alone.

She whispered to Lady Eliza that she would be back momentarily, and fled the room, escaping down the dark hall to the library, which overlooked the enclosed garden at the back of the house.

She had intended to come here anyway, to choose a couple of books to place by the bedsides of her friends, so they would have something to while away the hours should sleep desert them. It was one of her favorite rooms in the house, even if it was dark and small.

But no such task was possible at that moment, with her head buzzing and her mind racing. Sitting down in the dark stillness with a sigh, Kittie rested her head back on the cushion of the divan in the corner by one high bookshelf. She loved her friends, and it was going to be heaven to have them there for a couple of weeks, but it was going to be tiring as well. That was so partly, she supposed, because she had become so accustomed to solitude and quiet in the last three years. Where was the lighthearted girl who could visit all day, dance all evening, and play cards all night? She had been that girl once, when she was young and happy and married to a dazzlingly handsome young man.

Poor Roger. They had never been wealthy, but without his gambling they would have been able to make do on his small inheritance. Their poverty had worried Roger more than it had her, she supposed, at the time. But then she was young and foolish and fancied herself in love.

Had it been love? What was such an emotion? Could one love a man truly, or was all love an illusion based on fanciful notions of the nobility and perfection of the other?

She had fallen into almost a trance, staring at the dusty window and the sun streaming through, motes dancing in the warm beam. The door opened, and a figure backed in, and then turned.

It was the duke.

"Your Grace," Kittie said, leaping to her feet.

"Mrs. Douglas!"

Caught, as they were, both where they really shouldn't have been with a room full of their guests to be attended to, they both, unexpectedly, at the same moment, grinned.

"Are you, perchance, escaping, Mrs. Douglas? Do you find all the chatter a bit much?"

Kittie sighed. "I . . . I suppose that's what it is."

"Your friend is . . . persistent."

Kittie chuckled. Of all the things she had expected he would have to say about Rebecca, the word "persistent" seemed mild. "She is." In the dim light from the window, she could trace the youthful outline that was the base for the stubborn, powerful man the duke had become. She watched him as he circled, touching books in the bookcase, examining titles with apparent interest.

"I thought you told the earl that you had to attend to some household matter, though," he said, over his shoulder.

"I think I just needed a moment alone. I'm a little overwhelmed by all the socializing. We live a very quiet life here." She stood, thinking she ought to leave.

He turned, then, and stared at her. "I find myself in the unaccustomed situation of having to thank you, profusely, for your care of my aunt. I have been lax in my attentions, and I regret it. But it seems that you have filled the void admirably."

"She never blamed you, sir, for not coming up in the three years. And you have been most assiduous in every other way. Your letters were a comfort, and you never let a month go by without some attention or other. Mr. Lafferty has followed your orders, too, and has been very good to us."

"But I should have come up myself. If I had had any idea that she was truly going blind . . . but she concealed even some of the encroaching darkness from me when last I was here." His face was set in a brooding expression of melancholy. "I remember, now, that she seemed clumsier than normal that month."

"She is a very proud woman," Kittie said, watching uneasily as the duke approached her. "It would have been difficult to tell you, and she would have felt that you had . . . that is, your last visit . . ." There was no way to finish that sentence without referring to his wife's desertion and subsequent death.

When he finally stood in front of her, she looked up, directly into his eyes. She was a tall woman, but he towered over her easily by seven or eight inches, and it was an odd feeling, as if she was standing in a hole.

He took one of her bare hands in his and raised it to his lips, laying a soft kiss on the back. "Still, I want to thank you. I'm not without imagination and I know that this has not been an easy time for either of you. She is a proud woman, as you say, and so her descent into darkness would not have been accomplished without a good deal of anger and frustration on her part. It cannot have been easy."

Oh, this was terrible. As long as she could look at him and see disdain in his eyes and haughtiness in his manners, she could feel her emotions cool, the feelings she had built up in three lonely years as she read his warm letters and gazed at his handsome portrait receding, but now, with him being so kind to her, she felt all those warm feelings bubbling again, and she involuntarily moved forward until she was close to him.

And she could see in his dark eyes a blaze of responding feeling. Was it true? Was he attracted to her, as well?

How much more awful if that was true, for she was under no illusion. She was the widow of an unsuccessful gambler and with no distinction in her name or past. He was a duke, second only to the royal dukes in prominence.

She could never be anything more to him than a friend. She stepped back again. "I . . . I should go see about my friends' rooms," she said, hating the breathless tone in her voice, but helpless against the flood of warmth in her heart and through her body.

The door opened, and a maid scurried in to the fireplace. With just one glance at the other inhabitants of the room she went directly to her work, brushing out the ashes from the fireplace, and the moment ended. Kittie had to be grateful to the little maid, Maggie, and promised herself to make sure the child had a treat that Sunday.

"And I should return to the drawing room." He bowed. "I will see you there, Mrs. Douglas, when you finish your . . . household arrangements."

Seven

The gentlemen left soon after, set to tour the area in preparation for the hunting for which they had come north. The ladies spent a pleasant, lazy day getting to know their hostess, Lady Eliza Burstead, and she, them. As Kittie attended her in her chamber late that night, she pronounced herself well-pleased with the company; and she even had found something to appreciate in Hannah Billings. At least, she told Kittie, the woman spoke softly once she got over the notion that her hostess's impairment was hearing.

Kittie was still chuckling over that the next morning as she walked in the garden after a solitary breakfast with Lady Eliza. After the journey they had suffered, the ladies were having a long lie-in and were not expected to appear until noon or later.

The hours she spent on a September morning in the garden at Bodenthorpe Cottage were the finest Kittie had ever experienced, and she considered each one precious, like an individual gem to be treasured for its uniqueness. Every birdcall, each blossom, even the mist drifting over the stone garden wall, each sight was made more cherished by the knowledge that here, at the cottage, she was loved and needed.

Her early years were spent with her family in a small village in Devonshire; she still had a brother there, a busy lawyer with a large family, though they did little more than exchange letters once a year.

Her married years had been spent mostly in London and Bath. She had made many friends . . . or rather, acquaintances, during those cheerful, thoughtless days, but when hard times came they blew away like chaff on the breeze. All except Rebecca and Hannah.

Yorkshire was so very different from Devonshire, London, or Bath, and yet, though she had had no choice when she was offered a position of such great worth and had to come north to accept it, it had turned out that Yorkshire was very much more to her mature liking. She may not have appreciated its loneliness and isolation when she was twenty and newly married, but as a widow and a woman of thirty-one, it was very much to her taste.

She had wandered the moors and fells many a time, but it was to the garden that she always returned with a satisfied sigh. She had transformed it in the three years she had been here. Lady Eliza had never cared overmuch for gardening and had left it to her staff to keep it tidy and neat. But for Kittie it bloomed, roses climbing the walls of the cottage and daisies rioting in the garden beds, herbs scenting the Elizabethan knot garden and even the privet hedge thickening with glossy green leaves.

The cottage was enclosed by a stone wall several feet high. Against it, Kittie had planted more roses, and Lady Eliza had learned to love them, able to identify each by scent now, in her blindness. September was a mellow time of year, with thoughts turning to the winter ahead; it would be the second winter with Lady Eliza completely blind. They would need to find ways to amuse a woman of her intelligence, since she could no longer read or write.

Kittie wandered the garden, laying her basket on a

stone bench to receive the flowers she had cut for her friends' rooms and for Lady Eliza's bedside vase. She crouched down by one bush and examined it closely, worried by the yellowing of the leaves.

"A rose by any other name . . ."

She looked up to see the duke leaning over the wooden gate to the garden. She stood and brushed her skirts back into place.

"Don't let me stop you, Mrs. Douglas." He opened the gate and moved through, shutting it behind him. Bernard, the ancient male tabby cat, beyond anything but milk and friendship, brushed up against him, and the duke picked him up, cradling the old cat in his arms.

Kittie was arrested by the sight. Of all things, she would not have thought the duke was one to appreciate cats. Though she could picture him astride a hunter with a pack of baying hounds at his feet, she had not imagined him in his present guise, as a man stroking the old Tom, chucking it under the chin until it purred loudly.

"You are oddly silent, Mrs. Douglas. I'm sorry if I startled you."

"I . . . I wasn't startled, sir."

He stopped and put Bernard gently down in a patch of sunlight that leaked through the close trees, and the cat rolled over and struck a strangely inelegant pose, stretching out luxuriously after such a proper petting. The duke brushed off his elegant morning coat, ridding himself of Bernard's fur, and said, "I'm glad I caught you, actually, Mrs. Douglas. I have been deputized by my friends to come and ask the ladies of Bodenthorpe Cottage if they would be so kind as to join us for dinner tonight."

"I cannot say for certain, but I think the ladies would

be delighted." She tried to stifle a smile, knowing how Rebecca would greet the invitation.

"I am on my way inside to speak to my aunt. If you'll talk to your friends and send a message up to me this afternoon, I would be grateful."

"I am almost certain of acquiescence. I will send a message only if it is a negative."

He nodded approvingly, and Kittie waited for him to go inside. Instead, he lingered.

"What are you doing?"

She took a deep breath. Really, she was being ridiculous. She must learn to breathe normally in this man's presence. "I'm cutting roses for vases," she said, gesturing to the basket on the bench. "It is almost time to cut them back for autumn, but I like to enjoy all the blooms I can this time of year, before winter sets in. Last year was a hard one."

He strolled closer, off the pathway and toward her. "It must get lonely at times, here. I know my aunt, for some strange reason, has chosen to mire herself here in Yorkshire all year long. But you . . . why are you here?"

"I am making my living," she answered swiftly, not hiding the vexation in her voice. Really, what a question! Did the man have no common sense?

"But why did you not marry again after your . . . after your husband's demise?"

Impertinence. Just because he was a duke— "Until I can grow myself a suitable husband like a rose, then I must go where I may to live. If you have a stray gentleman around who would not mind a thirty-one-year-old widow of no means, no family, and no background to speak of, then I will be happy to marry again. But as long as men continue to be men, and prefer young, dowered women of title or gentility, then I will do what I must to survive."

Unexpectedly, a grin curved his mouth upward, and he laughed. "So, Bernard is not the only one with claws in this garden. Very well. I was, perhaps, discourteous in my close questioning. I will retreat." He bowed, then turned and strolled up to the house, whistling a jaunty air.

Alban was still smiling as he found his aunt sitting in the morning parlor, a sunny room with large windows overlooking the south garden. He entered and gazed at her.

She had heard him and stilled; then she said, after a brief hesitation, "Alban?"

"How do you do that?" He strode across the room in two steps and leaned down, kissing her cheek before taking a chair opposite her at the small table in front of the window.

"Nothing more than a parlor trick." She snorted. "Quite literally, since I am in the parlor. When, nephew, did you become a cheek kisser? You never were one before."

He gazed at her, examining the face he had known and loved for so long. He had thought of her as unchanging and unchangeable, but her hair was iron gray now, when in his youth it had been dark, almost black. And her skin was pursing around the mouth, showing the affects of age. He took her hand up and caressed it absently with his thumb. "I've missed you so much."

"Not enough to visit before now."

"I know, and I deserve that rebuke. I don't know what happened. Three years seem to have gone by in a flash. I suppose I was so tangled up in affairs in London— It has not been a good few years for our king and his family."

"No. You used to be close to him, Alban. Are you still, in his infirmity?"

"I'm afraid not. My last visit to him was awful, just

awful." Alban bowed his head and stared down at the floor. He had not intended to speak of such dark topics to his aunt, hoping to entertain her, but he had been mistaken. She didn't need coddling now any more than she did before she became blind. "He accused me of . . . of plotting with Napoleon to poison him and Amelia. Said I was to blame for her . . . for her last wasting illness. It was terrible." He passed one hand over his face.

"Oh, Alban," Lady Eliza said, her voice trembling. "I'm so sorry. I had no idea it was so bad. And he used to love you so, he treated you almost like another son."

Alban drew in a deep breath. "I can't help but think that that was my undoing. There are many who would not discourage his mad ideas once he had them in his head."

"You suspect they are deliberately poisoning his mind against you?"

"No. No, not really. I'm only saying that once the idea had taken hold, there are many who would be happy to have him focus his madness on me, rather than others in court."

"Mm, jealousy, as usual. It is what I do not miss about court life."

He made an impatient noise. "Scandal and gossip will always be there, but it's not so very bad. There is so much more . . . you're missing so much," he said, emphasizing his words with a pat of her hand. "And I have heard you were legendary for your wit and vivacity. Even Her Majesty remembers you fondly, and you know how few people she considers adequate even, outside of her precious girls and sons. I've never understood why you came up here, so far away from everything and everyone, and . . ."

"Alban, I had my own reasons. Perhaps they no

longer exist, but I did have them. And I've made a life for myself here."

He knew the tone too well to argue with her. He couldn't help but suspect a failed love affair, or maybe a love that was impossible for one reason or another. Perhaps the man was married, or maybe he had even deserted her. It was too long ago for him to know. To him, she had always just been his spinster Aunt Eliza up in Yorkshire, there for him in ways no one else ever was.

"I saw your Mrs. Douglas out in the garden," he said, releasing her hand and wandering the room. "She has made a wonder out of the gardens."

"She has a rare talent with flowers," she admitted. "Tell me, is she still as lovely as I remember?"

Alban flashed a look at his aunt. What did that question mean? As innocently as it was couched, it still had an odd, stilted tone to it. "If you like red hair."

"You always did, if I remember that serving girl you were infatuated with one summer. But Kittie's is not that red; it is more like a bronze color, isn't it?"

"It is, and she is beautiful, if you like tall, sturdy, prickly wenches."

Lady Eliza threw back her head and laughed. "Impudent devil," she rebuked him. "I think the earl likes her well enough."

"Hmm, yes. Orkenay has spent much of his time with her, hasn't he? Even though she is not the type of woman he normally is attracted to, from what I have seen." He rejoined her at the table. "Anyway, as I was going to say, I met Mrs. Douglas in the garden and relayed my invitation to her and her friends and you to all come to the house for dinner this evening. She said she thought it would be acceptable."

"Very good. You may go now, Alban."

The duke kissed her cheek again and stood.

"But you did not answer my question. When did you become a cheek kisser? You never were before."

"I thought I answered it," he said, moving toward the door. "We will be happy to see you ladies tonight, then."

"Evasive, impertinent rascal," Lady Eliza said.

"I heard that," the duke replied, as he exited.

"I intended that you should," she retorted.

The evening closed in early in September, and the air chilled. Swathed in their finest evening attire, Rebecca and Hannah, Kittie and Lady Eliza entered the duke's hunting box, though that humble appellation was too modest a description for the lovely house. As large and sprawling as it was, still it clung like a Swaledale sheep to the side of the fell and appeared to spring from the land, the deep gold Yorkshire stone of the walls glowing in the dying sunlight.

Kittie had seen it in all seasons and had toured the home, visiting it often, with and without her employer. The duke occasionally sent instructions, and Lady Eliza had, since her blindness, left it to Kittie to oversee the changes, so she was as familiar with it as if it were her own home.

But she had never seen it with the master of the house in residence, and it was a far different place, the great hall humming with servants and blazing with warmth from the enormous fireplace that warmed the echoing chamber. As the ladies' wraps were removed and carted away by serving staff, Kittie gazed around in bewilderment.

The mere presence of the Duke of Alban seemed to have infused the old stone walls with grandeur. The walls were covered in tapestries and the colors glowed in the firelight. The duke strode toward the ladies. He was dressed carefully in his evening best: his coat black and plain, but his waistcoat a gorgeous figured silk and his cravat fixed in place with a large diamond stickpin.

Kittie was suddenly happy that she had been goaded by Lady Eliza into wearing her best dress, a rather low-cut sapphire blue velvet gown with long fitted sleeves and white silk embroidery at the bosom and hem. Lady Eliza wore black silk, Hannah, green, and Rebecca was resplendent in her favorite gown, a ruby red velvet and satin. Rebecca had brought her maid—the girl was a marvel, she said, at styling hair—north with her, and that woman had taken care of Rebecca's own black locks and Hannah's mousy brown hair.

The duke, his manners formal, accompanied them into the withdrawing room, guiding his aunt on his arm. The gentlemen were there and came forward, each taking a lady by the arm. Mr. Norton renewed his acquaintance with Hannah, the earl took Kittie's arm, and Sir John bowed before Rebecca.

Kittie, watching, was amused by Rebecca's assessing look as she walked with the young man toward a seat by the fire. She privately thought that the baronet was more likely twenty-five or -six rather than in his thirties, as Lady Eliza had surmised, and that made him at least ten years younger than Rebecca.

Everyone chatted desultorily before dinner, and then moved to the dining room with their respective partners for the evening.

Kittie couldn't stop thinking of the duke's questioning her that morning. Was he so completely unaware that he didn't even realize that there were many women, and many more men, who had no other means of support than whatever they could sell their skills or abilities for? He was an intelligent man, and before meeting him, strictly on the evidence of his letters, she would have thought a compassionate one. Had he taken her in dislike for some reason?

She glanced down the table to where he was seated, with his aunt on his right and Rebecca on his left. He was assiduous in his attentions, and he and Lady Eliza spoke often.

"Would you like a drink of wine, Mrs. Douglas?" the earl asked.

"Hmm? Oh, certainly, my lord," Kittie replied, in the necessary way, as he took up his glass and held it up. They both sipped, her acquiescence freeing him to drink down his glass of red wine as they ate the beef course.

"I must compliment your seamstress, my dear; that blue is simply spectacular on you. It matches the color of your brilliant eyes."

"Thank you," Kittie replied, still eyeing the duke and his aunt.

Until she felt the hand on her knee. She gave a little gasp and glanced over at the man beside her. The earl smiled and winked.

Sir John's steady gaze was on them, and so she could not be as fierce with Lord Orkenay as she would have liked, but, teeth gritted, she muttered, "Please, my lord, release my knee."

With one lingering caress, he did so, merely murmuring, "I'm so sorry if I offended you, my dear Mrs. Douglas. I did wish to gain your attention, though, and I must say it is so obviously fixed on the duke, that I saw no other way."

"I wasn't staring at the duke, my lord . . ." She trailed off, for she had been, hadn't she? She glanced at her dinner companion in consternation.

He nodded, his pleasant smile masking a deeper meaning, she felt. "I only meant it as a warning, my dear, for Alban would surely take it amiss if you kept staring in that way. He's a most peculiar man in some ways, and feminine . . . er . . . *boldness* in any way is very disagreeable to him. "

"But I didn't mean . . . I wasn't intending . . . in short, Lord Orkenay, I was only thinking about something the duke said to me this morning."

"And what was that?"

"He questioned me very closely on the reasons behind my 'miring myself,' as he called it, in Yorkshire, and he asked why I did not marry again after my husband passed away. I found it most strange."

"Did you think there was a hidden meaning behind his questions?"

Kittie toyed with her beef. "I don't know," she admitted. "What hidden meaning could there be?"

"Does he think you are an adventuress?"

"An adventuress? What do you mean? To what end?"

The earl shrugged. "I suppose he is being careful of his aunt. Perhaps he suspects you of some intention toward his aunt of which he would not approve."

"What do you mean? I don't understand."

The earl, a faint, kind smile on his thin lips, patted her hand. He was elegantly dressed in charcoal gray, and his sandy hair, silvered at the temples, was perfectly dressed. Kittie didn't think she had ever seen a man more carefully and perfectly dressed and coifed. The duke was competently dressed, and his clothing was immaculate, of course, but it appeared that the earl was really the leader in fashion among the company of gentlemen that night.

"I would merely suggest that you be careful, Mrs. Douglas, where Alban is concerned."

She frowned. "Careful? Whatever can you mean?"

Orkenay shook his head. "I will say no more. Just be careful. I would not like to see a lovely woman like you hurt in any way."

"He is your friend, is he not?"

"Oh, I'm not saying he would do anything deliberate," Orkenay assured her, hastily. "He is the best of men and the soul of propriety, in most ways. But he is very haughty, you know, and if he thinks for a moment . . . but I will say no more. Just be on your guard in his presence, please."

Dinner, seeming interminable to Kittie, finally finished, and they all moved to the drawing room for coffee and sweetmeats. Rebecca, urged by Sir John, moved to the piano, and Hannah and Mr. Norton were engaged in examining a book of watercolor plates of Yorkshire.

Kittie was pleased to see her friends so well engaged, but she was undecided herself where her duty lay. She moved uncertainly toward Lady Eliza.

"Kittie, dear, come here," her employer said, holding out one hand.

Kittie gladly joined her. The duke stood by her chair.

"I have been telling Alban that I set you to overseeing the improvements to the house while he was gone, since I didn't truly think he wanted a blind woman choosing new paint colors for his bedchamber and other rooms."

"I must thank you, Mrs. Douglas," the duke said, with a bow. "Lafferty has praised you most lavishly. He told me that you have been valuable, gave it the woman's touch, I think he said."

Flustered by the praise, Kittie remained silent.

"I have not been here in some time, Alban," Lady Eliza said. "I would very much like to see the house again, but I would ask for both your guidance and Kittie's arm, as she can describe to me what she changed."

"I'm sure His Grace can provide the necessary explication," Kittie said.

"I would like your company, my dear," Lady Eliza said in a gentle voice that clothed the steel of her will.

"She means that she will have you, whether you like it or not," Alban said. "Such is the fate of a companion, is it not?"

"Yes," Kittie said, hearing the barb in his words but not responding. "I will certainly accompany you, my lady."

But of course the planned expedition could not be affected without an announcement to that affect, and equally as surely the other ladies expressed a desire for a tour as well. Lady Eliza's expression was one of chagrin, Kittie noted, and she wondered why.

But go as a troupe they would, into the great hall and up the winding stairs to the gallery, their progress slowed by Hannah's deliberate perambulation and Rebecca's determined admiring of everything, and the explanations of their respective swains.

Kittie had expected that she would be on the other side of Lady Eliza, supporting her in her progress up the stairs and along the gallery, but Lady Eliza changed her mind and demanded that Kittie be guided by the duke's strong arm. Knowing her employer as well as she did, Kittie suspected some subterfuge, but could not imagine what the aim was.

And soon she forgot to even wonder. Though nominally keeping up her end of the conversation, pointing out improvements affected by Mr. Lafferty and guided by herself, she had far too much time to note the strength of the duke's arm, his inimitable scent, the fine fabric of his jacket sleeve, and something more.

He was assiduous in his attentions to both of them and divided his time equally between them, careful of her comfort, supporting her as they climbed the stairs and his hand at her back as they walked the gallery. In that position she was almost tucked under his arm, and she realized that she had never quite felt so protected and sheltered. With her husband she had always, after the first weeks of marriage, had to fend for herself, for Roger, though cheerful and convivial, was not one to consider her comfort. And so she had learned to be self-sufficient. But there were times she longed to lay down her battle shield and rest, and there could be no better place than in the duke's arms.

And she was shocked by her own scandalous, outrageous thoughts. She could not keep thinking like that. She looked up at him, his strong jaw, the hooded eyes. What she felt was merely the residual attraction she might never entirely be rid of. And of course, her thoughts were not only improper, but foolish and fatuous.

No doubt the duke's wife had suffered the same sense of abandonment as she did once the novelty wore off. It seemed it was what happened in a marriage, men taking their wives for granted, and it could have accounted for the duchess's running away to find love with a paramour. Kittie had idealized the duke these last three years, but in person he was a much more formidable presence.

She stared up at him still. They stood at a wall, and he was explaining to the company at large that the painting in front of them was of his great grandfather, the fifth Duke of Alban. When he fell silent, Lady Eliza, from memory, described it, the rich tones, the quaint costume.

The duke caught Kittie's steady gaze.

"Have I told you how lovely you look tonight?"

She caught her breath, then let it out on a sigh. "No. But then I have not yet commented on your own sartorial grandeur."

He chuckled and rubbed her back with his free hand. She felt chills race over her skin. He cast her a quizzical glance. "I'm sorry," he said. "Are you cold? Shall I have a maid fetch your shawl?"

"No, I'm fine, thank you."

He rubbed her upper back, the skin naked to his touch. "You have lovely skin, like silk," he murmured.

She was wordless, but a warm flush passed over her body.

Lady Eliza finished her explanation, and the company moved on. Kittie detached herself from the duke, uncomfortable with the sensations his touch produced. The earl's words at dinner came back to her. He was warning her, but to what end? She turned and found Lord Orkenay's gaze on her, and their eyes met. He quickly smiled and turned away, but not before she caught the expression on his face.

It was one of troubled concern.

Eight

"This is what I've missed," Kittie said, as the three friends sat together in the morning parlor after a late and leisurely breakfast.

After the exertion of the night before, Lady Eliza had awoken with a head cold and was staying in bed with Beacon at her bedside to read to her, an unusual talent in a maid, perhaps, but one Beacon had perfected and appeared to thoroughly enjoy.

"I'm so happy we came up," Hannah said with a watery smile.

Reaching out around the table by the window, Kittie grasped both their hands.

They made a tight circle for a moment, and then Rebecca said, "Enough of this sentimentality. What think you two of the men?"

"Rebecca," Hannah said, with gentle reproof. "You are too bold."

Rebecca, her eyes widening, gazed at her and said, "And you speak who spent the whole evening whispering and cuddling with Mr. Norton? For shame, Hannah!"

Her eyes tearing up, the woman looked about to dissolve into a fit of weeping, but Kittie hastily said, "Hannah, you know she's just teasing! Mr. Norton is clearly smitten with you, but it was he who initiated

your close conversation. Even a fool could see that."
She cast a warning glance at Rebecca.

That woman rolled her eyes, but then turned to Kittie and said, "And you! Whom do you fancy . . . the earl or the duke? You can have your pick, you know."

"Rebecca, your imagination is running riot. Let us instead turn to you, and your swain, Sir John."

"A pleasant dalliance, don't you think?"

"Isn't he a little . . . pardon me, Rebecca," Hannah said, tentatively, "but is he not younger than you?"

Rebecca, her green eyes flashing, said, "Yes, a good deal younger. At least ten years, I hope." She leaned forward and lowered her tone. "Ladies, I am thinking, now that poor old William is gone, of taking a young lover to my bed."

Hannah cried out in alarm, and even Kittie gasped.

"Rebecca, you cannot mean that, you cannot!" Hannah choked out, her voice tight and strangled. Her pale face had gone white, even to her lips.

Kittie gazed steadily at her older friend. "Are you teasing again, Rebecca? Or . . . no, I believe you're serious."

"I am. Why should I not? I've been married twice, both times to men much older than myself. For once I would like to feel younger flesh meet mine before I'm too old to enjoy it."

Hannah fanned herself with her handkerchief and made tiny mewing sounds of horror.

Shocked, too, but unwilling to let her daring friend see how much, Kittie said, "You say that, but I doubt if you will actually do it. You're no courtesan, Rebecca, you're a lady."

"And ladies take lovers all the time. Do you not read the London papers? There is always gossip over 'Lady H.' and 'Lord B.' and their scandalous *affaires,* and so on. And sometimes they are even still married. No . . .

often they are still married. At least I have waited until my dear William was gone. And if I do take a lover, it doesn't make me a courtesan, for you know a woman with 'Lady' before her name will never be that."

"Did you not love your husband?" Hannah gasped out.

Cocking her head to one side, "Of course I did, in my own way. But who was speaking of love? William was very good to me, and I was a virtuous and faithful wife to him. But now, while I'm still young enough to enjoy it, I'm going to take a lover, and I'm going to enjoy myself."

Reluctantly, Kittie had to say that as shocking as it sounded, there was nothing untoward in what she was saying. When she was married and in society, there was much talk about what lovers men and women were involved with, and as long as the parties were discreet, no one thought badly of them for their amorous adventures.

And this was her friend, not herself. Rebecca was an independent woman, with an income of her own and a home to retreat to if she so desired. It made a difference in how she was perceived that she had those things.

"And so, Sir John is the man?" Kittie asked, trying to digest the notion.

"If I can catch him," Rebecca said, thrusting her determined chin out and nodding. "He is as pretty a young man as I have ever seen, and witty, too. But don't worry, Kittie, I promise we'll not carry on our assignation until I leave here." Not having even thought of that complication, Kittie was grateful to her friend for her delicacy.

"Come, ladies, be honest with me," Rebecca continued, including Hannah in her glance. "We have all been widows long enough. Do you mean to tell me that neither of you have thought of bedding down with a man again?"

Kittie drew in a sharp breath, reminded suddenly of the last moments of the evening the night before when the duke saw them to their carriage. He had helped the others into the carriage, but when it came her turn, he grasped her around the waist and lifted her, rather than just handing her in. His touch, so strong, sure, and intimate, had affected her pulse, which hammered erratically, and when she gazed back out at him there was a strange expression on his face in the moonlight, one of uncertainty.

Or was it just a trick of the light?

"Kittie! Did you hear me?"

"What? Oh, I beg your pardon, Rebecca, I was . . ."

"Yes," the woman said with a sly expression. "I know. You were thinking of a certain gentleman, no doubt. But which one, I wonder? The older, more polished earl, or the younger, more powerful duke? What a dilemma, to be sure, to choose between an earl and a duke."

"Now you are talking errant nonsense," Kittie said, sharply.

"But both men did seem rather taken with you," Hannah said, ever timid, but gaining in boldness by Rebecca's example. "Even I could see that."

"And *she* was completely taken up with her Mr. Norton!" Rebecca sat back in her chair and observed her friend. "Yes, I think you might be interested. Oh, I'm not suggesting a dalliance such as I am contemplating; you're far too conventional for that. But did you not say just last night, when we talked before retiring for the night, that you missed being married? I would say that for your purposes, the earl is likely the better possibility. A duke is perhaps too high even for someone as pretty as you. But an earl . . . and a lifelong bachelor, too. He may just need an heir or two and be thinking of setting up his nursery."

Kittie shook her head, but just then Oliver came in, bowed, and said, "The Earl of Orkenay requests your company, Mrs. Douglas. He bids me to pay his compliments to all the ladies, but to ask you if you will walk in the garden with him?"

Rebecca gave her a significant look, and Hannah murmured her encouragement.

Kittie turned to the footman and said, "Tell Lord Orkenay I will fetch my shawl and be out directly."

It did occur to her as she hurried outside that she would have liked him more if he had come in to pay his compliments directly, rather than sending Oliver, but what did she know of manners among such an elevated group as the earl inhabited? Among the upper echelons of the nobility perhaps this was perfectly acceptable.

She saw him before he saw her, and examined him. He was a nice-looking man, for all that he was ten or fifteen years her senior. His hair was silver, but his form was lithe and youthful, and his step was not weary in the least. Could she imagine him as a companion, or . . . or a husband?

How foolish of her, though, when all they had done was have a few conversations. Though she had to admit he had made his admiration plain, and had she not had far more foolish thoughts concerning the duke, and those based solely on his tender letters to his aunt?

The earl turned just then, and his gaze brightened. He came toward her as she approached him on the crushed limestone pathway.

"Mrs. Douglas, how lovely you look today!" He took her hands and held her away from him, looking her over in an admiring way.

She smiled, and yet could not help noticing that she

felt nothing when his hands held hers, not like her ab-
surdly wild flights of fancy just at the touch of the duke's
hands on her waist. How odiously idiotic she was.

She took the earl's offered arm, and they strolled
down the stone path among her roses. The air was
misty and cool, just the way she liked it.

"You must pardon my approach and request this
morning, Mrs. Douglas," he said, earnestly, squeezing
her arm to his side. "I would not in the normal course of
things send a footman to make my request, but my boots
suffered from the walk down here—it rained last night
and the path is rather muddy—and I did not want to
spoil the hallway or the parlor with my muddy boots."

"How considerate of you, my lord! I would never
imagine a gentleman of your status to be so . . .
thoughtful of the maids." It was, indeed, not merely
highly unusual, but in her experience, unheard of.

"I assure you, I'm the most domestic of gentlemen.
A stern look from my housekeeper and I quail, my
dear. And I am mindful that Lady Eliza's household is
small and taxed with extra guests; I could not add to
your own worries, as, I'm sure, the chief administrator
of the household. What impression would that make
on you? But my intention this morning is not to talk
of myself, but to speak to you of a matter very near to
my heart."

She glanced over at him quizzically. He guided her
to a stone bench, and they sat down.

Birdsong trilled in the air, and the breeze freshened,
ruffling the flowers and making the branches sway.
Lord Orkenay wrapped Kittie more closely in her
shawl. Roger would never have thought of such a tender attention; perhaps there would be consolations in
marrying an older man.

"I just enjoy your company so much, my dear," he
said, after a pause. "I have never met a lady quite like

you. You are a rarity, I feel, a beautiful woman who has no vanity, nor any pretense."

She was abashed; never had a man been so forthright in his admiration, but she honored his honesty. It was said without expectation nor with any demand in his tone.

"You will make me blush, my lord, with your kindness."

"No," he said earnestly, pressing her hand. "I'm not kind, I'm honest. I feel like my whole life . . . but I get ahead of myself. I will not push my suit too hard. It is sufficient to say, I think, that I consider you the most lovely, sweet, honorable woman of my acquaintance, and I wish to further our friendship."

Never had a gentleman said such earnest, sincere, and honorable things to her, and in such a fervent manner. She felt a little trill of anticipation to think that he might be seriously interested in her. No woman in her position could afford to do otherwise than consider her own future. "I'm honored by your esteem, my lord, and return the wish for friendship."

"Then I consider myself the most fortunate of men," the earl said, rising and laying one gentle kiss on her hand. "I must return to the duke and our companions, but I think you will see all of us before the day is out and I look forward to more conversation then."

He bowed and left her, but she sat in the garden for a while, wondering if the clear impression she had received—that he wished her to consider him a possible suitor for her hand—was justified.

And how did she feel about him if what she thought was true?

The afternoon had become overcast with a rumble of thunder in the distance on the other side of the fell, but instead of seeking shelter Alban paced the length of the Bodenthorpe Cottage rose garden and tried to pinpoint the source of his agitation. He would enter presently and visit Lady Eliza and her company, but first it behooved him to attain a measure of serenity.

So what was wrong with him?

It was true that he was not pleased with the way his visit to his aunt was proceeding. He had intended to enjoy the quiet and solitude of Yorkshire and the company of his beloved aunt. Finding that she was blind and had not seen fit to tell him about the momentous change in her circumstance had been the first blow. Learning that her companion, a Mrs. Douglas of no discernible family and with only a tenuous connection to gentility, was her trusted helper, attendant, and even friend, had added to his uneasiness. The little he had been able to ascertain about her in the days he had been here was that she was of gentle birth, but had married poorly, lived precariously, and had descended to the position she now held. But she was far too beautiful to be a paid companion to an elderly blind woman.

Every time he looked at her he felt the unwelcome stirring within him. She was not suitable for a mistress, though, because he could see how much his aunt relied on her. To take her away from Lady Eliza would be cruel and heartless, and yet, he could not have her as long as she remained in his aunt's employ. It was an impossible situation, and he had resigned himself to admiring her looks, enjoying her company—surprisingly, she was an intelligent conversationalist, for a woman—and nothing more.

He stood and stared up at the house. If only he could trust that Orkenay would be so circumspect. Ah! He had happened on the burr under his saddle. It was the thought of Orkenay, and how devoted he seemed to be to Mrs. Douglas, that made him uneasy. And that was

likely just because he suspected the earl would try to seduce Kittie Douglas away from her honorable employ.
He was worried for his aunt, that was all.

He nodded briskly and strode to the door, banging
on it with an unwarranted clatter. His aunt had no butler, so Oliver, her footman, opened the door and
bowed.

"Is my aunt in the parlor?"

"She is, Your Grace."

He strode in only to find the parlor full, with Orkenay, Sir John, and Bart already there, and the ladies
too.

"Alban," Bart cried, strangely cheery, his face flushed
and eyes glittering. "I knew you would head here eventually. It looked like bad weather was closing in, and so,
when you didn't come back, we thought we would join
the ladies for the afternoon. Your aunt was kind
enough to extend the invitation to dinner, as well."

"I was only gone a while conferring with Mr. Lafferty!
Is Boden so lacking in congenial pastimes that you
must turn to Bodenthorpe Cottage?"

"After all, Alban, you did," Sir John said, with a secretive smile.

"It is my aunt's home. I hope I can visit my aunt with
no accusation of any other motive being levied against
me."

"You are far too irritable, nephew. Come talk to me."

"Alban is just tired of company, perhaps," Orkenay
said, from his position winding wool for Kittie Douglas.

Alban shot him an irritable glance, but was caught by
the very homely nature of the earl's activity. He
stopped. "Orkenay, you are becoming domesticated,
like Bernard there," he said, indicating the fat, lazy, old
tabby Tom who adorned the hearth, letting his belly
spread as he lolled over on his back. "I shall broadcast
this about London, you know, and soon you will have

every tabby in every parlor all a-twitter that you are finally ready to settle on one woman."

"How mean-spirited you are today, Alban," the earl said, lightly. "But I think I would not object to being compared to that old Tom if I were allowed to have my Kittie," he added slyly, glancing at his companion, who colored prettily and ducked her head, winding her wool with ferocious concentration.

"How very precious." Alban sneered, unable to contain his vexation.

He was rewarded by a wide-eyed look of consternation from Mrs. Douglas, and he regretted his ill temper immediately. He was becoming a bear, but he didn't know what was wrong with him.

"Come here, Alban," Lady Eliza said, with a tone that brooked no nonsense.

He hoped he was man enough not to object to her hectoring. He sat down beside her.

"What is wrong with you today? I will not have you roaring at my guests nor even at your own guests, and certainly not at Kittie."

"My apologies, Aunt. I didn't sleep well last night."

"That is not an excuse. However, I will not spend our time together quarreling, even if you do deserve a thorough tongue-lashing. But know that I will not have you acting so poorly without remonstrance." She reached out for his hand and grasped it.

Gazing down at it, he noted that her hands were as bony and strong as always, and she had lost none of her fierceness of attitude. It was what he had always loved about her, her absolute indomitable spirit.

Why did he so appreciate it in her and abhor it in other women, condemning it as unwomanly? He supposed there was a vast difference in what one would want to see in one's relation, and what one would want to see in a wife or mistress. He turned in his chair and could see Orkenay winding wool, still, for Mrs. Douglas, to whom he was whispering.

"What do you know about her?" he asked, almost talking to himself.

"Of whom are you speaking, nephew?" Lady Eliza said, her tone forbidding.

He still held his aunt's hand. "I think you know I'm talking about Mrs. Douglas. Do not try to reprove me. You can no longer cut through me with your gaze, as you once did, anyway."

She tightened her grip and his hand went numb. "But I am still not a fool, Alban. You are being abominable today. Why? What is wrong with you?"

He was silent. What could he say? He had come north for peace and to see his beloved aunt. He supposed he had pictured a quiet bucolic visit with walks over the fells with his Aunt Eliza and the occasional hunting party with Bart and the others. Instead there was a veritable country house party, complete with flirting couples and the confusion of a gorgeous woman who stirred his blood but was unattainable by virtue of her relation to his aunt, who had gone blind since the last time he saw her. And he was being a selfish ogre.

He cradled Lady Eliza's capable hands in his own and examined her, the strong Alban jaw, the wrinkles now tracing lines down from her nose to her mouth, and the milky opacity of her once-clear eyes.

It had been a blow for him, her blindness, and he couldn't imagine what strength it had taken for her to face such darkness, and all alone.

Or . . . no, not alone, for it appeared that Mrs. Kittie Douglas had admirably become a bulwark protecting his aunt from the worst of the fear and loneliness. He should be appreciative of Mrs. Douglas instead of being faintly resentful and suspicious.

He would start anew. Taking a deep breath, he said,

"You're right; I've been an ogre and a bear and I will start again."

Lady Eliza nodded. "Good boy. Tell me what is happening in London; give me all the gossip. And tell me about the poor queen and her daughters and young George. I have heard that he is getting enormously fat and fancies himself ill. Is that true?"

Alban talked to her for a while as he watched the others. Bart was completely taken with one of Mrs. Douglas's widowed friends, Mrs. Billings. Alban could not see the attraction himself; the woman was well-enough looking, he supposed, but her pale eyes were often watery, and she seemed on the verge of tears. But Bart had been suffering himself of late from a depression of spirits. It would seem, strangely, that in buoying the despondent Mrs. Billings, Bart's own woes were forgotten.

And then there was Sir John, the mysterious young fellow who had somehow insinuated himself into the party heading north.

Lady Eliza at that moment squeezed Alban's hand and said, "Enough of court gossip; tell me of your friends. I know Bart well enough, of course. But Sir John . . . from his voice he seems a most pleasing young man, though he has been very circumspect with me when I ask him how he came to know you and why he decided to join you in Yorkshire."

Alban gazed over at the young man who was engaged in some silly word game with Lady Rebecca Severn. "He was one of the ever-present hangers-on in Brighton— new to the court this year but well received, for he is witty and congenial—and he seems a harmless young man. I had heard that he was attached in some manner to some government office, but if so, his duties are most light."

Lady Eliza pursed her lips. "But how did you come to know him?"

"Just as one of Prinny's court. He was always at the Marine Pavilion, but he really seems a pleasant young sprig compared to some of the other unwholesome chaps who worship at Prinny's swollen feet."

"Hmm. And the earl; is he as enamored of Kittie as it appears just from listening to the silly fellow?"

"Orkenay . . . yes, it appears his regard is genuine, but I cannot say with what end in mind."

Lady Eliza sat back in her chair, releasing Alban's hand. "I will not have Kittie hurt. I leave it up to you to find out what he intends, nephew."

"That is hardly my province, ma'am," he replied, though he had been thinking much the same himself just moments before. "They are both, after all, fully grown adults."

"There is just something about him that makes me uneasy," she said.

Alban was silent. He had to agree. There was something about the earl's behavior that made him uneasy, too, though he really was being the soul of propriety. Were his own feelings mixed up in the blend? For he had to admit, if he was honest, that the thought of Mrs. Douglas in the earl's arms was enough to make him cold with anger.

It was something to ponder; was Orkenay truly interested in Kittie Douglas, or did he see her as a dalliance? And what business of Alban's was it, either way? Well, Lady Eliza's concern had made it his business, and so he stood and motioned to the earl.

"Orkenay, could I have a word with you in the library, please?"

The earl stood up, a frown marring his pleasant expression. "What is this about, Alban?"

Rather than answer, Alban exited, expecting that the earl would follow.

He strode to the library and Orkenay did, indeed, follow him in.

"What do you mean by making a spectacle of me, Alban, as though I were a schoolboy called onto the mat?"

Alban gazed at the other man, undecided how to handle the necessary interrogation. He supposed this was a bad beginning, and he cursed his own impetuosity in dragging the man away from the company in such an abrupt manner. What exactly did his aunt want? It was certainly not in his interest to enrage the earl, though he had never seen Orkenay even mildly put out. This was the most angry Alban had ever seen him, and he seemed to be just perturbed.

"It has come to my attention that you are expressing an open interest in Mrs. Douglas. As my aunt's companion, her welfare is our interest."

Orkenay strolled around the room, turning objects over and disarranging piles of books on tables. "Are you asking me my intentions? How amusing. I feel as though you are her father, and I must tell you of my plans for the future."

A spurt of anger flared in Alban's breast, but he tamped it down. "So?"

"So? Mrs. Douglas is a damned fine woman, don't you think?"

"She is lovely, in her own fashion."

The earl whirled and jabbed one finger in the air. "Exactly! She is out of the usual way of women in London or Brighton. Very amusing."

"But she is not exactly a woman of breeding or gentility. I mean to say," Alban continued, frustrated by his lack of ability to express his exact meaning. "Mrs. Douglas is genteel, but there is no particular family history there."

Orkenay shrugged. "Who worries about breeding when a woman looks like her? She is a different type . . . earthy, physical, good country stock, I would say. Healthy young woman like that, locked away in Yorkshire for years with no male companionship . . ." He broke off and winked. "There is nothing so invigorating as a lonely woman faced with a man she has expressed an interest in."

Alban's hand clenched. What was infuriating was that there was nothing Orkenay had actually said that was untrue, by appearances. The earl's tone was one of one man of the world to another, and it was nothing that he had not said himself, in other times and about other women. But this time it offended him gravely.

"Orkenay, please remember where you are and that Mrs. Douglas is my aunt's paid companion, and therefore under the protection of my household."

Eyes widening, Orkenay drew back. "Alban! I'm shocked. Why would you assume that I mean anything but that Mrs. Douglas and I are enjoying the invigorating prospect of a mild flirtation?"

"Just see that you keep it to that." Alban strode to the doorway but turned back and glared at the earl in the murky light of the library. "Mrs. Douglas is, I am told, of a good family. Please don't forget that, and act accordingly."

"She is also an adult woman," Orkenay said. "With wants and needs I am more than willing to satisfy, at some point in time, near or distant. Don't *you* forget that, Alban."

Nine

Dinner and the evening had not brought any fresh reason for concern on Alban's part. It seemed that his words had had a salutary effect, and the earl was being very careful in his attentions to Mrs. Douglas. But Alban's stomach still churned and his mind still worked furiously on the problem.

He walked the woodland path alone the next morning. After an afternoon and night of rain, the dead leaves on the path were slithery, but the scent that arose was refreshingly countrified to his city-deadened senses.

What was wrong with him? Perhaps he was being unfair to Mrs. Douglas, but he couldn't help but feel that she had ulterior motives in immuring herself in Yorkshire with Lady Eliza Burstead. Was her past all she claimed, or were there scandals of which his aunt was ignorant? Had Lafferty really researched her as he declared? Was she truly simply an unfortunate widow?

Brooding, he came to the edge of the forest and found that, once again, he had made his way to the cottage, and there, once again, was Mrs. Douglas in the garden, cutting roses. He stood at the edge of the woods and watched.

She was graceful, there was no doubt of that, but with no mincing step or studied kind of grace. Rounded

and voluptuous, her auburn hair unbound and drap-
ing in glorious curls down her back almost to her waist,
her gown a simple print morning gown, she was more
beautiful than any woman he had ever seen, and his
heart thudded treacherously, his breath catching in his
throat. Ill with longing, he gazed in rapt stillness.

One single ray of sunshine broke through the
canopy of cloud and the wall of trees and shone on her
hair, lighting it to flame. She turned her face to the
sunbeam and her pale throat was exposed, a column of
white, like marble. Alban stared, capturing that moment in his memory, soaking it in as Kittie Douglas
soaked in the sunbeam.

And then the moment ended; she turned and
caught sight of him, standing at the edge of the forest
like some Oberon staring at his glorious Titania. Her
lips parted and she said something, but he couldn't
hear. On numb legs he lurched toward her, recovering
his composure enough as he approached, so he would
not look a complete ass.

"I'm sorry, Mrs. Douglas, I was too far away to hear
you," he said, breaking the spell with such ordinary
words. He leaned on the wall, drinking in the sight of
her so close, her ruddy curls beckoning his fingers, her
lush form summoning his body.

"I . . . I merely said, will you join us for breakfast, sir?"

"Breakfast?" He had lost his train of thought again in
staring into her eyes. How had he never noticed how
blue they were and large, fringed with dark lashes?

Pink mantled her cheeks and her breathing quickened. He imagined leaping over the wall, taking her
into his arms, and kissing her roughly and thoroughly.
Oh, for days gone by when he might have caught her
up in his arms, tossed her up on his saddle, and stolen
her away for a night of passion. He was enough of a sav-
age sensualist to find the idea enticing, and too much

of a civilized creature to think that it would ultimately serve anything but the briefest and most one-sided of passions. In the old tales of kidnapping and seductions no one ever considered the woman's thoughts or feelings in the matter, it had long ago occurred to him.

Like cold water dashed on him, such civilized reflections cooled his ardor. He was not a medieval knight, after all, but a modern man, to whom abduction was anathema.

"Uh, no, I have already eaten breakfast, but please, don't let me stop you."

"I've already eaten. But Lady Eliza is still at the table."

He chuckled. "Have you ever seen any woman who can eat as much as she can?"

"And yet she stays so thin . . . gaunt, even," Mrs. Douglas said, smiling and shaking her head in wonder.

"She seems to eat the most at that meal, and then not a lot for the rest of the day." The mundane aspect of the subject matter struck him at that moment. Never would he have, in the past, considered discussing his aunt's dietary habits with a woman he lusted after so fiercely.

Kittie stayed silent. Alban straightened and pushed away from the wall. "Does she still . . . does my aunt still go for walks in the hills?"

"She does, accompanied by Mr. Lafferty or myself. But"—she shyly looked away—"I think, Your Grace, she would consider it a special favor if you would walk with her occasionally while you are here."

"I was thinking the same thing." It was curious that he should not take her suggestion amiss; he did not generally bear up well under advice from any source. He moved toward the gate and opened it. "Mrs. Douglas, would you walk a ways with me? I feel we have not really gotten to know each other since I arrived, and I do want you to know how much I appreciate your devotion to my aunt."

Kittie laid down her basket and exited the garden, taking his offered arm. "She is a wonderful woman, sir, and even if she was not my employer it would be a privilege to know her."

Was she sincere? She had the look and sound of sincerity. Had he just become so jaded by court life that he could not recognize a good woman when he met one?

He had to admit the possibility, and to that end he would talk with her and walk with her. He led her down the path and away from the cottage. He noticed that she threw one long, lingering glance back, over her shoulder, toward the garden.

"Let's climb up to the fairy cavern and waterfall. I wish to see the improvements Lafferty has effected."

"I think you'll be pleased by the work. It's quite marvelous, really."

"Do you go there often?"

"No. I . . . I don't feel it is right to leave Lady Eliza so long. But this morning I know she is still recovering from her cold and is going to have Beacon read to her for a while in the parlor." She began the stiff ascent up the grassy hill, away from the copse and toward the rill that joined the beck, or quick-running brook, at the bottom of the fell.

"That isn't the way there," Alban called, trying not to stare at the enticing sway of her bottom as she climbed.

She glanced over her shoulder and smiled. "It is now. Mr. Lafferty agreed that for those who can manage the ascent, this is much quicker."

"You seem to have wrapped Stuart pretty snugly around your finger, Mrs. Douglas," Alban said, grunting as he climbed after her.

"Nonsense! He is just a sensible male and amenable to suggestion, not at all the usual sort."

And yet his land manager was known to be unusually stubborn, even for a Yorkshireman, and there was no other kind. It was contumacy of an unusual force that kept them surviving through bitter winters, spring floods, poor harvests, and unfair tax laws.

He wondered once again about the subtle seduction a smart woman could use to get her own way, and how Mrs. Kittie Douglas perhaps planned to use it in the next while on Orkenay. They didn't talk during the climb, mostly because all of their energy was devoted to ascending.

He followed her path, and when they came to Boden Rill and the fairy waterfall, as it had been called in his youth, he was taken by surprise, perhaps the intent of the new pathway.

They came out instead of at the top or bottom, at a spot about halfway up. Above them was a sheer face of stone shelves over which tumbled sparkling water, and below them the water hit the pool. It was exhilarating gazing down from a height of twenty feet or more, and dizzying looking up another twenty feet.

Kittie moved along the path and indicated wood steps up to a narrow stone shelf. "We . . . Mr. Lafferty and I, discovered another cave about halfway along, and with just these few wood steps, you can get to the stone path and explore it."

Alban grinned, leaning against the stone wall as he caught his breath. "Yes, Bart and I climbed up here once or twice. I wondered if our secret cave, as we called it, still existed in its seclusion. But you found it out."

She grinned back. "Will you go with me?"

"Of course," he said. "Why would I not?"

She picked up her skirts, showing an enticing flash of well-shaped ankle and calf, and they scaled the precarious shelf; within moments they were in the small cave behind the waterfall.

"Look," she said, her voice, hushed and awed, echoing back in the stone cavern.

Before them the sun broke through the trees just then, and, through the mist, a rainbow appeared, arching down to the pool below.

She lowered herself down to sit on the shelf, and he followed her example, watching her with interest as she gazed in awe at the spectacle until the sunbeam shifted and the rainbow disappeared. When it was gone she sighed and turned back to him, catching him watching her.

"Where did you come from?" he asked, almost to himself.

"Devonshire," she said, interpreting his question literally, though it had not been intended that way. "I was raised there, but when I married I moved to Bath first, and then to London."

"From Bath to London? Why?"

She stared down the rock face to the pool below. Her day dress was damp at the hem and her unbound hair, too, from the mist, tiny pearly globules of water decorating her hair like a misty netting, but she didn't seem to care. "I didn't question Roger," she said, with a shrug, "I just did as he bade."

"Roger . . . that was your husband's name?"

"Of course! Of whom did you think I was speaking?"

Her tone was sharp; why, he wasn't sure. Their walk had started on good terms, but now he wondered at that wariness.

"I was merely making conversation. How long were you widowed before you came to my aunt?"

"Two years."

"What did you do in that time?"

She bridled and stood, wavering. She stamped one foot. "My foot has gone to sleep."

He stood, too, and said, "You didn't answer my question."

Her eyes widening, she retorted, "I don't think it is any of your business. I can understand any questions you might have concerning my time here, but before is before."

Even more intriguing. She moved to push past him, but he caught her arm as she swayed back. She pulled her arm out of his grasp, teetered on the edge of the path, and he caught hold of her again.

"Mrs. Douglas," he said, his tone biting. "I would not advise you to move hastily. There is rock at the bottom and a deep pool, no one is sure how deep, but it is carved in sheer rock. The water disappears there back into the fell. Please be careful. If you fall in I will have to jump in and fish you out. If you wish to return to Bodenthorpe Cottage you need only say so."

"I wish to return to the cottage."

"Your wish is my command."

"Then you will need to move, sir."

He regarded her carefully, her flushed face and glittering eyes. What had he said or done to offend her? Or was there no offense, just guilt? He turned and made his way back to the safety of the path, and she followed, but her foot slipped on the damp mossy rock as she made the transition. He caught her once again and pulled her to him.

Her heart was pounding against his chest and her auburn hair tangled over his hands where they gripped her tight. Staring down into her eyes, with the sound of the rushing water and the cool shadowy green all around them, he was tempted by her full lips. She met his gaze, and there was a question in the clear blue and dark expanding pupils.

But he released her, and she passed him, and they made their way back with no further talk. Somehow he had ruined their tenuous connection just by asking about the mysterious two years between her husband's death and her tenure at Bodenthorpe Cottage.

Why?

Over luncheon Kittie thought about her morning ramble with the duke. Lady Eliza commented that she seemed abstracted. Hannah shot her worried little glances. Only Rebecca let her go in peace.

After eating, they all sat together at the luncheon table, discussing projects for their stay at Bodenthorpe Cottage. But Kittie found that her mind would still wander. The walk with the duke had left her confused. It had started so well, but he had shattered their comfortable companionship with close questioning. It had felt like an interrogation, not so much the questions, she supposed, as his tone, harsh and suspicious.

Maybe she had taken offense too easily, and she had certainly been hasty and precipitous in moving away from the waterfall. She never thought she would be the kind of idiot female to endanger her safety through pique.

But it began to seem that his only reason in asking her to walk had been to pry into her past. There was no great mystery there; she had laid her life bare to Lady Eliza, even telling her the sordid tales of Roger's gambling, but Lady Eliza had never made her feel as if she was prying.

But the duke . . . she had seen in his eyes as he made his farewell that he had gained only suspicion of her from their unfortunate discord. And she really had no one to blame but herself. She could have cleared up any suspicion, warranted or not, in two sentences, but it had been beneath her dignity. Or pride.

"Kittie! Kittie! The girl has not heard a word we have said to her this half hour!"

"I . . . I beg your pardon, Rebecca," Kittie said, awakening from her reverie with a start.

"Oh, it is no matter," Lady Severn said, airily, with a wave of her elegant hand. "When one is beset with beaux . . ."

"Rebecca!" Kittie cried and cast a glance at Lady Eliza. She would not have her employer know about her embarrassing infatuation over the duke for anything. It was hideously inappropriate, and she sorely regretted ever divulging to Rebecca her feelings. It had just been such a joy to see her friends again, that she and Hannah and Rebecca had stayed up late a couple of times and just talked long into the night.

"Rebecca is being droll," Hannah said, gently. "She often thinks she is wittier than she is."

"I would not be surprised by any male admiration Kittie was in receipt of," Lady Eliza said. "I have long considered her the sweetest of girls, and if my memory serves she is one of the most beautiful."

Kittie stared at her benefactress. An enigmatic smile tugged the woman's lips upward.

"She still is that," Rebecca said. "And I can tell you, Lady Eliza, that when we all were in London, many men regretted that she was attached to Roger Douglas. She could have had her pick of gentlemen far better financially set."

"Rebecca!" Kittie remonstrated, hurt by her friend's candid words. "I loved Roger sincerely, and he was a good and devoted husband to me!"

"But he was a poor gambler and a worse provider."

"That is uncalled for," Kittie said, her voice shaking.

"He loved me. You may have chosen a husband for reasons other than love . . ."

"Kittie, Rebecca," Hannah said, raising her voice. "Nothing shall be gained by squabbling."

"Mrs. Billings is right," Lady Eliza said. "I think that we should adjourn . . ."

Oliver entered the room just then and bowed. "My lady, Lord Orkenay sends his regards and requests permission to invite Mrs. Douglas for a walk."

"Really," Kittie said, with asperity, "can the gentleman not come in and pay his respects in person, first?"

Oliver turned to her and said, "He said that you would ask that, ma'am, and told me to say that he has something particularly on his mind that leaves him ill at ease and unfit for company, and that after he speaks to you about that he would be glad to come in and sit with the ladies."

"Go," Rebecca urged.

"I wouldn't, Kittie," Hannah said, her face set in worried lines. "He really is being most impolite."

Kittie turned to Lady Eliza. "My lady, what should I do?"

That woman, her expression an enigmatic mask, said, "Kittie, you must do what you will. It seems to me that Lord Orkenay has something particular he wants to say to you, as he said so eloquently in his message by Oliver, and that it will be swiftest to hear him out."

Reluctantly, Kittie nodded, then said, "I suppose." She turned to the footman. "Tell him I will join him in the garden in five minutes, Oliver. The day has gotten cooler, and I will fetch my shawl first."

Rebecca followed Kittie out toward the stairs. "My dear," she said, grasping Kittie's arm. "I'm sorry for what I said."

Kittie gave her a quick hug. "It's all right. I have long

known we have a difference of opinion about some things."

Holding her away, Rebecca stared into her eyes. "My fear is that you will not do what is best for yourself and your future for that very reason."

"What do you mean?"

"Just that the earl seems genuinely taken with you, Kittie, and I needn't say that he's a most eligible gentleman. If he should propose . . ."

Kittie protested with a quick exclamation and a movement.

"No!" Rebecca shook her lightly. "Listen to me. You would have to be blind . . . Oh! I didn't mean to say . . ." She shook her head, her dark curls bouncing on her shoulders. "I am being most incoherent today. What I mean is, he is clearly vastly taken with you. This particular behavior can mean nothing but that he is going to propose marriage, my dear, and if he should, tell me that you will at least consider it!"

Through the open doors Kittie could hear a clock as it ticked on the sideboard in the dining room, measuring the seconds and minutes. Life was moving on, every second of every day taking her closer to her own end, and as pleasant and mundane as her life at Bodenthorpe Cottage was, could she honestly say that she was living as she would have chosen? Lord Orkenay had expressed a preference for her, and in the intervening days had taken every opportunity to talk to her and get to know her. If he should truly be interested in her as a possible wife, as unlikely as that seemed, should she not hear him out?

"All right, Rebecca, I'll listen to what he has to say."

She retrieved her shawl and exited the house a few moments later, to find the earl pacing in the garden. She wanted to upbraid him for his discourtesy in again asking her to walk with him without coming in and pay-ing his respects to her employer, but something in his manner stopped her.

He glanced up and watched her approach. "Mrs. Douglas, how kind you are to indulge me this way. I must apologize once again for calling you out like this."

"I must admit I was surprised and a little disconcerted, my lord."

"And that is the furthest thing from my wishes," he said, taking her arm and guiding her out the garden gate.

He directed her down a path to the meadow, and she felt some relief that at least he was not taking her through the woods. Something in that action would have made her uneasy.

"I just needed to speak to you, and knew I would make poor company until I have had my say," he said.

Still puzzled as to his meaning, but not feeling any need to respond, Kittie stayed silent.

"Your silence I find encouraging. It tells me you will listen to what I have to say. I must preface my . . . well, my request, by saying that I have never met any woman so lovely as you."

Skeptical but unwilling to interrupt, Kittie still remained silent as they walked down a path that wove through the shorn grass of the hay meadow. She cast an uneasy glance back at the cottage, nestled snugly, barricaded from the world by stone walls. A curl of smoke puffed from a chimney and drifted on the September breeze.

"You are so very lovely, but with that you unite such a fine mind, ladylike demeanor . . . in short, you are perfection, my dear."

"I think, my lord, that no woman reaches such a state as perfection."

"And demure, too! You are far too modest, my dearest."

She shot a look at him, but his gaze was directed off in the distance, at a hill near the cottage. She started to look off that way herself, but he suddenly stopped her, turning her and clutching her shoulders in his tight grip. She would have been alarmed, but the expression on his face was still mild.

"Mrs. Douglas, I am a man of few words. I find you exceptionally attractive, and have come to adore your sweetness of countenance, your adorable modesty . . . in short, I have come to think that I cannot live without you!"

Dubious at first, Kittie was convinced that he truly was coming to the point. He was going to propose, and after knowing her only a week! What should she say? Should she ask for more time, or simply say they would need to get to know each other better?

"I . . . I don't know what to say, my lord . . . you honor me, but . . ."

"Do not answer yet! Oh, my little love, that you should know how my heart beats whenever I see you!"

The declaration seemed false, but Kittie, gazing into his eyes—he was a bit shorter than she, she had thought, but they were eye to eye that moment—could not imagine why a man would seek to attach her if not for love. She wasn't wealthy, nor did she have any future expectations. Perhaps it was just his theatrical demeanor that made it seem artificial.

"Kittie . . . if I may be so bold as to call you by your adorable given name . . . may I ask . . ."

"Yes, my lord?"

"Will you come back to London with me?"

"I beg your pardon?"

"Oh, for the words of a poet . . . come live with me and be my love!" He struck his breast with a free hand. "And I will . . . oh, I don't remember it at all. Always was a poor student of poetry. But you know what I mean.

Anyway, will you come back to London with me? I have
a lovely house in Richmond that happens to be vacant
at the moment. I would be happy to see you snug there,
and I can introduce you to such society . . ."

Stunned, Kittie tried to digest the earl's words.
"What . . . what are you asking?"

"Why, my dear, have I not made myself plain? I am
asking if you will be my mistress!"

Ten

Alban, when he asked about the whereabouts of his guest the earl, was informed by his butler of Lord Orkenay's walk to the cottage. Suspicious of his intentions, he pursued him there, but found only Lady Severn and Mrs. Billings in the morning parlor. He abruptly made his obeisance to both ladies, and then asked of Lady Severn where Lord Orkenay and Mrs. Douglas were.

"Why, they have gone out for a walk . . . just a few moments ago they left," Lady Severn said. "It was the oddest thing. Lord Orkenay would not even come in, for apparently he has something in particular he wishes to say to Kittie."

Alban did not miss the alarmed glance Mrs. Billings cast her friend. She would rather the woman had not said anything. "Really."

"Yes. They have gone walking. Toward the east meadow, if I did not mistake their direction once they were out of the garden."

That she spied on her friend did not shock Alban. Lady Severn was the kind of woman who had a need to know everything. He bowed, thanked her for the information, and said he would see them later that day with the gentlemen. He strode out of the house, exited the garden, and looked at both paths, the one through the woods and back to his house, and the one down the slope and into the meadow.

Inevitably, he took the one through the meadow. Kittie Douglas was, after all, his aunt's companion. He had the dual responsibilities of her protection and the protection of his aunt at heart, he assured himself as he strode.

Kittie, in shock at the earl's words, was helpless as he clasped her to his chest and covered her mouth with his. He tried to pull her down into the grass, but she twisted, unwilling to allow him such a freedom, even as she was paralyzed with the horror of his offensive request. His kiss continued for infinity, it seemed, and yet she could not move. He didn't appear strong, but he had her arms pinned to her sides.

When he released her, she put one trembling hand to her mouth, and said, "I can't have heard you right, my lord. I *will* not believe I understood. What . . . what did you ask of me?"

He smiled at her, his expression full of sly meaning. "My dear, I think you understand full well what I said. I asked if you would be my mistress. It is a very lucrative position, and far more entertaining than being companion to an old blind woman. And I promise, the *work* will not be onerous!"

Ashamed and horrified, afraid that she had done or said something that had led him to believe she would acquiesce to such an arrangement, Kittie opened her mouth to speak, but found it covered again with his. She struggled this time, but though not as large a man as the duke, the earl truly was surprisingly strong. He kept her against him, releasing her only after a long, deep, wet kiss.

His grip loosened, and Kittie pushed him away, finally, wiping her mouth with vigor. Cold with anger, she said, "I can't believe you think I would acquiesce, my lord, to such an arrangement as you suggest. What woman in the world would go willingly from a position of respectability to one of such disgrace?"

Clearly disconcerted, he said, "Disgrace? But, my dear, a life of ease is yours for the taking! I have told you, I would give you your own house in Richmond, wait on you, give you jewels . . . how can that be disgraceful?"

At first convinced that he was being unbearably base and that he must have known she would find his offer insulting, Kittie, gazing at him steadily, saw the shock on his face and the bewilderment. She backed away a little more on the path. "I don't know what it is like in your world," she said, her voice low and trembling with emotion, "but in my circle a woman who willingly goes to a man without benefit of marriage . . ." She trailed off, remembering that her friend Rebecca was considering just such a thing with young Sir John. So were her thoughts on the subject out of step with society? Was she exceedingly prudish? It had been several years since she had been in society, but she had seen much there, and yet—Uncertainly, she continued, "It is just not the life I choose for myself."

Hearing something in her tone that perhaps made him think she was softening, he took a step toward her. "I am a most considerate lover, my sweet."

Her stomach twisted at his intimate words. A cloud passed across the sun, and the shadows flitted over the meadow. "I don't think you understand," she said, trying to be reasonable and quell the anger that she felt over his invitation. "How can I benefit, ultimately? Without marriage, if you tire of me I lose everything, and my loss of reputation will then cause me much suffering, for once lost, no woman can regain it."

"But you will materially benefit, my dear, I have promised you that," he said, with an earnest expression. He moved toward her and held out his arms. "The house in Richmond . . ."

"Yours, sir, and not mine. When you tired of me, I have no doubt you would demand that I vacate the premises."

"But that might not happen for a long time," he replied. "You are very beautiful, and there is something more . . ."

Kittie turned away and began walking back to the cottage. She could listen no more to a catalog of her assets, as though she were being listed in a bill of sale at an auction house. The conversation had taken on the tone of a negotiation, and since she had no intention of ever acquiescing, it was pointless. He followed, she knew, but did not accost her again until they were almost at the garden gate.

"Please forgive me if I have offended you, Mrs. Douglas," he said.

There was such sincerity in his tone that she stopped and looked back at him. "You have, Lord Orkenay," she said, unlatching the gate. "But I cannot help thinking that you don't quite understand why."

"I admit, I have made this proposal before and the answer was far different from yours," he said ruefully. "You are a rare woman, Mrs. Douglas. I said it before and you have done nothing to disprove my statement."

Frowning down at her shoe and smudging it in the dirt as she thought, Kittie said, "There are many who would think I was mad for turning you down; it is a generous offer, sir, one I'm sure some women would thank you for. Others would think me mad for *accepting*. It is said, as I stated before, that feminine virtue is like a jewel; once cast away, it can never be recovered. But I am not one who happens to believe that a man and a woman enjoying each other out of wedlock is necessarily a sin."

"Really," he said, advancing on her.

"No, my lord, that was not an invitation," she said hastily, putting up one hand and blocking his movement.

He merely reached up, though, and tenderly pushed a stray curl from her bun back behind her ear and caressed her cheek with his finger, rubbing the soft flesh of her chin. "I know."

"But what I was saying is, that to become your mistress would mean, for me . . . oh, I don't know how to say it. Please don't be offended, my lord," Kittie said, not wanting to hurt the earl, who seemed to be only guilty of misunderstanding her wants. "But to come to you as mistress would require two things: an overpowering love or need on my part, and the absolute impossibility of a legitimate match on yours. But in this instance—pardon me again, my lord—I don't love you. And on the other side . . . sir, you aren't married or otherwise ineligible for marriage. There is no impediment to marriage for you. In fact . . . why have you never married?"

"I will tell you sometime perhaps. Not now. I need to go away and think," he said, his whole mien expressing dejection and even his posture dispirited. "I feel sure that you have underestimated your effect on me, my dear, and how hard this will be for me to accept."

Hand still on the gate, she watched him turn, as if to walk away, and then turn back.

"One thing, Mrs. Douglas . . . please, may I beg the favor of a kiss from you? I know I rather pushed myself on you last time, and I would erase it with one single solitary kiss from you given of your own free will."

"I don't think . . ."

"Please! As a great, a *very* great, favor, one I promise

to never ask again. I shall think you furious with me if you don't."

"I don't think . . ."

"Please! Just this once and I shall leave you alone."

"All right," she said reluctantly, anxious for him to leave and thinking to hasten that moment.

He opened his arms and she let go of the gate and walked into them. He kissed her, gently, this time, and yet it left her cold. What would she have done if his proposal had been a legitimate one, for marriage? Maybe it was lucky that she would never know. With all her fine-sounding words, she might still have been tempted into a marriage so inconceivably beneficial to her future.

With a sigh, he released her and with one final caress, walked away. He stopped, though, looked back, and said, "Make my apologies to the ladies. I'm sure I'll see you all later."

Alban watched from a window as Orkenay kissed Mrs. Douglas tenderly, cupped her cheek briefly in his palm and then turned to walk down the path. How touching! What had been agreed between them, the duke wondered, burning with anger. He had not even told the others he was there, resolving to wait until he was fit to see his aunt, after what he had witnessed in the meadow, but he couldn't tolerate not knowing what was going on. What had that scene at the garden gate meant? There was an intimacy in the earl's gesture that bespoke some understanding.

He heard Kittie move through the hallway and up the stairs, but couldn't bear to talk to her that moment. He would make some accusation, and until he knew the truth he didn't want to be precipitate.

He exited the cottage and raced into the woods after the earl.

"Orkenay," he shouted, once his acquaintance was in sight.

The man paused and glanced back. "Alban. Where the devil did you come from? Thought you were home this morning."

"I was, but I decided to visit the ladies. I heard you were out walking with Mrs. Douglas."

"I was." The earl began to walk again, along the shadowed path that meandered restlessly through the glade.

"Why?"

"Why was I out walking with Mrs. Douglas? I didn't know I needed a reason."

"Orkenay, don't toy with me," Alban said, grabbing the other man's arm.

"Whatever do you mean? You seem most odd this morning."

"I saw you!" Alban thundered, his voice echoing back to him strangely, and some bird fluttering, upset at the shout.

"Did you? You saw us . . . walking?"

"I saw you kissing! What the devil was that all about?"

"None of your business, old man, whom I kiss or don't. Mrs. Douglas is a very beautiful woman, as I'm sure you've noticed, and very much in need of kissing."

The earl's nonchalance was insufferable, and Alban longed to plant him a facer, but he allowed only one hand to ball into a fist at his side. He was much bigger than the earl and would surely hurt him if he allowed his ire free reign. "She is my aunt's companion. I'm sure you recognize that gives us some reason to inquire as to your motives in kissing her?"

"Hmm, 'us'? Are you truly inquiring for Lady Eliza,

or more for yourself? And really, Alban, motive? To kiss a lovely woman?"

"You know what I mean. What do you intend?"

He watched the other man's expression, the measuring gaze, the indecision.

Then Orkenay's chin went up pugnaciously, and he said, "It's none of your business, but Mrs. Douglas has agreed to go back to London with me once our visit here is at an end. She is to become my mistress. Ain't I a *lucky* fellow?"

Alban, stunned, stared at the earl wordlessly. If he had not seen the young woman kissing Orkenay so passionately in the meadow, and then again so tenderly at the garden gate, he would have thought it a lie.

The earl smiled and shrugged. "Now I have said too much, Alban, and she specifically asked me not to, not until she can prepare Lady Eliza. She feels responsible to your aunt, and grateful, and all that, and does not want to shock the woman. You do understand, don't you, and will not tell on the poor girl? She is the most beautiful young lady I have ever seen; I felt some encouragement from her, welcoming glances and all that, and so I asked, and she accepted my offer. I must say, I didn't think anyone would have seen us!"

If he didn't know better, Alban would have suspected sly triumph in the earl's tone, but no one knew how he felt about Mrs. Douglas, not even himself, for God's sake. But at that moment, his stomach was churning and he felt nauseated.

What in God's name was wrong with him?

He turned and started back to Bodenthorpe Cottage. He heard, but could not respond to Orkenay's shouted, "I say, Alban, what's wrong with you? Aren't you coming back to Boden?"

Instead he returned to the cottage and sought out

his aunt, who was sitting in the drawing room with Beacon, her devoted maid.

"Alban," Lady Eliza said, as he entered.

"Aunt," he said, shortly, and threw himself into a chair.

"Beacon, leave us, please. I will take tea with the ladies in a half hour. Tell Oliver that His Grace will be staying."

"No! I have to go back, but I do wish a word with you, Aunt."

Lady Eliza waved her hand and Beacon slipped from the room.

But Alban sat silent for a few moments, staring out the window on a day that suddenly had turned cloudy and breezy.

"What is wrong, Alban?" She sniffled, dabbed at her nose with a handkerchief, and leaned back in her chair. "If you are just going to sit and brood silently, I will have Beacon back."

"I'm sorry, Aunt." He sat up straight in his chair and reached over, grabbing her hand and giving it a squeeze. "I hope you're feeling better and are over your grippe."

She returned the gesture and then released his hand. "I am as well as can be expected. Now, I can feel your agitation, Alban, so don't try to deceive me."

"How well do you know Mrs. Douglas? And how much do you trust her?"

"I know her well enough to know her heart and I trust her with my life."

Alban sighed. Such an answer left no room for doubt, but who was being deceived, him or her? He knew that the earl was prone at times to exaggeration of his romantic conquests; if he had not seen with his own eyes the earl's encounters with Kittie Douglas, Alban would have thought the fellow was fabricating his story. And if it was only his own disappointment he had to consider, he would put her out of his mind as worthless, for any woman who would go to Orkenay as his mistress was not a woman who could ever interest him.

"Why did you ask, Alban? I think I have a right to know, since it is Kittie you are concerned with."

What could he say? He had been asked not to inform her before Kittie had that opportunity, and he had to admit that was fair. He didn't relish breaking that particular news to his aunt. And yet—

"I am just wondering how you came to know Kittie Douglas so well, that's all."

"And what is your concern in the matter?"

"You're my aunt! Your comfort and safety are of primary concern to me."

"You did not worry for the three years she has been my companion. Why now?"

"When I heard that she was a widow . . . that is, I pictured . . ."

"A poor, broken-down old widow-woman, sad and meek. Instead you find Kittie Douglas, lovely, vibrant, glowing." There was, strangely, fierce satisfaction in her voice. "She glows, does she not, Alban, like a flame." Lady Eliza turned her face to the window, though the light was gray and weak, giving little perceptible warmth. "And that worries you for some reason. Why? Is it because you wonder what she is doing here, when a woman like her could be anywhere, with anyone?"

It was so close to some of his thoughts that he stayed silent.

"Aye, I thought as much. You think she means to take advantage of me in some fashion."

"It had occurred to me."

"For heaven's sake, Alban, why do you not make an effort to get to know her? Walk with her, talk with her."

"I tried that this morning and we ended up quarreling . . . or almost."

"You likely questioned her as if she were a subject in the Spanish Inquisition. She has spirit; she would not take kindly to that kind of treatment. It is one of the things I admire most about her, that being a companion has not reduced her to some submissive little mouse. I could not stand that; I would despise her in a sennight. No, Alban, I mean talk to her as you would any other woman you wanted to get to know better."

Alban thought for a moment. What could it hurt? He felt that there was a puzzle there, and he hated unsolved puzzles. He would be pleasing his aunt and following his own inclination, and perhaps annoying Orkenay in the process, if the man thought he was trying to steal Mrs. Douglas away from him. That thought delighted him, though he wasn't sure a close examination of his reasons would stand up to his own rigorous standards of behavior.

He stood, leaned over his aunt, and gave her a smacking kiss on the cheek. "I will do that, old dear. I want to see what it is that makes everyone so enamored of your Mrs. Douglas."

Lady Eliza had a sly smile on her face as she reached up and patted his cheek. "Good boy. It's about time you heeded me. Now send Beacon back to me." She sneezed gustily and waved him away.

The weather turned brisk, as September entered its second half.

Alban, Orkenay, and Sir John hunted during the day and in the evening met with Bart at Bodenthorpe Cottage, where he seemed to be a permanent and welcome fixture. Bart had never enjoyed hunting, and without his father's boisterous presence had finally admitted it. Instead he spent his time with the ladies, though the obvious lure was Mrs. Billings. What he saw in her Alban could not conceive.

He had asked his friend that, in as tactful a manner as he could, but Bart had seen through his clumsy wording immediately.

"Because she is not to your taste, Alban, does not mean she is without attractions."

"I know. I'm not so dense as that, Bart."

His friend had struggled for words. They were in the library at Boden, a dark-paneled room with wine-colored furnishings and the heads of many slaughtered animals on the walls. "I can't explain how I feel inside, Alban, but I have long known very few people would ever truly understand me. I know you don't and that's all right. I can love you like a brother without us understanding everything about each other."

Such open speech made Alban uneasy. Even his aunt, whom he adored, had likely never told him that she loved him. But Bart continued.

"Hannah understands me, and I understand her. There is no need for pretense between us. Neither of us expects life to be easy, but despite what people may think of her excessive sensibility, she is strong under it all. She has had to be strong for her sons—she has two boys—and I respect that. And"—Bart looked toward the window—"I think she's beautiful. It shines in her eyes, and when I hold her . . ."

Alban made an exclamation, and Bart caught his eye and grinned.

"Yes, I've held her. I'm a man, after all, and she's a woman. Do you think we only talk?"

So it is serious, Alban thought. He gazed at his friend with wonder. Had Bart finally found his match? Of all the ladies he had ever met—and as a young gentleman of good birth, there had been many—why Hannah Billings?

"What is it that makes you . . . how do you know how you feel about her?" Alban was genuinely curious. He had been in love many times before, he thought, but what Bart felt seemed different somehow, and he wanted to know how so.

"I'm a better man already just for knowing her, Alban. I want to be with her, I want to make her life better, and I know that her life will be better with me in it. And I feel stronger. She needs me, Alban."

Uneasily, Alban wondered if they weren't just reinforcing mutual weakness, but when he clumsily tried to express his concern, Bart shook his head, his eyes sparkling. "No, you don't understand. That is the beauty of this. I care for her so much I will rise to new heights to buoy her when she is downhearted. And she has already done the same for me. It's as though in our care for each other, we will ourselves to be stronger."

Alban had clasped his hand then, across the library table. "Then that is all I could ever wish for you, my friend."

"Alban, I know you have not been so happy yourself, but . . ."

"No! Bart, I'm not you and I don't want to talk about it. Catherine is long gone, and Jacqueline's treachery is done."

"But after Catherine died . . ."

"No!"

The conversation had ended there. Alban would not canvass his problems with anyone, even his best friend. And it truly was over. Catherine had left him and then died with her paramour. Jacqueline, his treacherous mistress, had been selling secrets he told her to the highest bidder as well as going to other men's beds. But that, too, was over. He certainly didn't need to discuss it.

His promise to his aunt was often in his mind, and so he acted upon it, finding free time to talk to Mrs. Douglas with no other motive than conversation. Though she seemed wary at first, she soon relaxed, and to his dismay he found not only that she was physically attractive to him but also her mind stimulating and unexpected, her knowledge ranging over manly topics such as politics and economics. It seemed that she had spent some time in society, for she was well versed on the royal family's quirks, and even knew some of the same people he knew, society leaders and dragons alike.

It was disconcerting. She even proved to be a good rider, and, along with Lady Severn, accompanied the men on the hunt one day. Both ladies were bruising riders, though Lady Severn was the more daring.

In every way, as it proved. She and Sir John disappeared for a while and returned, tousled and laughing, claiming to have run some game to ground, though not a one of the company believed them. Even Kittie Douglas, her cheeks pink, seemed to know that they were up to more than hunting.

Which made him all the more curious about Kittie Douglas's apparent defection from his aunt into Orkenay's arms. She revealed nothing of her feelings or plans in company with the earl and even seemed to avoid him, though that may have been just so no suspicion was raised among the other members of the house party. Orkenay intimated as much, saying that Alban could not expect them to be making their connection obvious, when Kittie was trying to work up the courage to tell Lady Eliza that she was leaving. He implied that she may not want to say anything until their time of departure approached. She dreaded hurting her employer, the earl had stated, and was delaying the inevitable as long as possible.

It was driving him wild, not knowing what was true and what was false. He had never known Orkenay to be so patient when courting a new mistress, but it must be true. The image of him kissing Kittie Douglas so passionately in the meadow and so tenderly at the gate was seared in Alban's brain as proof of their intimacy.

He should have asked her himself. If she was going to leave Lady Eliza, it might as well have been for his bed.

Perhaps she would not be fit for society in the way clever and coquettish Jacqueline had been, but what a country mistress she would make, deposited in some cozy cottage near London, there at the end of the day for him to retreat to, talk to, and make love to! They could ride together, and then make slow, passionate love by the fireplace all winter long.

Finally, driven mad with wondering, he determined to find out the truth one way or another.

It was about a week after he promised his aunt he would get to know Mrs. Douglas. He had. She was intelligent, good-natured, lovely, delicate, and yet not weak. Now he wanted to know more, such as what she saw in Orkenay and why she had agreed to his proposition.

The day was a brilliant one after two days of steady rain. Puffs of clouds scudded over the high fells as he walked down to the cottage. Bart, he knew, was already there, but he had left Orkenay and Sir John behind, desultorily arguing over who was the more repulsive and manipulative of Prinny's many mistresses.

The woods were wet and the path slithery, but for all that he enjoyed the walk and congratulated himself on the inspiration that had urged him north. Other than wishing he had not invited Orkenay along, he regretted only that he had delayed his visit to his aunt so long, and that led his mind back, inevitably, to Mrs. Douglas. His aunt seemed as enamored of her as old ladies often got over younger women they viewed as daughter substitutes. But he had to admit there was nothing to actively dislike in Mrs. Douglas, and if it was not for her indiscretion with Orkenay, he might be singing her praises too.

The cottage was as always, nestled in the mist, stone walls lushly coated with roses and ivy. His aunt's groom, Jacob, stood with the reins of his aunt's ancient pony, Lily, in one hand, just outside the cottage gate. Lily was harnessed to the pony cart that Lady Eliza had used for many years, and that, apparently now, served Kittie Douglas.

That woman strode out the door of the cottage and, head down, rustling in her basket, moved down the path and through the gate to the waiting pony cart.

"Going into the village, Mrs. Douglas?"

He had the dubious pleasure of seeing her start and appear dismayed.

"Your Grace! Yes, I am on an errand for Lady Eliza. Just . . . just posting letters and doing some shopping."

"You are an early riser."

"Yes." She stepped up into the cart and took the reins from Jacob. "And now I must bid you adieu, Your Grace. You will find Lady Eliza at the breakfast table."

"Since I came to see you, Mrs. Douglas, I think I will go to the village with you. We can talk on the way."

Eleven

She did not look pleased, but made no demur. It was a novel sensation to be driven by a woman who knew what she was doing. Granted, Lily was the mildest of steeds, but on the rare occasion he had allowed himself to be driven by Jacqueline, who fancied herself a whip hand, he had regretted it and had come to believe that driving was a male skill not to be attempted by feminine hands.

But his aunt's companion made no extravagant demands of Lily, did not attempt to go faster than she was capable, and was careful and considerate on the way down the short slope into the village. Once there, Alban watched how she dealt with the villagers, and to a man and woman they all had accepted her as one of their own. Many of them had known him since he was a boy, but his elevated position still caused a hesitation, a formality in their address to him that had to be considered natural and perhaps warranted, though he remembered a time when they had treated him with more familiarity. But Mrs. Douglas they treated as a member of the community, telling her variously about Sunday service when they happened to meet up with some of the ladies of the village, and about the First Fruits harvest festival planned for that Saturday.

Kittie, for her part, was not having the relaxed visit

she usually had with the villagers, and there were one or two who seemed to catch her distraction. The morning's drive and errands were her way of getting a little time alone, away from the bustle of the household and her friends, love them though she did.

Instead, she was subjected to the duke's presence, and though he was the model of the perfect gentleman, she could not be comfortable in his presence when they were alone. It was easier with company, but so close, on his arm or by his side in the cart, she was agitated and, for some reason, apprehensive.

On the way back up the sloping path to Bodenthorpe Cottage she learned that her apprehension had just cause. The conversation seemed innocent enough at first.

"Are you enjoying all the company?" he asked, glancing sideways at her as Lily labored up the hill.

Poor pony, Kittie thought. Maybe the girl was past anything but some warm mash and a field to roam. They would have to consider a younger animal and let Lily retire. "Of course. I have missed Rebecca and Hannah since coming north."

"But the gentlemen, too. I think my friends have found the female companionship pleasing; would you say the same for yourself and the other ladies?"

"I think I can safely say that my friends are very much enjoying the male companionship," Kittie said, with a dry edge to her voice, thinking of Rebecca's behavior with Sir John the day they had joined the men on the hunt. She had been more circumspect since, but had made it plain that she was thinking of setting up young Sir John as her lover once they left Bodenthorpe for London.

"Yes, Bart and Mrs. Billings seem to have become very close very quickly."

Kittie beamed just thinking about it. Mr. Norton had

Hannah smiling so often, she seemed a new woman . . . certainly a happier one. It was charming to see, and warmed her heart. "He is a wonderful gentleman. I can't believe he has never married." She negotiated a tricky turn and set herself to try to enjoy the day more rationally. The duke was not an ogre to be trembled before; he was just a man, after all. It was foolish to be so agitated by his mere presence.

"I find it hard to understand myself, except . . . Bart is a rare fellow. He could never marry unless he felt satisfied that his marriage was helping someone, I think."

"You underestimate your friend and my friend's sincere attachment," she said, stung by his reply for reasons she didn't quite fathom. But it seemed to shift all the benefit from any possible match between Bart and Hannah in her direction.

"I don't think so," he said. "But she is, beneath her vapors, a shrewd woman, no doubt. She would be feeble-witted not to see that attaching and marrying Bart is her best guarantee of a secure future for her boys."

"I have to think, sir, that if Mr. Norton has remained unwed by now, when many ladies must have set their caps for him over the years, he knows what he wants and Hannah somehow fulfills his needs. Therefore, the benefit is not all on her side, but equally on his."

"Not equally. Bart would be just as well to remain unwed. But Mrs. Billings . . . she will gain greatly."

"You are speaking again in only material terms."

"Is that not one of the greatest advantages to a woman of marrying or attaching a man?"

"I pity you if you think that," Kittie cried, glancing sideways at the duke and resenting his obdurate, hard-jawed, opinionated attitudes.

"It is naïve to think any other way."

"Then is love not to be considered at all? Can a man

and a woman not just find that unique happiness together?"

"Love lasts only until the first conflict and quickly fades after that. Besides, I think if love was the basis for most marriages, there would be many more disinterested ones between wealthy ladies and destitute gentlemen, but one would be a fool not to consider the purse of their future spouse."

She bit back all the things she longed to say, that he was cynical and jaded, that he appeared not to believe in love, and that he was belittling that which he didn't understand. They fell into a silence she knew was mutually urged by aggravation with the other's views. He had kept his tone even, but he was clearly vexed by her defiance of his judgment.

They went a ways in that obstinate silence, but finally he broke it.

"Mrs. Douglas, I have a question to ask of you, and I hope you don't take it amiss. But it is important enough that I feel I must, even though I will be prying."

She couldn't imagine what it was, but she feared that it would be about her own feelings for him, for she often felt that she had shown her preference, blushing at his touch, becoming too vivacious in his presence, letting her glance linger and meet with his much too often. Even now, irritated with him, she was aware of a frisson of nervous attraction that hummed beneath her vexation. She swallowed. "I . . . I d-don't have anything to hide, Your Grace," she stuttered.

He cast her a shrewd look, his thick eyebrows shadowing his dark eyes.

Her heart thudding sickly in her breast, she waited, but he merely watched her for a moment. She wanted to stop the cart and run away. She felt like squirming in her seat like a five-year-old child, but she held the reins with what grace she could muster. Lily plodded on, and for once she wished the pony younger and livelier. They would be back at the cottage by now in that case.

"I have noted, over the past few weeks," he said, "a certain . . . softness or . . . how should I put this? Your behavior seems to me to be that of a woman interested in a man."

She felt ill. He had noticed.

"One particular man, in fact. I don't know how else to say this, so I must be blunt. Please, Mrs. Douglas, forgive me for this direct questioning."

She waited, dreading his question. What would she say? How would he consider her impertinence? Especially given what she now knew of his cynical view of life and women. Did he ask her just to put to rest any hopes she might have in his direction? How humiliating it would be if that was so. She must maintain her dignity.

"Are you leaving here with Lord Orkenay at the end of his stay?"

The question, so unexpected, pulled all the air from her lungs in a whoosh, leaving her breathless and gasping. Spluttering, she feared, like a hooked fish, she knew her face was turning a fiery red. She glared over at him and swiftly looked away, back at the rutted road, thankful they were almost to the cottage gate. "I c-cannot believe you would ask me that question."

He was watching her; she could feel his gaze, steady, impenetrable, judgmental.

"Will you answer?"

Resentment welled up in her bosom. She stared straight down the road. How dare he even think that, much less . . . but then the thought tripped into her mind on tiptoes, *What if Lord Orkenay said something about his invitation to me?* But no, if that was true, then he also would have told the duke of her absolute refusal, and the duke *had* merely said it was from his own observation. So he was just guessing and being unbearably discourteous, even if he was a duke and Lady Eliza's nephew.

"I don't think I will answer," she said, calmly, pulling the pony cart up in front of the cottage. Jacob hobbled out of the stable beyond the garden and took the reins from her as she clambered down, not waiting for the duke.

"What do you mean, you won't?"

She turned, watched him climb down awkwardly, his large frame unfolding from the pony cart like a jack-knife. "Just what I said." Her anger made her strong and she welcomed it like a fresh wave of cold air from the fell above.

He pointed a finger at her and said, "Orkenay is merely toying with you, Mrs. Douglas; he is used to much more sophisticated women, so if you think he will eventually make you his wife, don't for a second entertain the notion. If he ever does marry it will not be to a woman so far beneath him socially."

Tears of fury welled in her eyes, but she would not let him see how his arrogance affected her. She turned away from him and strode to the house, spilling packages out of her basket as she fled.

Alban returned to his hunting manse and reflected for the rest of the afternoon on Mrs. Douglas's behavior. If there had been nothing in what he was saying, surely she would have just told him that it was ridiculous to even think. He couldn't begin to figure out what the rapid shifts of emotion on her face had denoted, but he had read evasion at one point, being far too familiar with that from his experiences with Catherine and Jacqueline.

Catherine.

He sat in the library, nominally reading a letter from a London friend before getting ready to join the ladies for dinner at Bodenthorpe, but really reflecting on the morning's conversation with Kittie Douglas. Her evasiveness had strongly reminded him of how his wife had acted in the last days before her departure with her paramour, and how Jacqueline had behaved in the days before he discovered her perfidious treachery.

Women were not to be trusted, for in his experience men had the mistaken notion they were softhearted doves, when really, by necessity, they only looked out for their own benefit. If a woman could not or would not give him a straight answer, then he must suspect double dealing. He had sworn to himself never to be misled again.

Sir John poked his head through the library door and said, "I say, Alban, are you going to walk down to Bodenthorpe with Orkenay and me?"

"Yes, I suppose I am. If I ever want to see Bart again, I must go there, eh?"

The younger man grinned and stepped into the library. He glanced around and gave an appreciative whistle. "This is an impressive collection of books," he said, scanning the shelves, "for a hunting box. You must be a bibliophile."

"My father was," Alban said. He watched the younger man. "So why are you really here?" he said, on a whim, and was surprised by the other man's guilty start.

"Whatever do you mean, Your Grace? I came to tell you Orkenay and I are ready to walk down to the cottage."

"You know what I mean. Why did you insinuate yourself in this trip? You never went out of your way to befriend me until you found I was coming north. And you are no dilettante. I know there are political stirrings up here, insurrectionist murmurings and Luddite

talk. And I know that you have some position attached
to someone in government. I think you can trust me,
Sir John, if you have some other motive than just a
hunting holiday."

"Sir," he said, cocking his head to one side, "if I had
anything to tell you, I know there is no one in the world
I could more properly trust."

More evasion, Alban thought, with a sigh, but at least
this time he felt it had little to do with him. He stood
and stretched, setting his letter aside to be perused another day. "Let's go see the ladies. I wouldn't want to
keep you away from Lady Severn's side any longer than
necessary."

Dinner had been dull, Alban thought, with even his
aunt abstracted. They had retired to the small drawing
room, and Lady Severn was playing the piano, with Sir
John to turn her music for her, while Bart and Hannah
Billings sat together and talked. Orkenay sat down with
Lady Eliza and engaged her in an animated conversation about days gone past in London.

Kittie Douglas had placed herself in the shadows, almost behind Lady Eliza's chair, and had deliberately
chosen an activity, Alban noted, that was not a sociable pastime.

She knitted. He sat back in a large chair and watched
for a moment. Knitting. He was struck, suddenly, by the
knowledge that the flood of gifts he had received in the
last three years, all hand-knit goods purportedly coming from his aunt, must have been made by her very
own beautiful hands, for Lady Eliza had never knit a
stitch in her life.

And such intimate items! Stockings and woolen gar-
ments to be worn against the skin to fend off the cold

of a Yorkshire winter, all perfectly fitted to his large frame.

Candlelight glinted off her needles and highlighted her pale, quick hands. He had worn a pair of her well-knit stockings just that morning against the chill, and as he thought of such things, he found the notion to be faintly arousing, that she had been knitting away, creating items, reflecting on the right size for him, measuring, calculating.

She looked up, noticed his gaze on her and, her cheeks pinkening, turned her attention back to the work in her hands.

But she was aware, after that, of his observation and dropped a stitch on occasion, the rapid click of her needles slowing as she became clumsy under his regard. And that was more entertaining and gratifying than any mere conversation. He had never met a woman who so irritated him at the same time as she attracted him.

And yet it could not last, his opportunity to rattle her just with his steady regard. With a murmured word to Lady Eliza, who nodded, she swiftly stood, took up her shawl, crossed the room, and opened the doors out to the terrace. She slipped out into the night.

The cool air welcomed Kittie, whose cheeks burned with mortification that the duke could still, for all his boorishness earlier in the day, affect her by merely watching her so closely. His powerful physical presence haunted her day and night, and she would be glad— more than glad, rapturous—when he was gone.

It was merely physical attraction . . . it had to be that! She had certainly had inappropriate thoughts about him, unfortunately finding that his breadth of shoulder and muscular build made her preternaturally aware of the sinew and entrancing brawn that flexed and shifted under his well-fitted clothes. It left her quite breathless.

What was wrong with her? She flattened her palms over her flaming cheeks, feeling the heat even now as she paced to the edge of the terrace and gazed out over the moon-touched grass.

His rudeness that morning had left her cold, that was for sure. And yes, it had a salutary effect even now, many hours later. Who was he to ask such impertinent questions of her? She took in a deep breath and let it out slowly. Anger cooled her. Perhaps it was a good thing that the duke was not the courteous, generous, sweet-natured, loving man of his letters, for then she would surely make a fool of herself over him.

The terrace door opened, and someone slipped out, moving in the shadows. Oh, how she hoped it wasn't the earl or, even worse, the—

It was the duke. Did he follow her to make her miserable? Did he want to question her more? Bait her? Torment her?

He moved out of the shadows. "Mrs. Douglas, are you not coming back in? Lady Severn was asking where you were, so I said I would step out and see if you were all right."

Rebecca! Desperately inappropriate matchmaker. The woman, for all her practicality in her own life, had a romantic streak in her. The worst thing Kittie could ever have done was confess her attraction to the duke. She sighed in frustration and moved back toward the doors. "I will go in, then, and rejoin my friends. It certainly is rude of me to . . ."

"No," he said and put one hand on her shoulder.

She stared at it, unable to raise her gaze to his face. It was a big hand, with blue veins tracing across the surface and bristling brown hairs. A strong hand. A capable hand. Perhaps it was not good to concentrate so fiercely on his hands. She looked up into his eyes.

He circled her, leaning in and catching her scent. "You smell wonderful, like . . . roses."

As he circled her, she turned, watching him with uneasiness shivering through her to the marrow. His presence always powerfully affected her, and this night was no exception. The autumnal gloom of the stone terrace cast his hawkish features into harsh relief.

"You've been less than honest with me, Mrs. Douglas," he said, finally stopping in front of her.

She felt a jolt of trepidation, thinking he might be talking again about his friend, the earl, and that man's advances. "What do you mean?"

"I mean, you have been dissembling about the woolen stockings and other . . . unmentionables my aunt regularly sends me as gifts. You're the one who has been knitting them these past couple of years."

She sighed with relief. "Well . . . yes. But it would not have been seemly," she said primly, pulling her woolen shawl closer around her, "for me to have sent them to you myself, and you a stranger and a duke, and not even related to me. I merely sent them along with her ladyship's letters, without comment."

He moved to stand behind her and put his massive hands on her shoulders. She was not a small woman, but they engulfed her wool-clad shoulders which he caressed and squeezed. What was he doing, she wondered? His warm, moist breath bathed her neck, and she felt a moment of panic at the yearning it raised within her and the fleeting shadow images that chased through her brain of midnight thoughts and longings. Thanking providence that she was not transparent so he could see and hear how her heart thumped at his touch, she stayed resolutely still.

"I feel as if you know me intimately, for you know, never have my unmentionables clung to me so closely, nor been so superbly fitted to my form. The stockings caress my legs," he murmured. "The singlets mold to my chest like warm hands. How much do you know about a man's body, Mrs. Douglas?"

"I was married," she retorted, twisting out of his grip and facing him, reluctant to admit to the desire that warred with her caution. He was an attractive man and never had she been more aware of it than at that moment. "Or have you forgotten?"

"Mmm, yes. So you know men's bodies intimately."

"Only one man's body, Your Grace," she replied, keeping her tone acid. She squinted against the gathering gloom of twilight, watching him carefully and keeping a safe distance between them. In case he did not get her meaning she said, in a loud voice, "Only one man's body, and he was my husband."

He smiled and chuckled. "That's right, put me in my place." His slow gaze traveled down over her curves.

She should feel insulted, she thought, as a hot blush rose over her breasts and neck and up to her face. It was almost as if with just his eyes he stroked her intimately. But instead of being insulted, all she felt was this suffocating wave of hunger. She wanted to fling herself into his arms. How had she come to this pass? How had she come to want him so very badly?

And then a calm came over her, a trust in her own resolve. She found him attractive. If she didn't hold herself up as above certain behaviors, she would be sorely tempted to allow his wordless invitation—for surely the force of his personality bent toward her in such a way, with him looking at her as he did, could mean nothing but that he would like to bed her—to overcome her scruples.

But she would not. There were men, after Roger's death, who would have been happy to have her as a paramour, and even a few invitations . . . a few offers of "protection." But at what a price!

She would never hold herself so cheap as to acquiesce to such a bloodless arrangement. And especially with a man who had accused her of attempting to attract another man, and who had clearly shown he did not trust her. Kittie took a long, calming breath, and said, "I'm going in, sir, whatever you choose to do." She turned, wrapping her shawl around her shoulders, and reentered the drawing room.

Alban followed. How could he not? Wherever she went she pulled him behind her like a child pulled a toy along the floor on a string.

Why was he so damned attracted to her, and how could he overcome it?

The company had shifted some since he had exited. Orkenay now sat with Mrs. Billings and Bart, an evil grin on his face at the obvious discomfort of the two lovebirds.

Alban joined his aunt, sitting by her and taking her hand in his. One thing he had been puzzled about was explained when Lady Eliza said, "Orkenay was going to follow Kittie outside, but I made him stay with me. The man is so steeped in London manners that he could not be flagrantly rude." She chuckled. "But his conversation became rather disjointed, let me say. Finally he deserted me to plague Bart and Mrs. Billings."

Alban squeezed her hand. "And why would you have done such a thing, keeping the earl with you like that?"

"Because when Kittie said she was going outside for a breath of air, I knew you would follow. What did you two talk about?"

He gazed across the room at Kittie, who had joined Sir John and Lady Severn. Had she been expecting Orkenay to follow her, and is that why she went outside? It irritated him to wonder that.

"Alban!"

"I'm sorry. What did you ask?"

"What did you two talk about?"

"Oh. I . . . uh, I confronted her about her being the one who knitted me the underthings . . . the ones she sent me with your Christmas letter."

"Alban!"

He laughed at the outrage in her voice. Several heads swiveled in his direction.

"Why do you two continually bait each other? I should think the two people most important to my comfort, and whom I care for the most, would . . ."

"She has only been your employee for three years. Surely you cannot mean she has found a place in your heart equal to . . . well, equal to . . . Montrose," he finished, naming his cousin, her other nephew from her sister Eloise, long deceased.

"Montrose is my nephew and I love him, but it doesn't mean I have to like him. He is a silly ass, with little in the brainbox and less in his heart. He and Kittie are not to be mentioned in the same breath. Do not change the subject, Alban. Why do you and Kittie not get along? Is she not pretty? Is she not intelligent?"

Alban shifted in his chair and watched Kittie, who was playing a duet with Lady Severn, but in such a labored fashion that her friend was laughing at her. "She is all of that."

"Then what do you find in her to dislike?"

"Nothing. There is nothing at all to dislike in her demeanor, her appearance, nor, apparently, her heart." He just did not trust her motives nor her behavior, he thought, but did not say.

"And yet you do dislike her."

Lady Eliza said it with finality, and Alban saw no reason to add anything. What he felt could not be called aversion, since he was still very much attracted to her, even if he didn't trust her. It was a most annoying state of affairs. He had his own feelings on the subject, but he would not raise an old specter again, the ghost of Catherine, nor would he divulge his latest disappointment, the treacherous Jacqueline. It was more than that, anyway, but he also was not prepared to speak with his aunt about the possibility that she would lose her beloved companion when the men left. It wasn't up to him to break her heart.

"I had thought better of you," his aunt said, finally.

There was no response he could or would make.

Twelve

"Good night, my lady." Kittie blew out the candle by Lady Eliza's bedside. Beacon, who usually saw to their employer's nightly needs, was not feeling well, having caught her mistress's cold, and had been sent to bed early.

"Kittie," Lady Eliza said, catching at the younger woman's hand before she moved away from the bed.

"Yes?"

"Sit for a moment . . . that is, if you don't mind."

Kittie heard the tentativeness in her employer's tone and wondered what was concerning her. She sat up on the edge of the high bed, not pulling her hand out of Lady Eliza's grip. She wondered if her blindness made that physical touch more important to the woman, as an anchor in a dark world. With the candle blown out the room was only faintly illuminated by moonlight from a sliver of open curtain.

Lady Eliza was silent for a moment, but then said, "I have noticed that you and Alban do not get along very well. Why is that?"

How could she possibly answer? "It's not that we don't get along . . ." At a loss for words, she fell silent.

Squeezing her hand, Lady Eliza said, "I can feel the tension, my dear. I may be blind, but I have all my other senses. I fear that Alban has become . . . less trusting since the infidelity and subsequent death of his wife."

"He doesn't seem at all the man of his letters to you," Kittie admitted.

"He has always been, since his adolescence, a man of strong passions. Where he loves, he is unswervingly loyal. I wonder if the converse of that is other emotions—jealousy, mistrust, fear—have an equally powerful, though negative effect."

"Fear? I would never call the duke a fearful man, ma'am."

"I don't mean physical fear. Alban has never been fearful in that sense, but the other kind of fear is a loathing of the pain that treachery and rejection can inflict and a determination to avoid it at all costs. You weren't here when he last stayed, after Catherine's desertion and death. It was a terrible time. I hadn't realized he cared for her so deeply, for of course theirs was an arranged marriage."

"*Did* he care for her, or was it his pride only that was hurt by her elopement?"

"Kittie!"

"Pardon, my lady."

"No. You are entitled to have your own feelings. But you never knew him before this. I only want to . . . explain him to you. If only I knew how."

"You haven't seen him in three years. Maybe he's changed from the nephew you remember."

"I suppose that's possible." Lady Eliza laid her lace-capped head back on her pillow. "Love is such a powerful emotion, and when it is betrayed . . ."

Kittie was silent. The woman's words were said with personal meaning, she felt sure. Maybe she was reflecting on her own past experiences with love. That there was a painful story in her employer's past she had always felt, but she would never probe that wound. It wasn't her place.

"When love is betrayed, you feel as if everything you ever believed in your life is false . . . or at least suspect," Lady Eliza continued. "How can you trust anyone again, least of all yourself and your emotions, if what you believed of your beloved was false? Being wrong once alters how you think and feel. It changes who you are."

"But it isn't right to take that distrust out on those around you who are guiltless."

Lady Eliza turned her face away into her pillow. But then she turned back to Kittie and squeezed her hand. "Maybe you are right. But the Alban line . . . we are a strong and resentful pack, my dear. We hold on to our grievances, nursing them, letting them strengthen. It takes decades to forget a hurt, if it ever is forgotten."

"Perhaps certain members should learn to be more trusting."

"The Alban motto is *fronti nulla fides* . . . do not trust appearances, or something like that. We are a suspicious lot. And Alban *was* betrayed. He is not going to trust again easily."

"Then he's going to be a lonely man for the rest of his life," Kittie said, standing. There was too much in this conversation that felt personal, and yet, Lady Eliza had been talking about herself, too, it seemed, not just her nephew. She could not keep herself from it; she broke the silence at last and asked the question. "Tell me, ma'am, did you ever . . . were you ever in love?"

From the jolt of her fingers, twisted together with her own, Kittie could sense some dismay at the question. But she wasn't going to take it back. She stayed silent.

"Yes. But sometimes love isn't enough," Lady Eliza said.

The terrible sadness in her voice tugged at Kittie's heart. "Did he break your heart?"

She was silent for a moment, but then said, "We couldn't be together. There were . . . obstacles, grave obstacles. I knew it but I was stubborn enough to think we could overcome them. But then, when my darling Harry abandoned me for another . . ." She stopped and turned her face into the pillow.

"But you didn't let it embitter you." Kittie put one hand on the other woman's shoulder and squeezed. "You have given others so much, my lady, Alban and . . . and more, especially myself."

"Thank you for that, my dear. Maybe you had better go off to bed now. I am tired."

It was dark in the room, but Kittie's sight was excellent, and the gleam of moonlight caught the one tear that slid down Lady Eliza's withered cheek. "Good night, my lady. Remember that many around you love you. I know we're no replacement for your one true love, but I hope we are some small compensation."

"You are," she whispered. "Good night, Kittie."

Kittie slipped out and wiped a tear from her own eye. She and her employer had never spoken of such things before, and it added a new depth to her understanding of Lady Eliza. And a new determination to find a way to get along with the duke, who was precious and important to the woman, after all, and so should be to Kittie.

She entered her own room to find Hannah and Rebecca there, waiting.

"We're not leaving until you tell us what's wrong. You haven't been yourself almost since we got here, and we're worried."

That was Rebecca of course, but Hannah nodded vigorously in agreement.

"You're both here for a holiday, not to listen to my pitiful woes."

"But, dear, if you can't tell us when something is wrong, what kind of friends are we?"

Kittie gazed at Hannah, remembering the terrible time after Roger's death and her reliance on her dear friend, whom many dismissed as simply a weepy female. "You're the best of friends. I'm so glad Mr. Norton has seen fit to recognize all of your sterling qualities."

Hannah blushed, and Rebecca laughed out loud.

"She will not admit that they are anything more than friends, Kittie, can you imagine that? She refuses to see that Mr. Norton is completely smitten. I have never seen a man so obviously taken with a woman, and yet she will only say that he is very kind."

"Oh, Hannah, kind? His preference is clear! And truly . . . has he not kissed you? Admit it!"

Hannah pulled up her voluminous night rail and covered her face in confusion. "I don't know what to think," she cried, her voice muffled with material. "I've never met anyone like him."

"But we didn't come here to speak of our own amorous adventures," Rebecca said, turning her gaze to Kittie. "We want to know what is going on with you and the duke and the earl."

"That's right. We want to know what's wrong, for you don't seem like yourself," Hannah added, patting her gown down over her knees again.

Kittie slipped her shoes off and sat down on the bed. She had confessed to them her attraction to the duke, but had told them nothing beyond that. She sighed and gazed down at her gown, picking at the pattern. She had gotten out of the habit of sharing her thoughts and feelings in the years of virtual isolation in Yorkshire. She had been consumed with Lady Eliza's problem, her growing blindness, and the adjustments attendant upon it.

Was that so she could keep from feeling how lonely she was?

"Talk to us," urged Rebecca, reaching out and grasping her hand. "I won't leave here without knowing that you're all right."

"Nor I," Hannah said, grabbing her other hand.

Hannah and Rebecca joined hands, and the unbroken circle infused Kittie with strength and determination. She could trust these two women with her life, and if anyone could give her advice, it would be them. "The other day, when the earl invited me out walking . . . he didn't want just to talk, as I said when I came back, he . . . he proposed *carte blanche!*"

The other two woman gasped.

"He *what?* You? How absurd." That was Rebecca.

"Oh, how awful, my dear," Hannah said, squeezing her hand.

It all came spilling out then, all her humiliation over the offer, the shame and the fear that she had done something to make him think she would acquiesce.

"Of course you didn't," Rebecca said. "*I* have given him more reason to think that than you, goose!"

"And then," Kittie continued, her voice trembling, "just this morning the duke accompanied me into the village, and on the way back he asked me if the earl and I were . . . if we were leaving together at the end of his stay."

Hannah put one hand over her bosom. "Oh no! Did you tell him certainly not? Did you . . ."

"I hope you said nothing to him," Rebecca cried, her green eyes blazing with anger.

Kittie turned eagerly to her friend. "Yes! That is exactly what I did. I told him I had no reason to tell him anything. First, he was very insulting and full of insinuations. He has the lowest opinion of women and marriage and seems to think that all women are grasping and treacherous. And the things he said . . . I couldn't believe he would ask me such a question, for I'm sure if the earl had told him anything of the kind—and why would he, since I told him no?—then he would come right out and say that, but instead he just slyly insinuated that he had noticed a . . . what did he call it? A *softness* toward a particular gentleman and was I, perhaps, thinking of leaving with the earl at the end of his stay. I was insulted."

"But why would you not tell him the truth? That he had asked and you had declined?" Hannah asked, puzzlement in her soft gray eyes.

"Because it is not his affair, first," Rebecca said, fury in her haughty tone, "and second, how dare he ask in such a bold manner? What gives him that right?"

"Surely, though, it is best not to leave any lingering wrong impressions. You may have left him with the impression that you *are* leaving with the earl, b-becoming his mistress," Hannah said, worrying her lip with her teeth. "And Mr. Norton said . . . he implied . . ."

"What?"

Both women said it, quickly.

Hannah jumped nervously. "Bartholomew said that Lord Orkenay has been bragging to him, implying that he has reason to believe . . . in short, the earl has been hinting, though he has not said so outright, that Kittie and he are . . . are going to be together soon."

"You didn't say that before!" This cast a new light on things, and Kittie wondered to whom else the earl had been hinting.

"I knew it was not true and said so to Mr. Norton! I didn't think it even needed repeating, for I felt sure Kittie would leave no reason for doubt in anyone's mind."

"I think you may need to make sure the earl understands you, Kittie," Rebecca said.

"I think you're right. Could you, too, see if the earl has said anything to Sir John? I'm curious now as to what he has said and to whom."

"I'll find out tomorrow," she said, grim lines on her plain face.

"Kittie," Hannah said, her tone hesitant. "I was wondering if . . . that is . . . you said when we arrived how you felt about the duke, that you found him an attractive man. How do you feel now?"

Kittie reflected on their discord on the terrace that evening. "He is still the most attractive man I have ever seen. He is also the most infuriating."

"And you are still attracted to him," Rebecca said, with a sly wink.

"And I don't know why," Kittie admitted, clutching her hair with both her hands. "What is wrong with me, that even after that insult, I do not despise him?"

"Could it be that you see more than we do?" Hannah said, as tentative as ever when expressing an opinion. "You've read his letters, after all, and I think in his letters to his aunt he may have shown a more honest side than he does in person, for he isn't trying to hide anything from anyone there, do you know what I mean?"

Kittie thought about it. "Do you mean . . . he puts up a front with others to keep from . . ."

"To keep from being hurt again," Rebecca said. "Perhaps Hannah has something. It was the talk of London when his duchess deserted him and ran away with that courtier. It would have hurt his pride, certainly, but must he not have been hurt deeply, too, in his heart of hearts?"

"Lady Eliza said as much," Kittie admitted to her friend. "I don't know. He's a grown man. Can he not recognize what he's doing, then?"

"Men so seldom do," Rebecca retorted. "Show me a man who doesn't need a woman to point out to him the error of his ways, and I will show you a man who prefers other men."

"Rebecca!" Hannah gasped.

Kittie laughed. "Hannah, she just said that to shock you."

"I did not, I only said the truth. Hannah has just lived far too sheltered a life. Mr. Billings did not let her out of the house enough. Maybe her next husband will be more sociable and she can meet more interesting people."

Biting her lip to keep from laughing, for Hannah truly did look mortified, Kittie rose as her friends slid off the bed. She hugged each in turn, relishing their presence and drawing strength from the strong bond she felt with each of them. She was grateful for their support.

"Tomorrow," she said, "I'm going to make sure Lord Orkenay knows that I will never, under any circumstance become his mistress."

Sleep was not going to come easily that night, she knew, but the morrow would see her make some changes in her own behavior.

Alban restlessly prowled the house early, standing up in the gallery and staring at his forbidding ancestors, wondering if any of them had ever felt as confused as he did. His own emotions and compulsions puzzled him. Why was he so fixated on Kittie Douglas, when he could have any woman he wanted, as mistress or wife? He had been raised with the knowledge that his position as Duke of Alban meant that all of the distaff half of society was laid out for him like jewels on velvet, for his delectation. On one side were the sparkling, brilliant but cheap paste; those he could choose from to be his mistress. On the other side was the glittering array of society's diamonds, there for his selection as wife.

What happened when he wanted none of them, and instead of any jewel, preferred a rose growing wild in the bramble hedge? His illustrious ancestor gazed down at him, his bony, beaky nose raised in disdain at his great-great-grandson's common tastes.

Down in the great hall, a cavernous space decorated with game heads, he heard voices and, looking over the gallery railing, saw his butler give Lord Orkenay a folded note. The earl read it. From the foreshortened view above, Alban could not see his expression, but he heard the soft yes and noted the earl's sly demeanor. The man glanced around and then carefully placed the note, unfolded, in the silver salver on the ornate Jacobean table in the front hall. It was so calculated a move, begging for the letter to be perused. What did it mean?

When Orkenay left the hall for the breakfast room, Alban, unable to contain his curiosity, was about to descend to read the note when Sir John slipped into the hall, went directly to the note, picked it up, and read it. He tapped the note against his palm and put it back in the salver. Hesitating a moment, he picked it up again, began to fold it up, but then put it back in place.

How very odd, Alban thought, watching the drama unfold. When the young baronet left the hall, the duke descended, approached the note with trepidation, and picked it up. There was the faint trace of rose scent to it. Damn.

"My lord Orkenay," it read. "I have something of great import to discuss with you, and it cannot wait another moment. Would you please meet me in the rose garden of Bodenthorpe Cottage this morning? Respectfully, Kittie Douglas."

The page dropped from Alban's hand. What more

proof of a clandestine relationship did he need but a secret note? Though the note didn't really sound lover-like. He picked it up, read it again, and dropped it back in the salver. What he would not give to see that meeting, just to judge for himself what their behavior was to one another. The problem was he could too easily imagine what they would need to meet for. The gentlemen were leaving soon. If she was to go with Orkenay, arrangements would need to be made, plans confirmed. She might need reassurance, or information.

He could not eavesdrop, though. How humiliating was it to even consider that?

And yet there were Sir John's puzzling actions to consider, too. He had oft wondered about the young man's motives for coming north with the three older men. He had never particularly been a friend of any one of them. Bart had expressed his opinion that the young man was just looking to curry favor with so powerful a political figure as the duke of Alban, but Alban had his doubts. Undecided, he followed the two other men into the breakfast room.

An hour later, when Lord Orkenay yawned and made some weak excuse to go for a walk—alone, he made sure to indicate—Alban was determined not to follow. It was beneath his dignity. It was beneath him in every way imaginable.

And yet when Sir John, more convincing but still transparent to Alban, decided a solitary walk was just the thing for himself, too, it was too much for a man's curiosity.

It was farcical, he chastised himself, watching from a window as Sir John, with one quick look to the left and to the right, skulked down the same path Lord Orkenay had just traversed moments before.

And yet irresistible. It was a mystery now, not just

what was going on between Orkenay and Kittie Douglas, but why Sir John was interested.

Damn. He wanted to know what was going on in his own house. He should just ask, but he would be faced with evasion, no doubt. Or he could catch them all in the act and confront them. That sounded better. A confrontation just about suited him now.

He vaulted out of his chair and stomped to the front door, startling his butler and a maid conversing in low tones. They watched wide-eyed as he exited, and no doubt his actions would be the talk of below stairs. Not that it mattered in the slightest.

He hurried down the path through the woods, trying to overcome the feeling of being caught up in the farce at the end of the opera.

Ten minutes later, near the clearing, he slowed his pace, wondering where Sir John was stationed in his spying. There was the fellow; he had moved through the brush to a spot closer to the garden wall, and there, in the rose garden, was Orkenay and . . . Kittie. Alban felt his mouth go dry and a spot under his ribs hurt. What was it about her that made him feel as if he had just run a race? His pulse hammered, his throat constricted . . . he was acting and feeling like he was fifteen again and enamored of the village maiden to whom he had lost his virginity.

And like that first love, it was merely physical, he assured himself. She was beautiful, she was lush, he wanted to make love to her; it was as simple as that. They were talking. Orkenay reached out and grabbed her hand. She didn't shake it off. *Damn.* She was speaking with some earnestness and he was nodding. He reached up and pushed a stray curl behind her ear and Alban felt his blood go hot and pound in his ears. He had known Orkenay for years, but never had he seen the man so circumspect with a lady love. There was a tenderness in his gestures that surprised Alban.

Was Orkenay further along the garden path to love than he even knew? That Kittie Douglas was capable of inspiring love was no surprise to him. There was about her an aura of strength and yet sweetness, innocence and yet sensuality, that left a man breathless and aching.

Alban sighed and heard a rustling. He looked to his left and Sir John was staring back at him. When their eyes met, the baronet shrugged and melted back into the woods. He would have to have a talk with that young man.

When he looked back at the garden, his heart dropped into his boots. Orkenay opened his arms and Kittie Douglas walked into them and they embraced.

He had taken it better than she had expected. Kittie watched the earl walk away and reflected on their conversation. He told her that yes, he had still hoped to convince her to come away with him, and in fact was even more enamored of her now than he had been before, seeing her every day, talking to her, finding all her little ways irresistible.

Not irresistible enough for marriage, clearly, Kittie thought with some asperity. In truth, though, her mind would have told her to accept if his proposal had been of the honorable sort, but her heart would have forced her to say no.

She turned back to the house, relieved that she had left no further room for doubt—though she didn't think she had the first time—and that there could be no more misunderstanding. She need only enjoy the last week of her friends' visit now, and look forward to the long winter ahead.

That was a sobering prospect. She would need to order more wool from Judy Boxcroft and more books from the village library. But she wouldn't think about that right now. The gentlemen were coming that afternoon for a walk on the fells, and then back for an evening of music and cards in Bodenthorpe Cottage.

And she would see His Grace, the duke. It was a prospect both to flutter her nerves and give her reason to reflect on the frailty of the human heart.

Thirteen

"So you told him in no uncertain terms and he . . ." Rebecca trailed off as she looked past Kittie and smiled.

Kittie looked up. They were standing in the garden, awaiting their escorts, and the gentlemen were just arriving.

Sir John, his curly hair tousled by the breeze, went straight to Rebecca and whispered something to her. She chuckled and gave him a soft slap on the cheek. Mr. Norton, of course, headed straight to Hannah and took her arm, holding her close to him, secure.

Orkenay and Alban both headed toward Kittie and stood before her. How awkward.

"Mrs. Douglas," the duke said, "since my aunt has declined to accompany us, choosing instead to stay inside with Beacon, it appears that the numbers are uneven and you will have two escorts from whom to choose."

What could have been a humorous observation was said in such grim tones that Kittie didn't know how to respond.

"Nonsense, Alban," Orkenay said, taking her left arm. "Who says that we cannot *share* her?"

Alban stiffened, and Kittie frowned at the odd tone of the earl's words. Again, an innocuous sentence but one that seemed loaded with meaning.

"I prefer not to share a lady's . . . company with any other man," the duke said, and stalked off alone.

The walk proceeded, but though Kittie would normally have enjoyed the experience, she was left feeling unsettled again. She had felt calmer after her words to the earl that morning, but now she wondered, alarmed by his behavior, if he still had not understood her adequately. Though he would have to be a complete dunderhead not to.

"How has the hunting been, Lord Orkenay?" Kittie said, desperate to introduce some safe topic of conversation.

"Rather good, though I'm not much of a hunter. Most of my pursuit is confined to the boudoirs of London." He laughed at his own jest.

Alban glared at them, and Kittie began to feel angry at him again, though she had sworn to herself to try to get along with him better for Lady Eliza's sake. But really, his look had been impartially at them both, and the earl was the one making shabby jokes. She stayed silent.

"My dear, you must allow yourself to laugh once in a while," Orkenay said.

"I will when I find anything humorous, I promise."

"A shot! I am hit! You are a sure huntress, in truth, Mrs. Douglas."

They walked together through the woods, and up the fell, beyond Boden House. Kittie found an excuse to break away from the earl and stalked on alone. He lagged behind, not being as much of a walker as the rest of the company.

Autumn was fast approaching, stealing on silent feet across the fells and through the moors, turning the green grass to gold and the trees to crimson. A fresh wind whipped up the slope and tugged at her skirts as she crested the rise and stood looking down over the valley beyond the Boden property.

"You look as if you wish you were anywhere but here."

Kittie turned and stared up at the duke. The breeze lifted his dark hair off his forehead and out of his eyes. "Everyone wishes from time to time that they could escape their life and their choices, don't you think?"

He stared at her, his dark eyes riveted to hers. "Do you? Do you wish you could escape your choices?"

What did he mean? Why was he so intent?

"No," she said, afraid suddenly of his meaning. "I'm quite happy with all of my choices."

"Really."

He reached out and pushed one stray curl from her tidy bun back behind her ear. She shivered at the touch of his warm bare hand brushing along her neck. The caress felt intimate, tender, beckoning. It seemed to her that the earl had done much the same thing earlier that day, and yet it had held no meaning. But this . . . she swallowed. It was just physical yearning for a man's touch. Not just any man would do, clearly. It was increasingly odd how she could feel so antagonistic toward the duke and yet be so affected by his nearness. Was she holding herself apart, holding on to her anger toward him just to keep herself—and her heart—safe?

"But it doesn't mean I wouldn't make other choices if I had other opportunities," she found herself saying.

His thick eyebrows went up. "Really? And what other opportunities would you like?"

She felt as though they were speaking at cross-purposes. She was merely thinking out loud that perhaps she would like to marry again, if she ever found a man in her sphere who made her feel just a little of what she felt in the duke's presence, but she certainly could not tell him that. She had forgotten how delicious was that melting sensation when one was near a man one found attractive. How sweet it would be to fall in love again.

She looked away from the duke.

Like Hannah was falling in love, she thought, for that was so clearly what was happening. Mr. Norton and Hannah were on their own, looking over the rise at the valley below and speaking earnestly. The glances between them were warm, almost incendiary. Hannah rested her cheek on her beau's arm and he moved to put his arm around her shoulders and pull her close.

Sighing, Kittie glanced back up to the duke to find that he was watching the couple, too, and there was a strange look of yearning on his face, and yet so much doubt was expressed in his clouded gaze and set lips. Kittie marveled at the complexity of the man. It was perhaps a good thing he was so far out of her sphere, for if she released her emotions she would find herself wanting to soothe that worried frown and erase those stern lines that bracketed his hard mouth.

The earl, who had been climbing the rather steep hill behind them, crested the rise, puffing and huffing. He leaned over, hands on his knees. "All this for a bloody view? Pardon me, ladies, for my language, but I'm going back down to Boden for a drink." He turned abruptly and headed back down the hill.

Sir John and Rebecca, returning from a brief exploration of some rocky outcropping, both laughed.

Alban's expression relaxed for the first time, and he chuckled. He held out his arm to Kittie. "May I escort you, Mrs. Douglas? I have a feeling your erstwhile swain will be galloping on the way down."

She took his arm and felt again, reluctantly, the sweet tendrils of longing thread through her bosom. She must stamp out the tender bud of desire, for it was wholly inappropriate, and, she feared, unreturned. "Thank you, Your Grace. Let us proceed back."

How was she different? How was Kittie Douglas different from every other woman he had met in the last ten years?

He still could not answer that puzzling question.

They were all gathered at Boden that evening, his aunt well entertained by the witty Sir John and rascally Lady Severn as they sat together by the fire. Bart had apologized to Alban for being so oblivious to the requirements of company over the past weeks. With a rare jot of humor he said that now that he was completely in love and not just falling, he would endeavor to find more time to be a good guest. To that end he and Hannah were paired with Orkenay and Kittie, playing whist at a table by the window.

And Alban, alone, sat at his ease and stared at Kittie. She was gowned simply in pale green, but the cloth lovingly hugged her curves and the color accented her coil of ruddy curls that draped seductively down over one shoulder. She made him hunger for her, but he had yet to discover how she did it. That there was some seductive force at work he had no doubt, but what it was, was still a mystery.

He wanted her, and not just for her delectable body, but to tame her, to master her, to consume her. He wanted, for once, her gaze to soften while they spoke; instead everything he said seemed to antagonize her and she fought him, defied him. It was a novel and not welcome feeling to be at conflict with a woman he wanted so badly.

Their walk that day had left him even more confused, not only as to his own feelings but as to hers, too.

Was she signaling to him that she would be willing to change from the earl to the duke if he asked her to be *his* mistress? It had almost seemed that way when she had spoken of perhaps making other choices if she had other opportunities. Was he that other choice? Did he want to be that other choice?

His original reason for not pursuing her had been that he would not take her away from his aunt, affecting her comfort so devastatingly. But surely that reasoning no longer held, for he had no further doubt as to whether she was going away with Orkenay at the end of his stay or not. That little scene in the garden that morning was the confirmation he needed.

And so . . . should he bend his efforts at seduction?

They would only be there a little less than a week. Once she had left with Orkenay, he would not feel right about taking her away from the man, but he didn't think they had actually consummated their illicit relationship yet.

And Orkenay had flouted his host's request that he stay away from Kittie Douglas. That breach of etiquette alone had earned the man no consideration.

He would have to find a way to make up to his aunt for the heartache she would inevitably suffer when Kittie Douglas left her. That reminded him of what a tricky position he would be in when Lady Eliza found out that he had taken Kittie as a mistress. Would she be angry at him? Or would she understand, when he explained that one way or the other she would have been bereft of a companion?

Kittie had gotten up from the game and was bending over Lady Eliza, asking her something. That woman had her face turned up to her companion, and their hands were clasped. There was such love shining on his aunt's face that he was jolted from his contemplation. She adored her companion as more than just a valued employee; Kittie Douglas had become a daughter substitute, or even something more. She would never forgive him, maybe.

Sighing heavily, he knew in his heart that he just could not do that to her. He loved his aunt far too much, and it would be the merest bit of sophistry to pass off his actions as anything other than immoral, given how she felt about her companion and how he claimed to feel about his aunt.

Though the first breach of ethics would not be his, but would be Orkenay and Kittie's, surely.

He rubbed his eyes. In the deepest recess of his heart he knew he would never be able to conquer this desire he had for Kittie Douglas without having her at least once, nor would he be able to reconcile such an action with the care and consideration for his aunt's feelings that he claimed to himself and others was the basis of his actions.

It was a dilemma. A dilemma with no easy resolution, he feared. But while he was figuring it out, he could at least talk to her some more and try to gauge her feelings. He stood and stretched, then ambled over to his aunt.

Fourteen

"Alban," Lady Eliza said, stretching out her free hand to her nephew as he approached. "Tell Kittie that she must not mind me and must get some fresh air, if that is what she wants."

"Certainly . . . Mrs. Douglas, I concur with my aunt; you must get a breath of fresh air if that is what you require."

"She does; she was just telling me that she is feeling a little warm and headachy, and asked if I minded if she took a walk on the terrace." Lady Eliza smiled slyly and raised her eyebrows over her milky eyes. "Perhaps Alban will accompany you, my dear," she said, squeezing Kittie's hand.

Alarmed by such an obvious ploy to confine the duke and her to a close space—Lady Eliza was still concerned that her nephew and companion did not get along well—Kittie was about to spew a list of reasons why that was not necessary, but when she met the duke's gaze, she was speechless.

With a more open expression than she had ever seen, he said, "Will you allow me, Mrs. Douglas?"

"Go," Lady Eliza said, giving her a push.

The duke accompanied her to the terrace and guided her to a stone bench that overlooked the sloping lawn, silvery green in the moonlight. Candlelight from the room they had left behind spilled through the open drapes into a pool on the terrace stone.

The night air smelled of green things and a breeze rustled through the bushes, scattering leaves across the stones of the flagged terrace. He sat down beside her, radiating male heat in suffocating waves. He laid one arm across the terrace wall behind her.

"It's a lovely night," he said, his tone low and quiet.

A shiver raced through her. "It is."

"Why do you think my aunt sent us out here together like this?" he asked.

She turned to him, amazed by his perspicacity. She had long thought she was the only one who could see through the lady's sometimes devious machinations, but then she should have realized the duke had known her his whole life and he was, besides, an intelligent man. It was just that she had thought that kind of perception was a feminine province.

"I think she is concerned," Kittie said, driven to honesty, "by our seeming inability to get along as two rational adult people."

"Do you think we don't get along?"

She remained silent. She didn't know how to answer him, and since she had no real reason for her antagonism toward him other than his suspicion of her, she had nothing to say.

He touched her shoulder with his large hand, rubbing her shoulder blade with his thumb. It was a good thing he was not privy to her internal workings, for she was surely melting inside. She cast him a look of exasperation, and he stopped.

"Pardon me, Mrs. Douglas, for my familiarity."

She caught a secretive smile on his handsome face. Did he have some idea after all of how she felt?

It was a thought that shamed her back into speech.

"I am ready to be friends if you are, sir." She held out her ungloved hand and his engulfed it.

"I would like to be your friend . . . Kittie, if I may call you that as a friend. What a sweet name. How did you happen to be named that?"

"My mother's dearest friend was a lady named Katherine, but she died young. I think my mother always missed her, and so named me Kittie, her dear friend's diminutive denomination."

"My wife tried to convince her friends to call her Kitty, but to no avail."

Kittie held her breath. He had never mentioned his wife in her presence, and she felt if she breathed he would retreat back into his reticence. "Why would they not go along with her request?"

The duke's expressive mouth quirked into a sideways grin. "Her closest friend—a woman very much like your friend Lady Severn—said it was impossible to even consider because it was a little too apt. A kitty, she said, was a soft little creature that had the most unexpected needle-sharp bite when all you wanted to do was pet it."

Kittie smiled. "Was that true?"

Alban, grim again, stared off into the darkness. "I suppose."

"I . . . I'm so sorry for all the pain you suffered. It must have been a dreadful time," Kittie said, tentatively touching his sleeve.

"I don't wish to discuss it, Mrs. Douglas."

So, he had retreated to formality. "I was not discussing it, I was merely offering condolences."

"There are none needed."

What did that mean? That he wasn't sorry she was gone? "Condolences are never amiss. You must be sorry she is gone, and so my offering of sympathy is for your pain."

"There is none, ergo, your sympathy is wasted."

Infuriating man! He had clambered back into his hermit's cave and was brooding again, she could tell by the beetling of his dark brows and the grim set of his lips.

"Why do men do that?" she said, not realizing what she was going to say until her mouth was open. But, in for a penny—She turned to him on the bench and glared at him. "Why do men pretend they have no feelings, that they are cold and without human emotions? I don't understand it. I will *never* understand it. My husband did the same thing when his mother died, pretending he wasn't grieving, though he was."

His chilly veneer cracked. "Why, if we are to point fingers, do women insist on scrutinizing every little expression, every word, every minute detail of a man's speech, for meaning? Can you not for once just accept that we are telling the truth when we say we don't wish to talk about some things?"

"I accept that you don't wish to talk about it, but what I do not accept is that that is necessarily the correct way to behave."

"Oh, so even our behavior is remiss now? I could say the same. Women are prone to puzzling bouts of tears and hysteria at the most inopportune times."

"And men deliberately shut themselves off from all feeling, unwilling to do anything but . . . but bet on which snail will cross the path first, or which raindrop will hit the bottom of the window ahead of the others." She threw her hands up in the air and then clasped them on her lap. "Trivialities. Utterly inconsequential to life."

"Now you are being deliberately vexatious. What *some* idiotic men do has no bearing on the rest of creation."

They stared at each other, and Kittie wondered if this is what his wife saw when they argued, this implacable coldness.

He turned away. "There is nothing to be gained by opening one's heart, merely to have it stabbed and milked for every drop of red blood."

Kittie drew in a long breath. The raw pain in his awful words hung in the air like an odor. "Alban," she said, putting one hand on his sleeve, "that is what talking is for, to heal that wound so the soul can regenerate. If it were not for my friends after Roger died, I would have . . . I would still feel as empty as I did when he passed."

"But I would wager that he didn't betray you and then laugh about it," Alban grated out, his teeth clenched. "He didn't . . ." He shook his head and turned away, hitting his fist on the stone bench. "I don't wish to discuss this, Mrs. Douglas. It is over and done and in the past."

"Is it? Is it over?" Kittie said, gently. She removed her hand from his sleeve and gazed down over the moonlit grass. "Is it ever over? I loved Roger to the day he died. It wasn't until after that I found out how badly he had misused our funds, to the point of leaving me destitute. He gambled. I still don't know if he couldn't help himself, or if he just didn't care. If he had loved me as much as he claimed, would he not have made some provision, kept some money safe, as he promised?"

Slowly, uncertainly, Alban turned back toward her. "Do those thoughts plague you?"

"They did for a long time." She crossed her arms over her belly and hugged herself. "I had to forgive him and do my best to move ahead. For a while I wasn't even living. I was suspended in time; the rest of the world moved on, but I stayed caught in the trap of my . . . my own pain and grief." It hurt to think of that again, and how long she had wasted in anger and hopelessness and defeat. She felt his arm steal around her. How good it would feel to allow herself to let go for once. She swallowed and let his warmth steal through her.

But when she turned to him it was to find his lips so close, his warm breath fanned over her face, and she involuntarily closed her eyes.

The moment of his lips meeting hers was like the first heady fragrance of a rose, ineffably sweet, impossibly fragile. The warmth molded them together and every particle of breath was drawn from her body, consumed by a flame of need. She put her arms around his neck and pressed herself to the hard wall of his broad chest, her fingers threading through his dark curls and cradling his head.

A tiny part of her was asking, *pleading*, to know how this had happened. Why was he kissing her? Why was she allowing it? But the other part, the larger part that had longed for this delicious sensation, had hungered for it and imagined it a hundred times even before meeting him, urged her to surrender and give herself over to the powerful desire that wound through her body.

And then what?

She pulled away, and his dark eyes searched hers, the glaze in his a clear indication to her of his desire and how he imagined this would end. It occurred to her that he had kissed her to avoid thinking of what he needed to conquer, his anger and grief at his wife's desertion. Kissing her was one more way of pushing away and stuffing down difficult emotion.

How very male to let lovemaking override other more difficult emotions. Roger would always, when he wanted to avoid talking about their money problems or things she wanted to know, seduce her with his kisses and soft words. But she wouldn't be used that way, not now that she knew the price.

"I . . . I had better go back in," she said, rising and moving away.

"Wait! Kittie . . ."

But she could not turn back and listen to him. Vulnerable to his beguiling mastery of the art of seduction, she had to acknowledge her weakness for him and be strong enough to walk away.

Alban, unwilling to beg her to come back, watched her walk in and felt a thread of irritation wend through him. How could she just walk away when they both knew she wanted to go on? She was vulnerable to him, and it wasn't just his superior position as it was with some women. He had been a duke's heir and a duke long enough to understand the difference between a woman dazzled by his power and position and a woman genuinely entranced by his skill at seduction.

But she had walked away. Attracted to him, wanting him, she had still walked away. Women, as always, were a mystery to him.

The young baronet, Sir John Fitzhenry, slipped out the terrace door from the drawing room. "Lord, I want a cigar," he said, strolling across the flagged terrace as he took a couple from an inner pocket. "Would you like one, Your Grace?"

Alban took the proffered cigar.

There was silence for a few minutes as Sir John dealt with the complicated flint and tinder process to light their cigars. "Somebody will have to find an easier way than this to simply light a cigar." He grunted. "There must be something."

Alban shrugged. "It has always been that way. I don't see the need for change."

"Don't you?" Sir John said, glancing sideways at the duke. "I think there is always room for improvement in everything; don't you think so?"

Alban considered it, but it wasn't more ease in lighting cigars that occurred to him. Room for improvement. Had he been ignoring that need in his own life? He knew there were many people who wanted him to marry again, but he had not been able to come to any decision regarding that frightening prospect. He had vowed that his next wife would be a meek little miss fresh in her first Season. He wanted one who would be so awed by his position that she would never even consider feeling ill-used if he went his own way and did things other than how and what she wanted. Not like Catherine, who had wanted his time and attention.

And yet . . . it was possible that he could have prevented the whole calamity that his marriage became by just such a little attention. And therein lay his anger. He would never have the chance to mend it. Catherine had not only left, but she had died, and he found that outrageously unfair.

He should have prevented it. There were problems between them that he had ignored for far too long, and in the end they turned away from each other. He should have prevented her leaving, which would have prevented her dying, and so it was his fault, really.

Wasn't it?

"Your Grace? Is the cigar satisfactory?"

"Yes . . . uh, yes. Tell me, do you truly think that . . . what you were saying before. That there is always room for improvement?"

The younger man nodded. "Not that the old ways are not fine, but . . ."

"But change is necessary."

"For life, yes. Consider . . . we don't remain children, we grow and change, and so do our needs. Everything around us is like that, don't you think? We used to believe that it was all right to own other people and to force them to work for us. We don't do that anymore . . ."

"We do in our colonies."

"Yes, but change is coming there too," Sir John said, eagerly. "That is simply because people are resisting change. But soon there will be no need, because there will be better ways to harvest sugar and cotton. Manufactories . . . soon, work that took days will take hours. Stockings that used to be knit by hand are now knit on looms, swifter and better!"

Alban smiled at the zeal expressed in the young man's slim body, bent forward, his hands moving in the air as if to create pictures of vast, efficient manufactories. "Will it really make everything better? What about those who make their living from the old ways?"

"They'll be free to get a better education, to learn and study, to think and do better for themselves and their families."

They had moved far beyond the personal application Alban was placing on Sir John's statement about advancement being necessary for life. He saw problems in the baronet's theories, drawbacks to such an idealized world as he imagined, but he would not stamp on the young man's enthusiasm. Others could do that. Without idealists like Sir John the world would be a dreary place.

And without women like Kittie Douglas, a cold one. That unbidden thought danced into his brain, but he pushed it away. "If they can find a better way to light a cigar I will consider it miracle enough," he said.

Sir John chuckled. "I know I become overenthusiastic sometimes. It is a failing."

"No, never consider it a failing. There is time enough in your life for cynicism. Besides, I'm sure it is your enthusiasm for life and your vigor that Lady Severn appreciates so much."

The young man flushed. "She's wonderful, isn't she?"

"I suppose you could say that." Though he wouldn't.

"She is so intelligent and forceful. Like no other woman I've ever met."

Alban regarded him closely. "Why did you come north with us? Who are you following here, myself or Orkenay?"

Instantly the younger man retreated to his usual demeanor of calm, cool amusement. "Your Grace, why would I need any other reason to come north with your party than the excellent hunting?"

Hunting indeed, but what are you hunting? Alban wondered. *And why did you follow Lord Orkenay in his amorous adventures?* "I think I shall rejoin the others. Will you come with me, Sir John, or are you going to enjoy the night air for a while longer?"

With a sly smile, the baronet said, "I'll be in in a moment. Or, if Lady Severn comes out, in a half hour or so."

"I'll let her know you're waiting."

Fifteen

"I will admit she is a puzzle to me, your companion," Alban said to his aunt the next morning, as he took her walking along the high fell. His enjoyment in the walk was mostly in watching his aunt relishing the wind on her face and the striding walk they were able to share because of his own long-limbed frame.

"You have never been one to enjoy a puzzle. You always said they were tiresome and pointless, where Bartholomew would work at one for hours until he had solved it."

"Ah, we are to canvas my failings again, are we?"

"Why do you think I view it as a failing? When did you become so sensitive to criticism or even simple comment, Alban?"

They walked on for a while; he chose to ignore her question. She was leaning heavily on him, more so as the fell became steeper.

"Admit that she interests you," Lady Eliza finally said, sounding breathless. She stepped carefully, placing one booted foot deliberately before shifting her weight. "May we stop walking for a while, Alban? I dislike admitting it, but I am getting tired."

They stopped and sat on a rocky outcropping. Alban stared down the sloping fell at the zigzag of stony fences punctuating the sloping green and a herd of black-faced Swaledale sheep in the distance.

"She does interest you," his aunt repeated. "Come, Alban, do not be silent with me. I do not have my sight; please give me conversation, at least."

"All right! Yes, she does interest me."

"Would she not make some man a splendid wife?"

"Some man. She has great beauty of a certain kind, earthy and voluptuous. But she is very countrified and too plain-speaking."

"By that you mean contrary and stubborn, an indictment from you, indeed, who are the soul of compromise. There is more, though. You think she is not sophisticated enough for London," Lady Eliza said, her tone blunt.

"No, she's not. They would toy with her and then consume her like a cat does a mouse."

"Do not mistake her calm and lack of frivolity for simplicity. It is my opinion that Kittie Douglas could easily grace the most elegant of ballrooms, and would adjust her manner accordingly."

Alban eyed his aunt, wondering if she was implying something more than her words, on the surface, would seem to indicate. He had first learned from her that communication was never a simple art, built, as it was, from many layers of meaning.

"You do not reply," she said. "I will infer from your silence that you disagree. But you must allow that I know Kittie far better than you, having observed her over the three years of our acquaintance."

"However, some latitude must be given for your understandable affection for her and your . . . absence from London these twenty years or more."

"Really, Alban, I thought I would get a better argument than that. My affection has never blinded me to a person's faults—you should know that best—and yes,

I know I said the word 'blinded,' but without the slightest hint of other meaning. Nor can I believe London has changed so very much. It is likely the same treacherous, gossip-filled, inane, glorious, sparkling sewer it was when I left."

"Why does it matter if Kittie should grace a London ballroom or not?" Alban said. "She is unlikely ever to be in one. Her husband was a common gambler, from her own admission, and she is now a companion. I think that is the height she can expect to attain."

"I would never place limitations on Kittie Douglas, Alban. Given the right introduction to society, I think she could soar."

"Are you quite recovered, Aunt? Shall we go back?"

Lady Eliza stood. "I am not done yet," she said, with a grim cast to her lined face. She reached out her hand and caught up Alban's. "I want to climb higher. I shall not get another chance this winter, with you going back home within the week."

Determined not to quarrel, Alban stayed silent and took his aunt's arm. For the rest of the morning they concentrated on climbing and walking.

Later that day, back at Boden, Alban decided to confront Orkenay and demand a simple accounting of his relationship with Kittie Douglas. Nothing, though, was ever simple with the earl.

Orkenay was randomly shooting balls in the billiards room, smacking them into pockets with rapid skill. Alban strolled in, watched for a moment, lounging against the door frame, then picked up a cue stick.

"Shall we play?" he said.

"Certainly." Orkenay racked the balls. "Will you break?"

Eyeing the earl, Alban complied. A footman entered with a tray of glasses, and the earl requested brandy.

As the footman exited, Alban smacked the cue ball, and the other balls scattered wildly. "So, Orkenay, we shall be leaving in a few days."

"Yes. I confess anticipation at the coming departure. Not that your hospitality hasn't been all that it should, old man, but I have my reasons."

Stifling the instinct to badger the earl for information, Alban decided on a shot and took it, deliberately aiming to miss. "I can imagine," he said, straightening and watching his shot go wild, "that you have every reason to wish yourself back in London."

A smug grin on his lightly lined face, Orkenay examined the table and chose his angle. "If you are needling for information, Alban, you are to be disappointed. A gentleman does not divulge too much, and a lady never tells, you know."

And a gentleman also never broke his stick over the back of a guest, Alban thought. The earl's shot went wild, too, and it almost looked as though his hand were shaking. Despite his supposed calm, was he agitated about Alban prodding for information about his affaire with Mrs. Douglas? Lining up his next shot, Alban decided a change of subject might be disarming. "I think Bart is serious about Mrs. Billings. I would not be surprised if he had an announcement to make before we leave."

"Fool. He could do so much better."

Alban took his shot, aiming carefully, and watched in satisfaction as his target snapped into the pocket. Lining up his next shot, he said, "You mean he could do better than a lady who obviously adores him and thinks he is the only man in the world worth gazing upon?"

Chuckling, but with an expression devoid of humor, Orkenay replied, "No, I think that it is a bad match in every sense of the word. Marriages should not be made on the basis of fleeting feeling."

That it was much what he had been saying to Kittie Douglas lately did not escape Alban's notice. From another man it sounded cruel, calculated, and unfeeling.

"I mean really, Alban, how many times in your life have you fancied yourself in love? And if you had married the first girl for whom you entertained that feeling?"

"I would be wed to Maggie Shay, the village barmaid, who is now graying and portly and a grandmother."

"I think my point is proven."

Alban missed his next shot and strolled over to the table to pour himself some brandy. He refilled Orkenay's empty glass as the man took his shot. "So how should marriages be contracted? In the age-old arrangement? I can tell you from experience that that does not always work out well."

The earl pressed his lips together, but wanted to laugh, Alban could see it.

"Your mistake was not whom you wed, but how you treated her. You were far too indulgent, Alban. Women are very much like children; they need to know their limits. You should have beat her the first time she spoke to you impertinently. It is the only way women know they are loved."

It was not the first time he had heard that theory, and Alban should not have been shocked, but he was. The casual brutality of Orkenay's words was like a cold slap. And this man would bed fair Kittie? This man would have the pleasure of taking her home and being with her night and day, or any time he cared?

Alban tossed his cue stick on the table and faced the earl. "Orkenay, if I ever hear that you have hurt Mrs. Douglas or even raised your hand to her, I will come after you and kill you, I promise you that."

He turned and was walking away as the earl said, calling after him, "Alban, don't be ridiculous . . . one doesn't beat a mistress, just a wife!"

Alban's mood was black and thunderous, and the servants scuttled out of his way, clearly preferring to let his rare foul mood pass unobserved. He retreated to his library as dark clouds filled the sky, piling up above the fells outside his window. A few minutes or an hour later—he could not be sure which—Bart stuck his head in the door.

"Do you have a moment, Alban? I have something to tell you."

"Come in, old friend, though I have a feeling I won't be surprised at your news."

Bart strolled in and over to the window. He gazed out for a minute, then turned and stared into the gloom. "I say, is everything all right? You, sitting alone here in the dark . . . it rather reminded me of after Catherine . . . that is, after your wife . . ."

"I should not continue, if I were you." Alban took a deep breath and roused himself to sit up. He leaned over and turned up the lamp, shedding more light in the gloom inflicted on them by the lowering sky. Thunder rolled in the distance. "I'm not brooding, Bart. Come, sit and tell me your news, and if I should order the butler to dust off some rather fine champagne I have in the cellar."

Bart obeyed and sat in a chair near his friend. Simply, he said, "I have asked Hannah to marry me, and she has said yes, provisionally, of course, for I have yet to meet her two lads, and she will do nothing that would upset them."

Sticking out his hand, Alban said, "Congratulations. I have every reason to think you will be happy."

"Though you don't understand why," Bart said, with a return of that dry humor he only displayed on rare occasions. He took his friend's hand, and the two shook.

"It is not up to me to understand it, my friend, only to be happy for you and celebrate your good fortune. I'll ring and we'll drink to your happiness."

"No . . ." He put up one hand to forestall the order. "I . . . I have sworn off alcohol of any kind, Alban. Hannah has noticed—and I have to agree that she is right—that my mood becomes more depressed when I drink, especially brandy. She would like me to try for a while without anything."

"No brandy nor even champagne? Then what shall you drink?"

"She says she makes a wonderful lime cordial," he said, with a hint of laughter in his voice. "I say, I should take some of Mrs. Douglas's awful sweet cicely beer home with me; it would cure me of drinking anything alcoholic!"

The two friends laughed together, but when they sobered, Alban stared at him and nodded. "I'm happy for you, Bart. I've watched you two, and though she is not to my taste she is so well suited to you that I thank providence we came here."

"Alban, what about you? I have not been so blind that I haven't seen the way you look at Mrs. Douglas. Is she not . . . that is . . ."

"The future Duchess of Alban? Don't be an idiot, Bart," Alban said, tiring of the subject before it had been canvassed. "I could never marry someone like her. Although . . ." He stood and strolled to the window, gazing out at the high fells and the dark clouds scudding over the top. Thunder rolled again, and rain spattered the window, obscuring the view. Orkenay's hideous words came back to him. If she was serious about going to London with the earl it could mean trouble for her. But how to warn her when she would not even admit she was going to become his mistress? There was one course of action he had until that moment thought was unthinkable, but which now seemed to promise pleasure for himself and protection for Kittie. It might be the best thing he did for everyone.

"Alban?"

Called back to the moment, the duke whirled around and gazed at his friend, who had stood and stared at him with anxious eyes.

"Again, congratulations, my friend. I have a few things to take care of this afternoon. If I don't see you at dinner, forgive me. I have much to do before we leave."

"Certainly," Bart said, moving toward the door. His words were understanding, but his eyes still revealed his worry. "I have a few letters to write, to my family. I think I'll retire to my room. Breakfast tomorrow?"

"Don't expect me," Alban said. "I have some things to take care of, too, and may be busy."

Sixteen

The day had been dreary and thunderous, but the clouds parted late in the afternoon, and the sun came out briefly. After dinner, with the autumn light fading outside, Kittie knitted by the fire made necessary by the chill in the damp old house. Rebecca was playing the piano, and Hannah was just sitting, staring raptly at the fire, though she was supposed to be reading out loud.

Lady Eliza finally said, "Mrs. Billings, why do you not tell us whatever it is that keeps you so silent tonight?"

Rebecca stopped playing, and Kittie looked up. She smiled at Hannah's disconcerted expression.

"I . . . I don't know . . ."

"Hannah," Kittie said gently, leaning over and taking the book from her drooping grasp, "I think we can already guess, but why don't you tell us. Do you have some news that you can share?"

Hannah burst into tears.

Since it was not the most unexpected reaction, no one made a fuss. Kittie just supplied her with a clean handkerchief, and they waited out the storm.

"I'm sorry," she said, sniffing and spluttering. "I . . . I'm just so h-happy!"

Kittie set her knitting aside and knelt by Hannah, and Rebecca joined them. Lady Eliza listened intently, her head cocked to one side.

"And you're happy for what reason, my dear?" Kittie said.

"I'm . . . I'm . . ."

"Oh, Hannah," Rebecca said, "just spit it out for once and don't make us wait forever."

"I'm getting married," she said, clutching the handkerchief to her bosom. "Or at least I think I am, for Mr. Norton has asked, and I said I would if my boys like him and approve, though I know I don't need their approval, but . . ."

The rest of her words were smothered by the hug that Rebecca and Kittie enveloped her in.

"Congratulations, Mrs. Billings," Lady Eliza said. "I believe we are about to be joined by someone, Kittie."

As Kittie looked up, she saw the duke stroll in, and her heart thudded. Hannah, overcome by the emotion of revealing her impending nuptials, was guided away from the light by Rebecca; she would need a few moments to recover, and since she was afraid of the duke for some strange reason, though he had never been anything but kind to her, his presence would not help in the slightest. Rebecca escorted her from the room and toward the stairs, perhaps to repair the damage her tears had caused her complexion.

"Ladies," he said.

"Your Grace." Kittie dropped a curtsy, though such a formal gesture was not necessary. She had been flustered into awkwardness.

He strolled over, kissed his aunt's cheek, and sat down in the chair vacated by Hannah. "Have I interrupted anything?"

"Only an excess of sensibility brought on by the momentous announcement of Mrs. Billings's engagement," his aunt said.

"Ah, yes, Bart told me."

Lady Eliza held out her hand and the duke took it. It

was in the moments of his interaction with his aunt that Kittie saw in the duke the softer side, the loving man he could have been given other circumstances. She watched them avidly and he caught her at it. He raised his eyebrows.

"Are you happy for him?" Lady Eliza asked.

His eyes still on Kittie, he said, "How could I help but be, Aunt? If I have discovered anything in this life it's that love is rare, and should be snatched up whenever and wherever one finds it. He has found it in a most unexpected place, but Mrs. Billings' good character and his own sterling worth will ensure their happiness, if not quite on this same ecstatic level, at least comfortably for some time."

"Some would say his match is not very worldly."

"And they would be right, but in his case, I'm glad. He doesn't live much in society, Aunt. You know Bart; he prefers his books and his estate and his dogs. He will be a complete country gentleman, and her two sons will be the gainers for his solidity and kindness."

"So you think all the benefit on her side?" Kittie could not restrain comment.

"I don't think I said, nor even implied that, Mrs. Douglas. On the contrary, I think he very definitely benefits. He has shown a great deal of self-knowledge in his choice. He said himself that they're stronger for each other than they ever are for themselves."

"I wish that everyone had so much self-knowledge," Lady Eliza said.

The duke finally stared at his aunt, giving Kittie a reprieve from his searching look. What was he thinking? His dark eyes had never left hers, and he looked to be searching her soul for some answer. But she didn't know the question.

"I know you're speaking of me," he said to Lady Eliza, "and we've talked of this subject before. I think I

have made myself amply clear in every way possible."
His expression softened and he laid one large hand on
her arm. "Aunt, I promise I shall take steps to ensure
my own happiness, but you must let me do so in my
own way and my own time."

Lady Eliza sighed. She put her free hand over his
and rubbed it. With a final pat, she said, "I am very
tired, Alban, after that vigorous walk this morning. I enjoyed it very much, but I am tired. Would someone ring
for Beacon for me? I think I shall leave you two to talk,
if you will excuse an old woman."

Alban stood, raised her to her feet, and commanded
the footman to call Beacon to her mistress's aid. "Old
woman! I never thought to hear you call yourself that.
You're on the bright side of sixty, ma'am, and that, for
someone of your vigor, is a mere child."

She patted his cheek. Kittie rose, too, and Beacon
bustled into the room, fully recovered from her chill,
other than a red nose and tendency to sniffle.

"I had hoped to steal your companion away for a
walk, Aunt, if I have your permission."

Kittie gaped at him in alarm. What did he have to say
to her that he couldn't say in front of his aunt? And
why were they continually out walking and arguing? It
made no sense, and they hadn't advanced a whit in understanding each other, she sometimes felt, since they
first met. Even despite him kissing her.

Lady Eliza had gone still. "You have my permission.
Kittie, take a shawl; it is getting cold outside."

"Do I have no say in this? Perhaps I would prefer to
accompany you upstairs, ma'am, and see you safely to
your bed!"

"Do not be ridiculous. My nephew is a handsome rascal and you are a pretty young woman. Even if all you
do is walk and talk you will enjoy it far more than
watching me snore, which is what I believe I shall be

doing in about five minutes. Go! That is an order. I shall tell your friends on my way to bed." On Beacon's arm, she walked toward the door. She summoned Alban to her for one moment, whispered something to him, and then gave him a little push. "I shall see you tomorrow, Kittie," she called, as she walked from the room.

"Oliver," Alban said to the waiting footman, "Mrs. Douglas's shawl, please."

"I'll get it," Kittie said, with an exasperated sigh.

She wanted him, and he wanted her. She was leaving his aunt's employ anyway with the earl, who would be cruel to her eventually, no doubt, and who would certainly not treat her well when he was done with her. Alban knew all these things, and they had aided his final decision. It was a happy case that his inclination and her good were best served if she abandoned her plan of going with the earl to come to him instead. She was not a fickle woman, though, and would need to be convinced.

She liked him, was attracted to him, and would enjoy their time together. That should make her defection from Orkenay much simpler.

As they strolled outside, he said, "I have something to show you. Something you may never have seen, even in three years of living here."

Twilight was well advanced, but Alban knew the way well. He guided her down a long dark path through the wooded glade, taking a path not well traveled. She shivered at his side and he pulled her closer, under the protection of his arm.

The cabin was tiny, just one room, really. It was a huntsman's shack once, but years ago he had had it fitted for comfort as a retreat after Catherine's death.

And then he had never taken advantage of it, seeing it for the first time with Mr. Lafferty just that afternoon. Now it beckoned to them, candlelight in the windows showing a warm golden glow.

"I have seen this before, but never been inside." Kittie gazed at it as they approached and then looked up at Alban. "Mr. Lafferty said it was an abandoned huntsman's home."

"It was, but it has since been transformed. Come inside."

Kittie gazed around her as they entered. It was just one room, but the opulence was staggering: wood paneling, oak trim, a fireplace of gracious proportions. There was a table to one side set with dishes and wine goblets, ruby glass glowing richly in the candlelight.

Alban slipped her shawl off her shoulders, and indeed it was warm enough that her bare arms were not in the slightest chilled. He must have had servants here for hours, cleaning, setting the table, bringing food and wine, laying the fire.

"I thought we'd have a late supper and talk. I know you spoke of how we seem often to be at daggers drawn, and I wanted to make it right before I leave."

She turned and gazed at him suspiciously. His words were so smooth, his manner so polished. He guided her to the table and they sat, drank wine, and ate fruit and cheese, oysters and delicious sweetmeats. They talked about many things, but never anything of import.

What did he want? Or was she shamefully suspicious?

After eating, he guided her to a spot near the fire where a shaggy fur rug softened the cold of the marble hearth. He was solicitous of her comfort, but that wasn't new. He was ever kind and thoughtful where any woman was concerned, she had oft noted. He didn't particularly care for Rebecca, nor for Hannah, but he

was better than patient with them, showing a real regard for their comfort and desirous of their ease.

She therefore sat on the floor by the fire, threading
her fingers through the luxurious fur of the rug and
relishing the warmth of the fire. Why should she not
just enjoy instead of always being suspicious of his motives? The fine wine had left her feeling mellow and
contented, and when he sat down by her and toyed
with her hair, she turned her face into his hand,
cradling her cheek there. "You're so kind, sir," she
murmured.

"Not kind," he said.

"But you are." She gazed up at him into his dark eyes,
searching them.

He drew her closer and pulled her to his chest. "Kittie," he whispered. "Don't look at me like that. I feel
as though you're . . . you're looking for something I
don't have, something I never will. Looking for some
man I'll never be."

"No, no." She framed his face with her hands, rubbing her thumbs along his jawline. "I don't think you
know yourself well enough. I don't think you really
know—" She broke off, not sure what she was trying
to say.

He folded her into his arms and pulled her down
until they were reclining on the rug. He was too close;
she closed her eyes, and his mouth covered hers in a
hard, smothering kiss, which changed and became
gentle, as if he were reining in fiery emotion. She sur-
rendered to the moment, letting rich sensuality wash
through her, feeling his mouth suckle hers, noting the
hard line of his lean body against her plump form, letting her body soften at the shattering knowledge that
he was hardening against her thigh.

He wanted her. He wanted to seduce her, and this
whole night was dedicated to that, she thought, the

rich food, the opulent surroundings, the warm fire, just made to heat naked flesh.

And she could just surrender. She tried to tell herself it would be all right in the morning, that she would be happy she had given in, for once, to her most secret desires. He pulled her closer, almost under him, and his voracious kisses left her limp with need.

But it was no use. Morning would always come, and her life would go on, and she would have to face Lady Eliza, and worse, her own image in the mirror, and explain how she had let her judgment of what was right for herself be seduced with wine and kisses.

She pulled away and sat up, rubbing her mouth, righting her clothes. She must look like the veriest tumbled wench. She touched one hand to her hair to find it was pulled from the pins that held it fast.

"Kittie," he said, but didn't continue. Instead, his eyes glazed and his motions jerky, he stood and pulled her to her feet. Taking her hand he led her to the shadows in the corner of the room where a sumptuous bed, dressed with linen and lace, waited.

How planned, how calculated was this seduction. She jerked her hand from his. "I think," she said, her tone brittle in the overheated room, "that you have me confused with someone else, Your Grace, someone who would climb into that bed and . . . and spread her legs for you."

Like a slap, her words rang out, and the drugged glaze was gone from his eyes in an instant. "*What* did you say?"

"I think you heard me; I won't repeat myself. But if you think I will be your whore, you're very much mistaken." Her anger building, she stomped across the room, grabbed her shawl, and stalked to the door. She stopped and stared back at him where he stood, dumbfounded, by the big bed in the corner. "I thought we had a friendship, but *you* apparently thought it was all a prelude to my becoming your mistress. You're no better than your good friend, the earl."

And with that, she left, finding the path with some difficulty, and stumbling down it.

For all his presumed gentlemanly attributes, he didn't follow her, and she took a long and weary hour to find her way in the dark what had only taken them twenty minutes to traverse in the light.

Seventeen

Huddled in her bed with the candle still glowing, Kittie pondered what had happened. She had been propositioned by a duke. Well, that was a step up from *carte blanche* from an earl, wasn't it?

But it had been such a lovely evening before his attempt to lead her to the bed; she had thought they were finding a way to talk without the verbal jousting they often resorted to. Why did he have to ruin it? Though he likely thought he was doing her some honor.

She jerked awake from her half slumber at the tap at her door. "Yes?"

"It's just me, Kittie," Rebecca said from the other side of the door. "May I come in?"

"Of course."

Rebecca swished in, her grand night attire floating around her in crisp waves. She hopped up on the bed, and it creaked. "So . . . what happened? You were gone quite a while with the magnificent Duke of Alban. Did you . . . ?"

Kittie felt her cheeks redden at her friend's bold, if unfinished, question. "What do you mean?"

"You know what I mean or you would not be blushing." Rebecca thrust her homely face close. "Did he bed you?"

"He tried. I said no, then I left."

"Foolish woman! I would have said yes in a trice and had him on his back before he changed his mind."

"Rebecca!"

"Oh, don't worry," she said, with an arch glance and wicked grin. "I know he doesn't like me, so I shan't steal him away. But oh, if I could!" She clasped her hands together and rolled her eyes. "He is marvelous, very medieval. Don't you feel that? All that restrained power. And such a very *big* man!" She shivered dramatically.

"Rebecca."

"Big in every way, I would bet."

"*Rebecca!*"

"Don't be a Miss Prunes and Prisms, Kittie. Can't you at least admit that you were tempted?"

"Yes." She sighed deeply and let the sensual, slumberous feeling wash through her once again. "Oh, yes, I was tempted." She threw herself back on the bed and stared up at the bed canopy. "I wanted to." She sat back up and stared at her friend. "If you can believe it, he had a little cabin set up in the woods, with candlelight and rugs and wine and . . . and a bed, very luxurious, very sumptuous . . . heaped with cushions and pillows and a white lace counterpane."

"Good Lord, all that trouble and you said no?" Rebecca practically shrieked and gave a little hop, making the bed creak again. "He was being everything delicate, knowing you would not want to do anything under the same roof as his aunt, and knowing you would be uncomfortable at Boden, with his friends nearby. I think you are out of your head, my dear, and I don't mind telling you that. I would toss my little fish back into the river in a trice if I thought I could reel in such a giant catch."

"You would abandon poor Sir John? I thought you liked him." Kittie smiled for the first time in hours.

"I do! But men like the duke don't come along every day."

"I know."

"And really, you didn't think he would eventually propose or anything, did you? He's a *duke*!"

"I know that!" Kittie said. "You don't have to remind me that he's too good for me."

"I ought to slap you," Rebecca said, her green eyes ablaze. "Too good for you? No one on this earth is too good for you. I only meant his status is such that he will have to marry a duke's daughter or at the very least an earl's. It is what is expected of him. But how much more spectacular that he chose you to bed!"

"We do look at things very differently, don't we?" Kittie said, shaking her head at her friend's logic. "And I really didn't mean that he is too good for me in that sense. If I truly thought that, then I would be grateful for his . . . invitation."

"And you're not."

Kittie shook her head.

"You're insulted by it, aren't you?"

Kittie didn't answer for a moment. "Rebecca, I am, but don't take that to mean . . . don't think that I feel that you and Sir John . . ."

"My dear, don't upset yourself unduly; I am not so sensitive as to worry about your opinion of my relationship with Sir John. My situation is unlike yours, and so we cannot react the same way, especially since we are such very different women, in different circumstances and with different feelings. Sir John is going to visit me at my home; we will have a glorious time, and then I will release him to swim away," she said, her hands and fingers fluttering together like a school of small fish heading upstream, "the better man for what I have taught him."

Kittie giggled, Rebecca laughed out loud, and the two women fell into each other's arms. But Kittie's laughter soon changed to tears, and Rebecca cradled her to her bosom, stroking her hair.

"My dear, I was loath to say this before, but . . . but you haven't done the unthinkable, have you? You haven't fallen in love with the dratted man?"

Her sobs subsiding, Kittie wiped the tears from her eyes and straightened. "No. How can you love someone who doesn't respect you? But I very much fear I could. I should be grateful for tonight, for it saved me from the abyss."

Rebecca reached out and stroked back Kittie's hair. "My dear, you should be married. You really should. And . . ." She stopped and shook her head. "Love is the strangest thing, my dear. Tell yourself what you will, I think you must be a little in love with Alban, or you would not be so hurt by what you deem his lack of respect."

"I thought we were friends, at least," she said, her tone mournful.

"You are thinking as a woman does, my dear," Rebecca said, "that in wanting to take you to his bed he is showing a lack of respect for you."

"Well, yes. He should know that I am not the type to become his mistress, or even his fleeting affaire. How could I go back to Lady Eliza with a clear heart after spending the night with him? This differs vastly from you and Sir John, Rebecca, for I am his aunt's paid companion! It changes our relationship. He has all the power, and I have none."

Rebecca nodded. "I think I see. You reasserted your power last night, though, by rejecting him, did you not?"

Kittie nodded. "Yes. I hadn't understood truly, until now, but I felt that in our vastly uneven positions, he was . . . was trying to take advantage of my poverty." She sighed and looked down at the bedcover, plucking at a loose thread. "And I thought we had the beginning of a tentative friendship. Not an easy one, but a friendship, still."

"You have to learn to think like a man and you will see that respect, friendship, and lovemaking are not exclusive of each other in his poor brain."

"But I'm not in his brain and I'm not a man, and so must conduct myself as I will. As I feel."

"Of course. You did the right thing, my dear. But he meant you no disrespect."

"Then he is a fool. He's a fool not to see what his invitation would imply to me."

"He's just a man, for all that he is a duke and with some intelligence, it appears. The poor dears really have little knowledge of what women think and feel and want. Why should they? They have been raised to think that the planets revolve around their groins."

Kittie gasped, and then laughed out loud. How good to have a friend like Rebecca, capable of the absurd, but of sound advice.

"I have decided that in future," Rebecca finished, "I will just ask for what I want. It seems the simplest way."

Kittie thought about that. "Perhaps you're right. In this case, then, I shall tell the duke to leave me alone. They're leaving in two days. I should just tell him I don't wish to see or speak to him again."

"Is that really what you want?"

"One part of me . . . the part I intend to listen to."

Rebecca gazed at her for a long minute. "I think I understand more than you think I do."

"Don't, Rebecca," Kittie warned. "Don't think you see things that aren't there."

Her friend took her hand and squeezed it. "I'm not."

"I just have to make it through the next two days, and then I can return to my duties to Lady Eliza with a clear heart. She will need me all the more, for I have no doubt there will be some return of her depression when the duke leaves."

"Kittie . . ." Rebecca started, then stopped.

"What is it?"

"Let me matchmake for you. Visit me at home and let me find you a husband."

"Oh, no, I don't think so. Your and my idea of what is a good husband might not correspond, you know."

"Good Lord, don't judge by poor old William." She twisted her homely face into a grimace. "I was young and desperate and he was my best choice. At least he was clean and kind and good-natured. Much better than some I was presented with as possible husbands, let me tell you. But I know what you need."

Alarmed, Kittie gazed at her friend. "I think we'll just leave things as they are. I'm quite content."

"I would never say you are content, my dear. My personal feeling is that you would have been better off if you had allowed the duke to at least have his way with you once."

"Rebecca!"

"Kittie!"

They stared at each other for a long moment and then laughed, two friends who would never understand the other's viewpoint, but loved each other anyway.

But when Rebecca was gone, she took out the velvet sac and once more read the letter from the duchess to her husband. If she had been the duchess, how differently she would have handled their difficult marriage. With the power of a wedding ring she thought she knew very well what she would say to the duke about his autocratic ways and austere manner.

She snuffed the candle and curled up on the bed under her covers, but didn't sleep. She could only too well imagine how the night would have ended if she was married to the desperately attractive and undeniably arousing duke.

Alban spent a long morning with Lafferty, ordering the changes he wanted made to the property and the work to be done on his aunt's home. He had thought of some improvements that would aid her in her perambulation of her house, and even his own. If he couldn't convince her to come to London, or to his home in the country, then the least he could do was make things better for her here in Yorkshire. Independence was so very important to her, and he wondered if he could even find a way to make it so that she could walk up to part of the high fell again, with little help from her companion or maid.

And yet in the back of his mind the scene from the previous evening was replaying itself, over and over, and each time he got to the point where he led Kittie to the bed and she reared back as if he were an adder about to strike.

He couldn't understand it. Was he repulsive to her? He thought not. He knew there was more than a little attraction between them. But she had been insulted and even seemed shocked. His whore. She said she wouldn't be his whore. The word had sounded so ugly coming from her perfect mouth, and any arousal he had felt had dissipated as if he had been showered in icy water.

But what else did she think was going to happen when he took her to the cabin in the woods? All he wanted was to make love to her, and he thought that away from Bodenthorpe Cottage, her inhibitions would be loosened.

She didn't think . . . he frowned down at some papers in his hands. No. He abandoned any thought that she had anticipated a proposal of a different sort.

He made his way to his aunt's home later that day, determined to see Kittie and to apologize if he had offended her. He didn't think he had a single thing to apologize for, but something was bothering her that she would say such offensive words, and maybe in the light of day she would tell him what. Surely she could not feel any loyalty to the earl, when *he* was so clearly willing . . . or was that the problem?

After all, he had never made his intentions clear. She could have thought that a tumble was all he was asking, and that she would be better off to be faithful to the earl, who was willing to offer her some sort of settlement or allowance. Maybe that was what she had meant when she said she was not his whore. She was not willing to have a simple one-night tumble. He should just tell her that he would be happy to offer her much better terms than the earl, for he was a generous man.

He entered the house and made his way to the drawing room. His aunt was where he saw her the first day, with a stream of sunlight on her lined face.

"Alban," she said, as he entered. She turned, and her expression was grim. "What did you do to Kittie last night?"

Put on his guard by her harsh tone, he said, "What do you mean?

"Don't be evasive. She is a different woman today. What did you do? What did you say to her?"

He took a seat. "I . . . kissed her." That much was true, after all.

"And? She is not a child to be so agitated by a mere kiss."

He thought resentfully that her agitation might have a completely different source. After all, the men were leaving in two days. If she intended to leave with Orkenay, then she should be telling Lady Eliza now. She *should* have told her earlier. But how could he reveal that to his aunt if she didn't already know? It was unconscionable, and he still felt some doubt as to whether Orkenay was being completely honest, but if Kittie was not involved with the earl, then what did the scenes mean that he himself had witnessed?

"I would ask her, Aunt, if you want to know what is bothering her. I think you might find it has nothing to do with me."

The others entered then and he had to stop, but he watched Kittie, wondering if he could get her alone and ask her outright what was going on, and make his offer. She wouldn't meet his eyes. Lady Severn did, though, and glared at him severely. Only Hannah Billings was her own dithery self in his presence.

The other gentlemen soon joined them, and he watched Orkenay and Kittie for any sign of collusion, but at the end of the day he was in as much of a quandary as before. The next day was the same, with Lady Eliza still not aware of her companion's future defection. When was she going to tell Lady Eliza? And when would he get Kittie alone to ask her to leave with him instead of Orkenay?

They were all spending the afternoon together one last time. Lady Severn and Sir John were giggling together in the corner, and Hannah and Bart had retreated to Bodenthorpe's gloomy library to work out the details of their impending separate travels, when they would see each other again, and how Hannah would introduce him to her boys.

Lord Orkenay, Lady Eliza, Kittie, and the duke were left, then, in an uneasy group, ostensibly chatting, but really suffering more silences. Finally Alban could stand it no longer. He stood and said, "Mrs. Douglas, I have a wish to speak to you privately. Will you come with me?"

"I say, Alban," Orkenay said, bolting to his feet. "That is the outside of enough. You cannot just . . ."

"I think he can, Orkenay," Lady Eliza said. "Sit down, if you please, and regale me with some of your scandalous gossip. Kittie, go talk to Alban."

Alban saw an obstinate expression tighten Kittie's lovely face, and she was about to deny him, he knew. "Please," he said, finally, his voice hoarse. "Please, Mrs. Douglas, I have something of the utmost importance to speak with you about."

She didn't want to. She would rather have done anything than be alone with him. As she rose, she darted a glance over to Lady Severn. The two exchanged looks and Lady Severn shrugged and mouthed a word; Alban couldn't make out what that word was.

But she went with him. As he led her out of the house and toward the garden, he tried to take her arm, but she pulled it away. Really, she was taking her odd resentment to ridiculous heights.

Once outside, with the cool breeze riffling over them and the sky threatening showers any minute, he wondered how to go on. With the night the conflict had begun, he supposed.

"If I offended you in any way the other evening, Mrs. Douglas, I beg your pardon."

She stiffened, and her hands clenched to fists; he thought she was going to turn and go back to the house, but instead she stared at him searchingly.

"If you offended me? *If?* You truly don't know why I left?"

She was controlling her ire with great difficulty, and he scrambled in his brain to think what to say. "I . . . I know it was . . . well, I was precipitate, I suppose, in my haste to be with you."

"Not precipitate," she said, biting off the words like pieces of thread. "Deluded."

He frowned. "I don't think I understand."

"I'm sure you don't," she said, and sighed. She strolled to the garden wall and gazed over it, up the slope, past the woods, to the ridge of the high fell beyond. She turned back to him. "I suppose I shall have to put this in simple words so you will understand. I know there are many women who would have accepted your . . . *eloquent* invitation to bed, but I am not one of them."

Ah, now he understood. It was as he thought. "Mrs. Douglas . . . Kittie," he said, moving toward her and putting out one hand. She moved away again, walking over to a stone bench. "Kittie," he said approaching her again, "I suppose I didn't make myself clear. I was devastated that what I did made you feel like a . . . what you said that night. This was not an invitation to one brief interlude." He knelt by her side and took her hand. She would have pulled it away, but he clutched it to his breast.

"No, Kittie, hear me out." He stroked her palm, and for the first time he understood how much he wanted her, and how much he hoped she would take his offer. Kittie and him, together, in a little cottage away from London. He could make love to her, finally. But more than that, they could walk and talk and laugh by the fire, and argue passionately and then make love again.

She stilled, sighed and then said, "I suppose I should listen."

So anxious he was, he blurted it out, unprepared. "I want you to leave with me instead of the earl."

"What?"

Good, that was encouraging. She wanted to hear

more and had not pulled her hand away. "I know your scheme to leave with Orkenay; he told me all about it. But I want you to reconsider; you don't know him very well, Kittie. He's not a good man, not a kind man. He . . ."

She wrenched her hand away, stood, and stormed toward the door, stopping only when she was several feet away. She turned and glared back at him. "How dare you even imply, how can you say . . . believe . . ." She shook her head and whirled to go into the house, but changed her mind. Slowly she turned back and stalked toward him. "I am not your whore; I am not anyone's whore."

"I know that. But, Kittie, I never said . . ."

"Then what else would I be? Oh, yes, you have a delicate name for it in your upper crust circles, don't you? Courtesan. Is that not what you call them, the ladies you pay? The ladies you use and trade among you, or discard once they become too old for pleasure? Cyprians? Birds of paradise? And do you think I know nothing of that life that I would voluntarily subject myself to the indignities of the position, of being solely dependent upon you and your continuing desire for my body?" Her chin went up and her mouth tightened. "I was a society wife once, Your Grace, and I saw much more than I ever acknowledged, and heard much more than I ever wanted. I heard about the children of such squalid arrangements . . . even our own royal dukes and their army of unnamed offspring."

A flare of anger ripped through the duke, and he stood, his ire controlled for the moment, but not willing to bear much more of her harangue. "I was doing you an honor."

"An honor? An honor? By being willing to *pay* for my favors? I hardly think so. And that you thought I would abandon your aunt . . ."

"Orkenay said . . ."

"I don't *care* what he said. What about the evidence of your own eyes and ears?"

"I saw you kissing him," Alban said, pushed beyond endurance. "I saw you kissing him passionately in the meadow, and then again, more sweetly, by the garden gate. What was I supposed to think?"

"Why didn't you just ask me?"

"I did."

"You merely asked me if I was going away with Lord Orkenay."

"And you wouldn't answer."

They glared at each other across a yawning chasm of mistrust and harsh words. Kittie saw in his eyes the residue of old pain and past betrayal, but that was his burden to bear. It was not her task to help him see that unless he could let go of that old hurt, he would never have happiness again. She wished him well, but she was not in a position to come to his aid.

She took a deep breath, calming herself. "Perhaps I should have just told you outright when you asked that I would never have considered going away with the earl. I didn't think I should have to, and I *know* I shouldn't have to now. If you had just told me what you had seen, had asked me what it meant . . ." She pressed one hand over her left breast. "If you had listened to me as we spoke, every time we spoke, you would know my heart now. I care for Lady Eliza and would never abandon her like that. Not for the earl. Not even for you. I don't know how you could even have imagined I would." With that, Kittie turned and walked into the house and retreated to her room.

Eighteen

The air was heavy with the promise of rain and the scent of roses dying. Alban sat alone wondering at his sense of desolation. Nothing was different in his life. He would be leaving on the morrow and not a thing had changed.

Or everything had changed. Which was the true statement?

Perhaps it was just that he was accustomed to feeling that he was in the right about things, that he was taking the moral road. But now he had hurt someone he cared for. Cared for deeply. And worse, made her feel that he didn't respect her, though he did.

She wasn't leaving with Orkenay.

His aunt, on Beacon's arm, was guided out to the garden, and Alban, coming out of the fog of his contemplation, moved to take her arm.

"Come back in half an hour, Beacon," she said. "Alban, guide me to the bench and let us talk."

The maid gave one long, cool look through the evening shadows at the duke and then moved to reenter the cottage.

"You didn't have to come out here after me," Alban said. "I would have come in eventually."

"What I have to say would not wait. You have hurt Kittie unforgivably. She wouldn't say how, but she is very upset."

"Why do I have the feeling I'm about to be chastised for some failing?"

"Because you know me well," she replied.

"Let's not argue. It's my last day."

"You are not dying, just going back to London. Or wherever."

"You sound angry at me. Why is that?"

"Because I am."

"Why?"

"Because you are a fool. And not just any kind of fool, as my father used to say, but a damned fool."

"Aunt," he said, with warning in his voice. He would not be spoken to like that by anyone, not even her.

"No, do not try that tone with me. I am very angry with you, Alban, and you will hear me out."

He sighed. There was nothing to do but listen, and she would not let it go until he had.

"When you came, what did you think of Kittie Douglas when first you met her?"

"That she was very beautiful and had a sweet, country manner."

"And what do you think of her now?"

Alban couldn't answer. How could he? How could he say that she had left him in turmoil, that she had made him reevaluate every moral he had ever thought he had, and some he had never considered? And that he was ashamed to be thrown into such disorder by a woman.

But more ashamed to have hurt that woman.

"You will not answer."

"I don't know what to say."

"Say the truth; say you love her."

He shook his head, stood, and paced away, glaring off into the dark woods. "Don't be ridiculous!"

"Why do you not just be a man, admit your feelings, and ask her to marry you?"

Enough. It was enough and more than enough. He came back, sat down, and took both of her bony hands in his own. He restrained his ire, reminding himself that this was his aunt, the woman who had a right to tell him how to live his life, if anyone did, by virtue of her steadfast support and love. "I know how you feel about her, so I will not say things as bluntly as I could."

"Why not? You should ever be honest with me, Alban. I am with you."

"Then I will; she is not of an appropriate class to be my wife."

"So, is that why you have tried to make her your mistress?"

"Is that what she told you?"

"Fool!" Lady Eliza shook her head. "You don't know her in the slightest if you could even think that. She would never divulge such a thing, and would never tell me anything that would make me think less of you. I always knew you were blind in some ways, but I thought that at least you could be honest with yourself. You are the Duke of Alban. If you cannot marry where you want, who can?"

"Perhaps you have a point, Aunt, or at least you would if you were right about the rest of it. But I'm not in love with Kittie Douglas, and I never will be. I care for her, but I am not in love."

"Then this conversation is over," Lady Eliza said, standing. "If you would be so kind as to call for Beacon I will go back inside."

"Aunt, don't leave this way. We'll be going early tomorrow morning. This is the last we'll see each other for some time. I'll try to come up next summer, but it will depend on some things."

Lady Eliza sighed deeply, and said, "I know, Alban. I

have enjoyed your visit here, and I hope you will continue to write, even though . . . well, you know Kittie reads all of your letters to me. And writes my words to you. I hope that won't stop you from . . . from writing."

"Of course it won't." He engulfed his aunt in a rare hug, and felt her bony frame as she clutched him to her. He hated the tension between them, but her suggestion that he was in love with Kittie Douglas was absolutely ridiculous, almost as ridiculous as her urging him to take her as a bride.

But he was exultant that she wasn't leaving with Orkenay. And it made him wonder why the man had lied so steadily and convincingly about her plans. What did he hope to gain?

He hugged his aunt fiercely. As he looked over her head, he saw, through the window, Kittie gazing out at them. It was a rare moment of absolute clarity.

She stood hugging herself, her arms wrapped over her stomach, and her expression wavered between pain and acceptance. And he knew that he had lied to his aunt about one thing. Perhaps he *was* a little in love with Kittie Douglas. But it was nothing the winter season and gaiety of London wouldn't cure. It was the merest preference and the lingering desire to make love to her. That was all it was.

His aunt said as she turned and took his arm, "I still think you are a damned fool if you do not marry Kittie."

"You are entitled to your feelings, Aunt, but I must do what I feel right."

The house felt so lonely, Kittie thought, drifting disconsolately from room to room. Rebecca and Hannah had stayed on a few days after the men, but then Rebecca traveled south with Hannah to help her get ready to introduce her sons to Mr. Norton. Poor Hannah badly needed the bracing effect of Rebecca's presence, because without her friend she would have sunk under a morass of fears and tears.

Autumn had closed in, and though it was just October the first snows had already fallen. She stood and stared out at the garden where she and the duke had argued so passionately the last time she had seen him.

"Kittie," Lady Eliza said, coming into the room and feeling her way over to her favorite chair. "I have had a thought. If you would like to go to your friend's wedding, I can make shift with just Beacon for a few weeks."

"No," Kittie said, turning away from the window. "I have no desire to go to Hannah's wedding." Especially not since the duke was sure to be there, as Bartholomew Norton's best friend. "And there is no surety of a wedding yet, after all. Hannah will marry no one without the approval of her sons, and the boys might not like Mr. Norton."

"Then they would be great fools, and she more so for not grasping happiness."

Kittie didn't reply. Grasping happiness sounded rather desperate, but maybe that was what one needed to do in this world. If that was the case she would stay unhappy, because she was not the grasping type.

Days passed. Then weeks. Life settled back into a steady rhythm, and though she and Lady Eliza got along just as well as ever, she knew that within herself there was a restlessness, and her employer felt it, too. The letters came steadily from the duke, but they had a stilted quality that Kittie regretfully concluded was because he knew she was reading them to his aunt.

She didn't send him any more knitted stockings or singlets. Snow came and stayed, and Christmas passed. And in those weeks and months, Kittie acknowledged what was wrong with her. She wanted to get married again. When Rebecca had first offered to matchmake, she had dismissed the notion out of hand, but from there the idea had taken root. The desire had started as an itch, and grew to an almost unbearable urge. Lady Eliza, sensitive to much more that went on around her than that which one could see, seemed to know something was wrong, and one day in February, with a determined expression on her strong-boned face, she badgered Kittie until finally she was forced to admit what was bothering her.

They were sitting together in the drawing room, and at her employer's urging, Kittie finally said, "I . . . I'm so envious of Hannah! Isn't that terrible? I have never known her to be so happy as she is now, in her letter, now that she and Mr. Norton are finally wed."

Lady Eliza nodded and sat back in her chair. "Thank God you are finally being honest with me, Kittie. I thought you would never just say it. There is nothing wrong with a woman your age wanting to be married."

"But it sounds so ungrateful, my lady. I have such a good life here, with you, and . . . and I love you sincerely!"

She had never said it before and she saw Lady Eliza's lips tighten, as they always did when she was trying to deny emotion.

"And I, you, my dear, but just as a child's love for their parent does not preclude the desire for an establishment of their own, so this does not mean you are ungrateful, just a normal woman. The question is, what do you want to do about it?"

"Do? Why . . . there is really nothing to be done, ma'am. My situation is the same as it was when I took this position four years ago."

"I know that. But you have an ally now. Let us talk about it and think about it. I think you will find I have a few ideas for your future."

Nineteen

Alban shrugged himself into his greatcoat, held by one of the exemplary footmen his club employed, and accepted his hat and stick from two others. Another had been dispatched to ensure that his carriage would be at the front when, in a couple of minutes, he descended the marble steps from the dimness of the wood-paneled hallway. "Is it raining still, Manchester?" he asked the senior footman.

"No, sir. It has cleared, and promises to be a marvelous evening for so early in spring."

"March is so often indecisive," Alban said. He heard a voice he recognized and turned. The back of the fellow just receiving his hat from yet another footman was familiar. Was it—"Sir John Fitzhenry! What are you doing here?"

The young man turned with a smile. "You mean, how can I afford a club so exclusive as this? I can't. I was just visiting His Grace the duke of . . . well, I am visiting an acquaintance here." He strolled toward Alban as he spoke.

"And how is Lady Severn?"

Sir John smirked. "Last I left her, she was as fine as she always is."

"And that would have been . . . ?"

"At the end of January, Your Grace, if you must

know." He looked down at his hat and turned it around. "We have parted ways, though my wishes for her good health and happiness continue."

"I didn't think a young fellow like you would be satisfied with a woman like that for long," Alban said.

"A woman like that? What do you mean, sir?"

Shrugging, Alban said, "You know . . . older than you by some years and . . ." He couldn't say it. To say she was plain would be truthful but discourteous.

"You seem to be under some misapprehension. I wished to continue our special friendship, but Lady Severn very kindly but firmly dismissed me after our months together. I think . . . it is my belief that she has someone else in mind for her next, uh . . . conquest." His tone was amused but reflective as he added, "Someone younger."

Alban shook his head and clapped the younger fellow on the shoulder. "I'm sorry for my clumsiness, Fitzhenry."

"Let me be clumsy in return, then, sir, if I might," the baronet said with a sly smile. "It is bandied about that Lord Orkenay has left England for the Continent."

"Yes."

"With a very intimate friend of Your Grace's."

Alban sighed and did up his coat with his free hand. "Yes. Orkenay, apparently in some trouble with gambling debts, disappeared with my former paramour, Jacqueline. Why does every person I meet feel compelled to inform me anew?" He stopped and cast a suspicious look at the baronet. "And why, I ask again, were you following us up to Yorkshire last autumn? I never got a satisfactory answer out of you, nor anyone else, and I did ask around once I returned to London."

"I know, sir. I was informed of your queries." Sir John chuckled and started toward the door, held open by Manchester. "It was the most idiotic bit of tomfoolery

I have ever been a part of. Not even worth canvassing. I am leaving just now, Your Grace, as I must be elsewhere in one hour, but I will tell you a story as I go, if you are walking?"

"No, I'm not walking," Alban said, following the younger man. "In London? In March? I would not consider it, but I am going to some awful ball a relation is giving and that I am honor-bound to attend. I could drop you somewhere if you would like."

"I would very much appreciate it, as it appears to have begun to rain."

"Again," Alban said. "It stopped for a while, but this is March, after all."

The two men exited the club and climbed into Alban's waiting carriage. Sir John gazed around at the luxury of the interior, the velvet and brass and mahogany fittings. Running one gloved hand over the squabs, he said, "Oh, to have your position and wealth, sir, and I know that makes me sound hopelessly grasping, but I would have made Lady Severn stay with me if I could have. Not that jewels or furs would have done so, but I could have made a better show." He shook his head and sighed. "I don't suppose it would have made a jot of difference in the end. She will do what she will. I am certainly the better man for having known her."

"Better?"

"More experienced, certainly, and the value of a woman of a certain age who is not afraid to tell you what women like . . . it is inestimable. I find I was under some severe misapprehensions about the fair sex's desires in the boudoir."

Alban chuckled. "Yes, I remember one ecstatic summer, and how thoroughly I learned that same lesson. You were going to tell me the story of Lord Orkenay and why you were so interested in him." Interrogating young Sir John helped him forget for a while the emptiness of the evenings he was spending, and how much he dreaded this, in particular, a ball at the home of a relation who always plagued him to choose from among her acquaintances a new wife. He had decided he was not ready to wed.

"Yes . . . Lord Orkenay. It reflects poorly on many things, myself included. I suppose you know that I am employed by our government in a capacity I would prefer not to elaborate upon?"

Alban nodded and sat back, waiting for more.

"Last summer, at Brighton, I was watching Lord Orkenay. We were troubled by some of his secret activities and acquaintances, and by his closeness to Prinny. There has been much trouble in the north, with the Luddite uprisings, and when Lord Orkenay so assiduously made sure he was included in your trip north, we thought he was going to use that excursion for another purpose. In short, as ludicrous as it seems now in retrospect, we suspected Lord Orkenay of being a revolutionary."

Alban burst out laughing and had to hold his stomach, it hurt so bad. "You suspected him of being a Luddite? How amusing. The man could not care for anything past his next drink, conquest, or bet."

"Or revenge," Sir John said, leaning forward.

"What?"

"Do you *still* not know, then? The earl was infuriated when you stole *la petite* Jacqueline from him two years ago. He had been poised to retain her inestimable services when you waltzed in and made an irresistible offer, which she then, apparently, rubbed his face in. He had been looking since that moment for an opportunity to exact revenge on you, and when you went north, he thought you were going with some other motive. When he saw your . . . uh, reaction to Mrs. Kittie

Douglas, he thought he had found you out. From then on, his sole purpose was to steal her from you."

"So that was why he . . ."

"Tried to seduce her? Yes. But of course, with her feelings for you so strong, he was . . ."

"What did you say?"

"That the earl tried to seduce her?"

"No, after that."

Sir John lapsed into confused silence.

Alban, his stomach twisted into a knot, said, "You said something about Mrs. Douglas's feelings for me. What did you mean by that?"

"Uh, well, Rebecca told me that Mrs. Douglas was terribly in love with you."

"She must have been mistaken."

"How could she be? They spoke of it intimately. She has known Mrs. Douglas for many years, and says she never saw the lady so in love. Rebecca was furious with you for . . ." Sir John colored. "Your Grace, I have forgotten my manners."

His heart hammering so loud he could almost hear the echo in the dim carriage, Alban said, "No, be honest. I will hold nothing against you, nor the excellent Lady Severn, whom I begin to think I should have befriended."

Frowning, his smooth brow furrowed, the younger man stared down at the floor. "Rebecca said that her friend confessed her turmoil after your . . . after you and she spent those hours in the . . . the cabin in the woods."

Alban felt his stomach clench. That explained Lady Severn's steady glare at him the last two days of his visit. He had forgotten the feminine impulse to talk over every problem or anxiety with intimate lady friends.

"She said," Sir John continued, "that Mrs. Douglas's feelings for you were rather a jumble. She was angry that you . . . that you were attempting to seduce her. She felt it indicated a lack of respect and a misunderstanding of her character. And yet . . ." He took a deep breath and fixed his gaze, his expression flustered, on the lamp bracket. "And yet she was tempted, she told Rebecca, because her feelings for you were so powerful. If you had been just a little more . . . more patient . . . or . . ."

When the baronet lapsed into embarrassed silence, Alban didn't urge him to speak on. He had heard all he needed to know his own heart. She had cared for him, and he had thrown away her regard as if it were dross. How pigheaded and miserably inadequate had he been that even when his aunt pointed it out to him, he still refused to see. And how arrogant that he could not admit those feelings even to himself until he knew that they were reciprocated.

"Your Grace, this is where I need to go."

The carriage had stopped and the baronet was opening the door.

Brought back to the present, Alban muttered, "Yes, yes . . . uh, thank you, Sir John."

"Thank you, sir, for allowing me to go north with you last fall. I went for one reason, but as it turned out what I learned was that women are more fascinating than I thought. And that a plain woman's favors are every bit as valuable as those of a beautiful one." He grinned, his face youthful and unlined in the lamplight. "Lucky fellow who has Lady Severn's attentions now."

Alban smiled as Fitzhenry dismounted and shut the door behind him. As the carriage pulled away from its stop, though, his expression sobered. He had spent the long winter months trying to ignore or deny the urging of his heart, but now it seemed that he might have to go back to Yorkshire, and more quickly than he had intended. Even if there was no hope for him, he could not leave things as they stood with Kittie. How badly must he have hurt her by behaving as he did if she truly had loved him? Those tender feelings might be dead now, killed by his own repulsive inadequacy, but he had to try.

But first there was this wretched ball to attend. Perhaps he would just go home after all. He knew what lay ahead of him that night, and it was endless hours of tedium while young lady after young lady was paraded before him. He had known for some time that no simpering virginal schoolroom miss would ever do for him now. He wanted a woman who had experienced passion, who understood love . . . who could inspire him to yearn for her as he did for Kittie Douglas.

He would decide by the time he got there whether he could bear to enter the ballroom. Family loyalty demanded that he attend, as he did every year, but personal desire was urging a return to home and bed— bed to think about Kittie and feel all the new sensations coursing through him.

She had cared for him and like a fool he had thrown her away, had misused her, had underestimated her worth. He covered his face with his hands. He surely didn't deserve her, and that was merely the barest truth.

Twenty

Byron, Byron, Byron.

Kittie had been in London just one week, long enough to have a few new dresses and to have met some of Lady Eliza's oldest friends and acquaintances, and she was already heartily sick of the name of Byron. By the kindness of one of those friends, Kittie had the two cantos of *Childe Harold*, and had read them aloud to her employer.

Lady Eliza snorted at Byron's seeming self-condemnation at his familiarity with "Sin's long labyrinth"—for though the poet insisted on distancing himself from the hero of his tale, most thought it was his own world-weary self he spoke of, at the ancient age of twenty-one—and had merely laughed at anyone at his age thinking those old sins had not been well covered by many others.

Kittie was intrigued by Byron's undeniable ability, but didn't understand the fervor surrounding the man himself. It was the rage to be dying of love for him, and girls Kittie had met—including the daughter of the house they were staying in, a second cousin of Lady Eliza's—sighed over him or burst into tears whenever his name was mentioned.

It was ridiculous. And so Kittie told herself over and over, as she sighed in wasted desolation over the Duke of Alban. She was not in love with him. It was tedious to be in love with a man who did not feel the same. She would not *allow* herself to be in love with him.

Coming to London would have seemed to be a foolhardy project for one who had no wish to see him again, but she had learned in Alban's last letter that he didn't intend to be in the city until April. They would be back up in Yorkshire by that time, Lady Eliza had promised. Though knowing how her employer cared for her nephew, it was unfair to press for an early retreat.

And now she was at a ball. She glanced around herself in wonder, at the glittering candlelight, the elegant decorations, all gilt and white, and at the beautifully gowned and plumed ladies. It was a surfeit for the senses, a banquet of sight and sound and odor, sometimes pungent odor.

It had been many years, since before her husband died, the last time she had attended a ball. And then Roger would disappear into the card room for hours, and she would be left with friends to dance, and occasionally to fend off the improper proposals of men who wished to become her "intimate friend," as they so often styled it.

"Why are you standing here alone looking so forlorn?"

Kittie smiled at Rebecca, who approached her, her face pink from the exertion of dancing. She stopped and fanned herself energetically, all the while looking around.

Happy that her employer had managed to obtain an invitation for Rebecca, Kittie smiled at her friend. "I am not looking forlorn," she replied. "I just . . . I don't know anyone yet."

"We can soon remedy that. I already have. Where is Lady Eliza?"

Kittie indicated a group of women seated in a bank

of velvet seats. She was the center of the group—mostly old friends—and many chattered at her, touching her hand, plucking at her gown to get her attention, whispering to her on occasion.

"Why don't we join her for a moment," Rebecca said. "I have something to ask her, and then I demand that you dance with some of my acquaintances, for I'm being run off my feet."

They made their way through the growing crowd to the chattering group of women surrounding Lady Eliza. When Kittie made her employer aware of her presence, Lady Eliza clutched at her hand.

"Could we walk just a little ways away for a few minutes?" she gasped. "I am finding all of this noise distracting. The street noise of carriages and vendors and horses was enough, but this—After the quiet of Yorkshire, this is going to take some time to become accustomed to."

With Kittie on one side and Rebecca on the other, they moved to an archway partially filled with potted palms. The hubbub around them melted into a soothing babble, no particular words or voices distinguishable, almost like wind rustling through the trees in Yorkshire.

"This is a little better," Lady Eliza said, clutching Kittie's hand. "I am afraid I underestimated the effect of my blindness, both on myself and on my acquaintances. I was quite inundated with well-wishers."

Her tone was dry, but Kittie sensed the edge of panic. "I won't leave you alone again," she said. "I thought you would be well entertained renewing all of your acquaintances."

"Oh, I am, my dear. Please don't feel you must hover over me all evening. I brought you to London for a very specific reason, you know, and that will not best be served by dancing attendance on me."

She referred to her project of finding a husband for

her companion, and Kittie sighed, regretting she had ever mentioned her discovery of her own loneliness. It was ridiculous, when considered, that an employer would so go out of her way to get rid of the companion she claimed to value. Kittie knew it came from the goodness of Lady Eliza's heart, but it had been many years since she had anyone make such a fuss over her and it was disconcerting, to say the least.

And she really wasn't sure anymore that she had a heart to give to another husband.

"Don't worry, Lady Eliza," Rebecca said. "I have a vast acquaintance, old and new, and they will be happy to engage dance partners for her."

"I wish you would not concern yourself, Lady Severn," the older woman said. "I am seeking information on the most likely prospects, and will be guiding Kittie accordingly toward those most eligible."

"But I feel certain she'll easily find a husband if she will appear at her best, which is on the dance floor, where men can see her."

"However, exclusivity is not to be frowned upon as a method of inflaming interest. She must not appear common, or . . ."

"Are you saying my acquaintances are common?" Rebecca said, bridling.

"No one is saying anything of the sort," Kittie at last intervened. It was amusing at times, but fatiguing when two such managing women got together on a project close to both of their hearts. She appreciated their efforts, but occasionally felt a little like a bone being tugged at by two determined terriers. As she sighed and glanced around, her eye was caught by a beautiful older woman, gowned exquisitely in peacock blue silk. Her hair was white and piled atop her head, with curling tendrils drooping on her long neck. She lingered nearby, gazing at Lady Eliza and biting her lip, wishful, it seemed, of approaching, but held back by something.

"Do you know that lady, Rebecca?" Kittie asked, nodding toward her.

Slewing her glance around, Rebecca caught sight of the lady and said, "Yes. Or at least, we've been introduced. She looks like she wishes to come over to us, doesn't she? That is the widowed countess, Lady Montressor."

Kittie heard a sharp intake of breath beside her. "My lady?" she said to her employer. "Are you all right?"

Lady Eliza's lined face had paled. Her grip on Kittie's hand tightened. "Perhaps we ought to . . . go back to my friends. And, Lady Severn, I defer to your judgment; introduce Kittie to whomever you please."

Kittie was about to fall in with her employer's desires when she saw the lady in blue hesitantly walking toward them, gaining speed as she approached.

"Eliza," she said, reaching out one hand. "It is I, Harriet . . . do you remember . . . well, of course you remember . . ."

Lady Eliza had gone still, but her tight expression had melted into one of confusion, pain, and uncertainty. "Of course I remember, Harriet. How could I ever forget?"

Lady Montressor stretched out her hand and touched Lady Eliza's cheek. Kittie watched in puzzlement. Rebecca, with a knowing smile that broadened, had dropped back after a nod of recognition at the other lady.

"My lady," Kittie said. "Should I . . ."

"Oh . . . Kittie," Lady Eliza said in an odd choked voice. "May I introduce you to Lady Harriet Montressor? We were . . . we were friends many years ago."

"My lady," Kittie said, dropping a curtsy.

"More than just friends, Eliza," Lady Montressor demurred, her eyes fixed avidly on the other woman's face.

"Whatever we were ended with your marriage, though," Lady Eliza said, reproach in her tone.

"It has been many years, Eliza. Can we not . . . could we just talk for a while?"

Kittie watched her employer's face, the doubt, and then the quick decision.

"Of course. You see what the years have done to me, Harriet. I will need to take your arm if we are to go somewhere to talk."

"I heard about your misfortune, Eliza, and my first thought was sorrow for you, of course, but then I knew that if anyone had to be afflicted, you would find a way to triumph." There was trembling in her tone, pride for her old friend, and pain.

"You knew about my blindness before you sought me out?" Lady Eliza said coldly. "I am not to be pitied, Harry."

"I sought you out and then found out about your blindness," Lady Montressor said gently, searching Lady Eliza's face. "And I would never dare pity you. No one who knew you ever would. Please . . . let's just talk."

Kittie watched the exchange, puzzled at first, but then gradually coming into knowledge. Of course. Harry! Harry of the love letters. Harry of the past.

Harry, whom Lady Eliza had loved and lost to another.

Kittie exchanged glances with Rebecca, who nodded to her.

"I . . . I will be with the other ladies when you need me, Lady Eliza."

The woman nodded. Lady Montressor took her arm, and they strolled away, their heads together in conversation. Kittie watched them walk away, shock melting into understanding, and puzzlement giving way to hope for her friend.

Family duty won over personal preference. Alban strolled into the ballroom and sighed at the inevitable stir. He would, as always, pretend not to notice the women primping their daughters and the ladies preening. He would find his cousin, make sure she knew he had attended, and then leave.

The heat in the ballroom already was like entering a smithy's forge, or so it seemed to one who enjoyed more the coolness of green space or the quietude of his men's club. He glanced around the expansive ballroom, thinking that his cousin had outdone herself this year, with an elegance to the decoration that was new. Perhaps she had hired someone to make this transformation.

His gaze was drawn to a corner of the room by something familiar in the set of a lady's shoulders and the color of her hair. Her back was to him, and she was hunched over, speaking to another lady, their heads close together, but it looked like . . . was it—It was! His heart thudding, he quickened his pace, bumping into several ladies and having to apologize, losing sight of his objective, and then seeing her again through the crowd.

His Aunt Eliza was deep in conversation with another woman, a white-haired lady who looked vaguely familiar to him, but whom he couldn't place. Blocked temporarily by the movement of a group of people, he was halted in his tracks, and he turned, looking for another way through the crowd.

And that was when he saw Kittie Douglas on the ballroom floor, dancing the waltz with a well-to-do widower whom Alban knew was on the lookout for a wife. He stared, feasting on her exquisite beauty, her coppery hair glowing in the candlelight and dressed with pearls and plumes, and her white neck adorned with a pearl and diamond collar he thought had the look of his aunt's long-ignored jewels. Her gown was dark green and cut low to expose her pale bosom, and the widower was greedily devouring her with his eyes, it seemed to Alban's jealous gaze.

And then she looked away, her glance cool, her gaze unfocused. Until she saw him. Their eyes locked and she visibly started. He hoped she trembled. He wanted her to be astonished and as shaken as he was. He stared at her, remembering every curve and how she had felt in his arms. He tasted her lips, inhaled her delicious scent and caressed her skin. Swaying back, he watched her trip on her partner's feet, right herself, and then look away, spots of flame red burning on her cheeks.

She hadn't expected to see him.

Gathering his wandering wits, for he must look the greatest idiot, standing in the middle of the ballroom with his mouth gaping, he made his way through the crowd to his aunt.

"What in God's name are you doing here and why didn't you tell me you were coming to London?" he demanded as he approached the two women.

Lady Eliza looked up and reached out her one free hand. The other was locked securely in the other lady's grip, and he glanced at her, recognizing Lady Montressor, a great beauty from many years before. He hadn't even known she and his aunt were acquainted, but they appeared to be very close . . . intimate friends, in fact.

"Alban," his aunt said. She stood, as did Lady Montressor, but the women's hands stayed entwined.

"What are you doing here?" He took her in his arms and hugged her. She finally dropped her friend's hand

and returned his embrace. He nodded and murmured the other lady's name in acknowledgment of their acquaintance. "Not that I'm displeased, but for God's sake, why did you not tell me? I could have arranged travel and you could have stayed at my London house."

Just the thought of Kittie Douglas under his roof made his body ache. He felt a rush of blood to his head and other regions, and the light-headed sensation returned.

His aunt firmly put him away from her and reached behind for Lady Montressor's hand. "I knew you were going to be out of town for part of spring, and did not want to concern you. My objective was to visit my cousin and rejoin life. And . . . and I have become reacquainted with old friends, too."

Puzzled by her tone, he glanced from his aunt to the other woman, who was blushing, but with a beautiful smile on her unlined face. "I didn't even know you knew Lady Montressor," he said.

"We were friends many years ago, until her marriage," his aunt said, simply. "Have you seen Kittie?"

"I have," Alban said. "What do you mean by dressing her like a . . . as though she were looking for a husband? She is gowned and bejeweled and doesn't look at all like a companion should."

"Good," Lady Eliza said with a wicked smile. "Then she looks just as she ought. I think she has every right to get married, and if she should catch some gentleman's eye, then I wish her to have her chance at happiness. I think everyone should have their chance at happiness," she finished, squeezing her friend's hand and tucking it close to her.

Alban swallowed and sought a chair. He sat down. Kittie with a husband. He would need to become accustomed to that thought, for there was not a doubt in his mind that she would have suitors. Her beauty alone would be enough to ensure that, but she united with loveliness a temperament most men would find alluring and a disposition amenable to marriage and satisfying even the most discriminating man's desires.

Every desire, even the most carnal and erotic.

Fury boiled in his veins and when he looked up to say something to his aunt, he saw on her face undisguised triumph. He had been brought to heel, and she knew it. He couldn't bear the thought of her with a husband, and yet could not imagine wedding her himself. Or could he?

His brain humming and a headache pounding through it, he gazed around him at the couples, some married, some flirting, some engaged already, though it was early in the Season. Which among them were happy? Any?

And who among them would be happy ten years from now, those who had satisfied society's strictures as to the propriety of their bride? Or the ones who had followed their hearts?

"Your Grace," Lady Montressor said. "I will ask to be excused, if you will be so kind as to sit with your aunt for a while. I have social obligations, but then I . . . I'll be back, Eliza. We have much to speak about still."

Eliza sat back down opposite him in a gilt chair, an enigmatic smile on her lips. He regarded her for some minutes, and then said, "Please don't imagine I have forgotten your last words to me."

"What were those?"

"You said I'd be a damned fool if I didn't marry Kittie."

"I have changed my mind. I think she is too good for a stubborn idiot like you. You are incapable of appreciating her."

So, his aunt was in one of her ferocious moods.

Alban sighed and sat back, but a moment later bolted to his feet as Kittie approached.

"Your Grace," she said, with a formal curtsy. "I understood from your last letter before we left Yorkshire that you were not to be in London until April."

He glanced at his aunt. "I informed Mr. Lafferty about my change of plans some time ago. And there is likely a letter to my aunt sitting at Bodenthorpe Cottage at this very moment with the same news. How very odd that Lafferty didn't tell you."

Kittie looked at Lady Eliza, too, with a considering gaze. "Hmm. Yes. I am so happy you and Lady Eliza will be able to visit."

"I was just saying," Alban continued, "how strange it was that she didn't have you write to me and let me know you were coming. I could have had the town house ready."

"I told you," Lady Eliza said. "My purpose was not to visit you, but my cousin, whom I have not seen in many years."

"Yes. So you said." He turned his gaze back to Kittie and let it linger over her magnificence. "You . . . look lovely," he said, simply, the words inadequate to his meaning.

"Thank you. Everyone has been most kind." She touched the pearl-and-diamond choker.

"Your partner in the waltz seemed quite enamored of you," he said, unable to alter his tone. It sounded resentful, and he knew it but could not stop himself.

She stiffened. "He was very kind. I'm amazed how kind all the gentlemen have been, and how very complimentary. I didn't expect such amiability. And respect."

"You should," he said, releasing his jealousy and letting his anger go. "You should expect every good wish on your behalf, Mrs. Douglas, and the respect a gentleman reserves for every true lady. You have a right to it, and I can't imagine a person alive who would not wish you well."

She met his gaze and there was a glimmer of moisture in her eyes. He remembered what Sir John had told him just an hour before, about her confession to Lady Severn, and he wondered if it was true. Had she cared for him? And did she still?

Idiot that he was, would he ever again have a chance with her, and if he did, what would he do with that chance?

Twenty-one

A sleepless night followed by a restless morning during which all he could do was wait until an appropriate time for visiting was not conducive to a good mood.

Every noise on the streets grated on Alban's nerves as he walked from his own town home to that of his cousin's, only a half mile away in the tight confines of the "good" section of London. The drizzly weather suited his irritability and the leafless trees his somber mood.

If he had followed his heart the previous evening, he would have swept Kittie Douglas away and asked her to marry him, but now in the pearl gray light of a dreary day, he was undecided. He had sworn never to marry again if it meant allowing himself to care. But was that reasonable? Was it even wise? How had that philosophy served him so far?

When Jacqueline had betrayed him it had been a blow to his *amour propre*, but not to his heart. He didn't love her and had never thought that he did. But when Catherine deserted him for another man it had hurt deeply. He had felt like a raw wound for years after her death.

Coming to his cousin's home he mounted the steps and applied the knocker. Millhouse, the butler, bowed low and admitted him.

"I don't wish to disturb my cousin, Millhouse; I know after these affairs she always spends the day in bed with a headache. I was really wishing to speak with my aunt, Lady Eliza. Is she about?"

"Yes, Your Grace. She informed me that if you called, she would be in the conservatory with her maid, Beacon."

"Thank you, Millhouse. I can find my own way," he said, handing his hat and stick over to the man.

He strolled through the house, the bustle of servants pronounced in the wake of such a grand event as a ball. While a workman in grubby clothes replaced a door that had been removed to make a larger space for the ball, two footmen were laying a carpet in the parlor. Maids bustled about and the butler, after disposing of the duke's hat and cane, returned to his position overseeing the work.

Alban moved toward the south wing and the conservatory, a small but gloriously crowded greenery with an eclectic collection of rubber trees, orange bushes, and orchids. He entered and heard Beacon's voice droning on. Then his aunt's stern voice.

"Beacon, it is poetry. Young Lord Byron, for all his self-absorption and idiotic melodrama, has a way with words. But you make it sound like a grocer's list."

The maid squabbled back and Lady Eliza groused some more, but then stopped as he approached. "Alban, is that you?"

He bent over her, kissing her cheek. Beacon curtsied and disappeared discreetly, and Alban took her chair. He examined his aunt with interest in the clear green light of the sunny conservatory, noting her high color and something in her air, a heightened excitement.

"London agrees with you," he said. "You should have come years ago."

"I didn't have reason; now I do."

"To find Kittie Douglas a husband," he said, bluntly. She stayed silent.

He stood and walked away, staring at the misty glass of the conservatory windows, stretching above his height and arching in convex splendor. It was like gazing into fog, staring at the misty glass, the condensing water running in streams down to puddle on the stone floor. Turning back, he said, as he returned to sit down, "Suppose I admitted that the thought of Kittie as my wife . . ."

"Do not start," Lady Eliza said, her tone harsh. "I meant what I said last night, Alban. I no longer think you deserve her. Marry Kittie? You would be *lucky* to marry such a woman as Kittie Douglas. A woman so shrewd, intelligent, elegant, sophisticated—truly sophisticated and not as you and your friends think of it, with a fraudulent French accent and the morals of an alley cat—loyal and honest. And she doesn't fit into society? If you can even say that, then you are more of an idiot than I even thought you. Kittie Douglas has such a winning, unique and fully formed character that anyone who speaks to her for ten minutes is charmed by her. Quite frankly, she can do better than you; she can attract a man who will truly appreciate her. You would marry her and then for the rest of her life she would have to thank you for your condescension. She is a proud woman and that would destroy her."

Taken aback by his aunt's vitriol toward him, her favorite nephew, he said, "You think I would behave in such a beastly manner?"

"I don't think you would mean to, but our family is a proud race. I know myself . . . pride has kept me from happiness before."

"You looked happy last night," he said, staring at her, wondering what lay beyond the harsh expression.

Her look gentled. "I was."

They both fell silent. Alban locked his hands together and stared down at them.

"She would be out of place in my life."

"You saw her last night; again I say, can you still think it?"

"But she has no family, no background that is congruent with becoming a duchess. People would be cruel to her."

"People are always cruel. If one has love . . ." Lady Eliza stopped, and her mouth twisted. "Life is hard, Alban, but love . . . love helps. I wish . . . if people were stronger, if they worked together, if two people in love could just overcome their fears . . ."

She knew what she was talking about, Alban thought. Someone had disappointed her once, and she regretted the wasted time.

And then the fear overwhelmed him, and he sank down, his face in his hands. "What if . . . what if I let myself love her and she left me? I just can't face that kind of risk again," he mumbled.

"Then you are risking more by your fear. You are risking learning later that you could have been happy and threw it away. Kittie is not Catherine. Alban, you know I only want what is best for you. Despite my harsh words, I still want you to have Kittie. I think you love her."

"But how does *she* feel?"

"I don't know. Why don't you ask her?"

"There you are, Eliza!"

Alban turned. Lady Montressor was coming toward them. He glanced at his aunt and saw her face bloom with soft pink color. She stood and held out her hands, and the other woman took them; they embraced.

Lady Montressor greeted him but then turned back to her friend. "Shall we go for that ride? I so want you to meet my son, Alexander. I've told him all about you and he is eager to meet you."

"All about me? Harry, you have not told him *all* about me."

The two women laughed, and Lady Montressor said, "Well, not everything, perhaps."

For the first time with his aunt, Alban felt outside of her life. It was disconcerting.

"You're leaving? I thought we would spend the day together."

Lady Montressor opened her mouth, but his aunt said, "I am sorry, Alban, but I have plans. How about tomorrow? I will be free then."

"All right," he said. He walked behind the two ladies as they left the conservatory. Beacon was there with her mistress's bonnet and cloak.

His aunt stopped and turned. "Alban," she said, stretching out her hand. He took it and squeezed it.

"Go to Kittie. Please. She has the pink room and salon. Go to her. Talk to her. I know there are a hundred men in London who would consider themselves lucky to have her as a wife, but not a one of them would make her as happy as you could."

"I thought you said I didn't deserve her?"

"But she *does* deserve you." She gave his hand a last squeeze and walked away arm in arm with Lady Montressor.

Alban turned and gazed up the long staircase. It would shock the house terribly, but he knew what he had to do. He mounted the stairs.

Kittie, curled up in the window seat of her sitting room, knit a complicated piece with white wool, checking it every once in a while to make sure she was getting the pattern right. Hannah, married just three months, was already with child and as happy as could be imagined, which meant, according to Rebecca, that she dissolved into tears thrice a day rather than twice. As a gift Kittie was knitting a coverlet for the baby's cradle.

Lady Eliza was going out with her friend for the afternoon, and had archly said she did not need a companion for that time. There were times, now, in the last twelve hours, when Kittie did not even recognize Lady Eliza as the woman she had come to know. She seemed giddy, happy, like a younger woman.

Kittie didn't know the whole story, and she would never ask, but it was enough to know that Lady Montressor was the "Harry" of Lady Eliza's past.

She heard a bustle in the hallway and cast her knitting aside. She was about to rise when her room's door opened and Alban strode in, saying over his shoulder, "It's all right, Millhouse; Mrs. Douglas will not object!"

He turned and they stared at each other.

"Tell the butler that you don't mind my . . . my presence."

Kittie swallowed and looked over the duke's shoulder. "It's all right," she said. "His Grace may visit. Leave the door open, if you please."

"Being careful of your reputation?"

She tried to decipher his tone, but gave up. That was a pointless exercise with someone as infuriatingly opaque as the duke. She stayed silent and stared at him, drinking in his appearance, which always made her stomach flutter, and his intense demeanor.

Finally, as he gazed at her with no apparent intention to ever speak, she said, "If you mean to disconcert me then you will fail."

"I didn't mean to unnerve you, Kittie. I've thought about you so often over the winter and I'm just getting my fill. It was quite a shock seeing you in the ballroom last night."

Embarrassed, Kittie said, "I don't know why Lady Eliza pulled such a hoax. If Mr. Lafferty did tell her you were to be in London, she didn't tell me."

"She had her own reasons. Don't you know what they are?"

Stiffly, Kittie replied, "I am beginning to think I do. And I'm sorry. She's wrong to . . . to think . . ."

"Is she?"

Kittie stared at him, perplexed by his behavior. She had seen him in many moods, but never with the combination of nerves and eagerness he betrayed by his jerky movements and intense stare.

"You're silent," he said. "I can't blame you. I was . . . the last time we were private . . . in the cabin in the woods, I was inexcusably forward and . . ."

"You thought I would become your mistress!" She put one hand over her mouth. In her agitation she had to turn away from him and the look in his eyes; it was indescribable, as if he had been caught at something he shouldn't have, and strangely, it attracted her. As compelling as she found him in his usual manner, very much a man who knew what he wanted and was willing to do what he had to to get it, this uncertainty was appealing. She longed to reach out and ruffle his thick hair, pull him to her, but it was a false sense of closeness, she thought, and she would not be fooled by it.

"I did. And you called it something much worse last time we spoke. I'm sorry for making you feel as I did. It was wrong of me, and what was worse, I didn't understand your anger."

She glanced at him. "But you do now?"

"I . . . think I do."

Not convinced, she crossed her arms over her bosom and said, "So, why was I insulted?"

"You . . . would never consider being anyone's mistress."

"And . . . ?"

His eyes widened. He thought for a long minute. "Uh . . . it offended your morals?"

"More than that."

He shrugged. "I don't know."

She sighed and turned away, fussing with her knitting, bundling it and putting it into the cloth bag she carried it in. "I thought you knew me better than that. *That* was what upset me. And I thought you respected me more."

"But I do respect you! Why would becoming my mistress mean . . ."

"You just do not understand!" She whirled and stared at him. "How can you not understand?" She advanced on him and stood toe to toe with him, looking up, realizing how very much taller than she he was and backing away one step. She stuck her finger in his chest and prodded. "How can you not understand?" she repeated. "It's so simple. If you really cared for me you wouldn't want me as just a mistress. Mistresses . . . they're temporary; it means you don't think enough of them to . . ." She stepped back more. "This is a waste of time."

"No, Kittie, don't walk away."

"Why not? Your Grace, I accept that you meant me no harm and no insult when you attempted to seduce me with the intent of making me your mistress." His eyes widened, but she continued. "I know you thought that it was a good offer for one such as I, and in material terms, you're probably right. I'm far down the social scale from you, and that is what determined your behavior."

"Kittie, I . . ."

"I'm not done. I am no one's whore, and I don't accept that you had seen enough of my behavior to believe that I would come to you that way. You didn' even consider your aunt! How could you do that? How could you think it?"

"But Lord Orkenay . . ."

"You are no fool, sir, and I think you knew the earl well enough to know he would lie if it suited him. I think you wanted to believe him because of the light it cast me in. I was available then, with no need for any commitment or caring on your part."

His expression was blank, and she wondered if he would walk out and never speak to her again. Perhaps. But she had said what she needed to and would not start regretting it now.

"If you think that of me," he said, his tone resentful, "then we have nothing further to speak of. I beg your pardon most humbly for taking your valuable time." He bowed and turned to go, but stopped and didn't walk to the door.

She waited. Time hung, suspended, though it seemed to go on outside the door. Servants hustled past the door with barely a side glance of curiosity. Millhouse's stentorian voice could be heard directing workmen down in the great hall. The duke heaved a great sigh, his broad shoulders rising and falling.

Then he turned back to her.

"I almost let you drive me away, Kittie."

"I wasn't trying to drive you away."

"Weren't you? Are you sure?"

His expression was different, his gaze more open, his eyes unclouded. He walked toward her and stood, looking down at her. With one large hand he caressed her neck and twined a stray curl around his finger, letting it spring away.

"Why would I do that?" she asked, her voice breathy and almost unrecognizable, even to herself.

"Because I hurt you," he said. "And you don't want to

be hurt again. It's exactly why I have been avoiding the truth for so long."

She stayed silent. That he should see something she didn't see in herself shocked her too much to speak, even to deny it.

"I was callous and wrong to think I could have you that way. You're right about that. But I had fooled myself into thinking it was all right." He took in a deep breath. "That you should be flattered I wanted you so much."

She would have turned away at his words, but he put his hands on her shoulders and held her steady.

"No, Kittie, I have to say this. I wanted you, and I deceived myself about it. I thought that having you as my mistress would be enough, but I was terribly wrong and I know that now. I underestimated how much I . . ." He stopped, his whole body trembling. He was on the edge of the chasm, the opening to the abyss, and if he said the words he could never take them back.

And he was going to jump and be damned to the consequences. "I've been so selfish," he said, "in every way. Kittie, I love you."

Her eyes widened, and he knew she didn't expect to hear that, of all things, but he had no desire to take it back. No matter what happened, he didn't want to take it back. It was the simple truth, and now it was in the open.

"You don't know what you're saying," she whispered.

"I do."

"Are you sure?"

"Yes. And I'm sorry I did what I did . . . treated you the way I did. Please, forgive me?"

He was appalled to see tears glimmer in the corners of her beautiful blue eyes.

"Drat you," she said, sniffing.

"What did I say?"

She just shook her head, mute.

"Kittie, I'm just telling the truth. I've had a lot of time to think about it. The whole winter."

She stared at him. It had not escaped his notice that she hadn't yet told him how she felt.

"Kittie, look into my eyes and tell me you don't feel the same."

She just shook her head again, but her whole body trembled. He could feel the tremors through his grip on her shoulders.

"You do! I know you do. And I love you and have since last fall. I was too proud, too stubborn and too . . . damn it! Too *frightened* to admit it. Kittie, say something!"

"I'm afraid you don't know what you feel. Before you say any more, I have something of yours that I want you to have back."

She pulled away from him and disappeared into her bedchamber, returning with a black velvet sac, which she handed to him. He took a seat in the window seat, undid the knot, and spilled the contents out.

A letter fell out and a small painting on ivory, a miniature. Of Catherine. He turned it over in his hands and picked up the letter. As he unfolded it, Kittie said, "I found these things some time ago in the drawer of a bureau in the guest room when I went looking for some stockings that you left at Lady Eliza's . . . to find your size, you know, to knit you stockings."

He read the letter. How angry Catherine had been, and how bitter! He had forgotten all about this and the miniature, taken to Yorkshire when he retreated there after the awful news of her death reached him. He gazed at the painting.

"If I had been a better husband she wouldn't have left as she did. I . . . let pride keep me from speaking of things. And if I had been a better husband, she would be alive now."

She sank down on the window seat next to him and when he met her eyes, they were pleading for something, he knew not what. "You don't know that. You were only one part of the problem, I think. She could have fought for her marriage. I would have."

"Sad mementos," he said with a sigh, and slipped them back into the velvet sac. "I cared for her so much, but in the end, I didn't . . . I couldn't give her what she needed. If I had been a better man or she a stronger woman, we could have found a way."

Kittie heard the sadness in his voice, but there wasn't the pain that would have signified a heart still broken. Was there a chance for them?

It was her turn to take a chance, the way she knew he had by telling her his feelings. She still couldn't quite accept that he truly loved her, but maybe—"When you came to Boden last fall, I think I had . . . I had built you up to be someone beyond what any man could live up to. Your letters to your aunt were always so kind. I read them, and looked at your painting, and I . . . I fell in love with this perfect, loving, giving, kind man, this . . . this demigod who had been cruelly abandoned by the woman he loved."

He was staring at her avidly, devouring every word. She couldn't look in his eyes, for his expression was too raw, yearning, drawing her in.

"But when I met you," she continued, "I saw the cracks, the faults. I unfairly blamed you for being a man. And then that night . . ." She looked down at her hands, twisting together in her lap. She knew she didn't need to say what night she meant. "I wanted to stay. I . . . I wanted to just stay and . . . and make love with you and forget about whatever would come on the morrow. I still don't know if I made the right decision.

Should a woman give herself to a man that way, if that's what she truly wants, or should she be strong and insist he make promises to her that in the heat of the moment he may make and regret later?"

"I think you did the right thing. If you had any doubt at all in your mind, you did the right thing. And why should you have stayed when I wouldn't be honest and honorable?"

He understood; he truly did.

"I love you!" she cried, before she could even think, before she could remember to be careful.

His eyes widened, and he slipped off the window seat to one knee in front of her. "Kittie, I adore you. I love you. I *trust* you. Will you marry me and be with me always? Love me forever?"

"I will. I will!"

He stood and pulled her up into his arms and enfolded her in love. She felt it thumping in his heart and emanating from his soul. He buried his face in her neck and whispered.

She pulled away and gazed into his eyes. "What were you saying?"

"I said my aunt is going to be relieved. I think she thought she might have to box my ears if I didn't do the right thing."

"Do you really think she wanted this, us marrying?"

He laughed out loud. "I think she might have asked you yourself if she could have. The things she said about you, the praise! One would have sworn she was half in love with you herself."

She gazed at him. Did he know about his aunt and Lady Montressor? Interesting idea, but she thought not. He was not an imaginative man, and it would likely never occur to him to think of her that way, in love at all, but even more shocking, in love with another woman. They would have time to discuss it later, and as much as he loved his Aunt Eliza, his inevitable shock would soon give way to happiness for her, she felt sure, just as it had with her.

"So," she said, "was your proposal motivated by fear of your aunt, Your Grace?"

"Please find something to call me other than 'Your Grace'! *Anything* else." He pulled her to him again. "I was always afraid of her, but mostly because I wanted to make her proud. I wanted to live up to who she thought I could be. I feel she might have passed on that expectation to you."

She framed his face in her hands, staring into his deep brown eyes. "You never have to be anything for me but honest and honorable. I don't expect perfection. You're a man, my love, just a man."

"Thank heavens," he murmured, pulling her closer. "And I think I like your new name for me. I would rather be your 'love' than anything else. And just a man."

Molded against him, she could feel the very clear evidence of that statement, and she sighed, nestling against him.

Hoarsely, he whispered, "You won't require a long engagement, will you?"

"Not if you don't," she said, breathless.

The next kiss was destined to be long, but neither of them had any reason to wish it shorter.

ABOUT THE AUTHOR

Donna Simpson lives with her family in Canada. She is currently working on her next Zebra Regency romance, which will be published in February 2005. Donna loves to hear from readers and you may write to her c/o Zebra Books. Please include a self-addressed stamped envelope if you wish a reply.

BOOK YOUR PLACE ON OUR WEBSITE AND MAKE THE READING CONNECTION!

We've created a customized website just for our very special readers, where you can get the inside scoop on everything that's going on with Zebra, Pinnacle and Kensington books.

When you come online, you'll have the exciting opportunity to:

- View covers of upcoming books
- Read sample chapters
- Learn about our future publishing schedule (listed by publication month *and author*)
- Find out when your favorite authors will be visiting a city near you
- Search for and order backlist books from our online catalog
- Check out author bios and background information
- Send e-mail to your favorite authors
- Meet the Kensington staff online
- Join us in weekly chats with authors, readers and other guests
- Get writing guidelines
- AND MUCH MORE!

Visit our website at
http://www.kensingtonbooks.com